The Private Undoing of a Public Servant

'Funny, is it, Cabinet Minister? Funny that you're rolling around a stranger's flat in a flowery apron, drinking from a doggy bowl? Funny that you are about to know pain of the likes that has not been administered since you were twelve years old, caned for cheating in school tests?'

'No, not that,' you cry. 'I'm not into whips and stuff.'

'Oh yes, that indeed. Miko and I are specialists in pain. And don't you think you deserve it, writing that filth and thinking such disgusting things about your colleagues? You, who are so high and mighty, Minister for Public Policy. Imagine your secret thoughts coming out during prime minister's question time!'

You make a lame attempt to struggle out from under me, but I know you are inhaling my scent and so, so grateful to have my sex near to you that you know, and I know, your efforts are all a sham. I love having my thighs clamped to your ears, and I decide to go one further. I lurch forwards so that I am completely covering your mouth and much of your nose. You are calling out your delight, although it is quickly muffled. You continue to touch yourself; I can feel the familiar rhythm of your hand pumping up and down behind me.

The Private Undoing
of a Public Servant
Leonie Martel

BLACK LACE

Black Lace books contain sexual fantasies.
In real life, always practise safe sex.

This edition published in 2006 by
Black Lace
Thames Wharf Studios
Rainville Road
London W6 9HA

A version of chapter one was previously published by
Black Lace as a short story in *Wicked Words* 7.

Typeset by SetSystems Ltd, Saffron Walden, Essex

Printed and bound by Mackays of Chatham PLC

ISBN 0 352 34066 5
ISBN 9 780352 340665

In memory of Jhonn Balance (1962–2004)

'Angels are bestial, man is the animal'

You can email the author at
leoniemartel@hotmail.co.uk

Contents

1 **Clawing at the Temple Doors**

Je suis une belle dame sans merci. I tread softly and reverently on a path to exalted dominance yet I am wise enough to know the universe does not revolve around me. I become flushed with power when I stand in authority before the likes of you, but I am humbled by the awesome majesty of the forest at night, all of its creatures and the impermanence of things. You would do well to learn some of my humility, yet you share with others of your kind a reluctance to acknowledge your mortality and insignificance. You still think man a paragon of animals; that his obscene proliferation somehow entitles him to a saturation of privilege whereas I believe the lives of a thousand baby humans are not worth that of one Arctic wolf.

We are satellites on different orbits, you and me – a Cabinet minister and an unknown woman with a criminal history. We should never have met. But in moments like this, when your tears are moistening my pillow, and your strangled croaks herald your imminent bliss, I realise how fortuitous our collision was. You give meaning to my desires, and justify my actions. You have made flesh what were once fantastical abstractions. And I am bringing you inch by inch closer to the internal life you have striven to ignore and which will torment you until your last gasp unless you pay it some attention.

You see, you have cultivated a staggering conceit and woven a tapestry of lies that has eased your climb to the Cabinet but not your slumber in the small hours. But the beast of the wild unconscious will not be kept at bay with a best-practice initiative or a committee of policy excellence. He will slaver and snarl and claw his way to prominence, his fiery breath singeing your brain to wake you in the still hours of the dark. You have never experienced self-doubt but you soon will. You will sweat. You will know fear.

My status is contradictory; the absence of mercy is actually doing you the world of good. I have your best interests at heart, I really do. A good dominant should always keep a tiny reservoir of empathy for her charges; she will bestow something approaching tenderness in those moments of catharsis. To see you trussed like this, bent over on the floor, hands tied, exposed, with my shoe in your back, brings a flood of sensations to my already dizzy head. You are so deserving of what I am giving to you yet, 24 hours ago, you could not have imagined that such a thing would be happening. Especially as the early stages of our meeting showed all the hallmarks of a textbook seduction – man meets attractive woman in a bar and buys her a drink. Who would have thought you'd seen in the dawn gagged and bound on my living-room floor?

Like all men of your age and standing, you are vulnerable to the attentions of a pretty woman; such a thing props up your masculinity, even though you are not so gullible as to think them genuine. You know the type of woman that zeroes in on men of power. Predatory, designer clad, status obsessed, she craves to look sleek in the soft amber glow of four-star hotel lobbies. You can use her if you like – it's a fair trade. She gets the trinkets and you get a thoroughbred ball-breaker hanging on your arm. But supposing you pick unwisely and are lured to unfamiliar territory, out of your comfort zone? What happens when those attentions exceed your boundaries and experience? Do you run away? Well, you haven't so far. Do you phone your wife and beg forgiveness? No, of course not. You're the king of deception and the cloak and dagger. Do you call the police or storm out in a temper? No, you have done neither of those things because I have touched something in you that no one has acknowledged before and you're not sure how to respond. I have shown you just an inkling of the bounty on offer, even to wretches like you, when you are allowed into the realm of the exotic.

Like a character in a fable from old Arabia, who has been led into a dark cave concealing untold riches, all it needed was the conjurer's 'open sesame' and an ancient door creaked ajar to reveal a blinding golden light. And there, inside the secret chamber lurked a treasure chest spilling jewels you wanted to bathe in. It's the magic kingdom, my grey little parliamentarian. And you have endured great suffering to get here.

Writhing in shame on my carpet, you implore with your eyes to be allowed release. When you kneel up, your head is level with my thighs and you do your best to nuzzle into their warmth. You can smell the female musk – heavenly scent – and you strain for contact. How gratifying to see reverence from one more commonly used to wearing a supercilious smirk. Flushed with arrogance, you need taking down a peg or two. You are not so well known that those outside the House would recognise you in the street but most UK citizens with an awareness of current affairs will have heard your name attributed to one of the more dull political features.

I have bagged myself an MP. And what a perfect specimen of life deferred you are. Just over fifty years old, in the depths of your midlife crisis, you are the epitome of the career politician. Toed the party line, didn't stand in the way of progress when modernisation swept you to power. Always put in the hours, got on to a select committee here and there, did meticulous research. But none of it has brought you joy. You have hung on to your regret until it has festered and stunk: your schoolboy fantasies that still linger; the egomania of the young man that has warped into disdain and resignation; the private dreams that were once within your grasp but shoved aside for that inexorable climb up the greasy pole. You've never had any fun, and that realisation sticks in your craw like a cold chisel. But the secret self doesn't go away because you have matured. Instead it will nag you like an old fishwife until you empty the bin.

You never rolled down hills drunk on cider with your mates, bunking off from lectures. You never wore fancy dress on magic mushrooms, hitch-hiked to the Greek islands or got loved up in Ibiza in the 80s. When your fellow students were getting loaded and rocking out to Led Zep you eschewed it all as too hedonistic. You had the hair and the loon pants but you never had the stomach for where the wild things were. And now the wild things are all but extinct and cloned conformity has the cultural dominance, it's all coming back to haunt you – the ones you never did.

I knew what was going to happen the second our eyes met last night in the bar above WH Smith in Victoria station. You were cradling a pint of bitter, sat at the bar, passing time until the 18.20 arrived to take you home. I recognised who you were and I wanted you, desperately so. Not because of your status – it doesn't impress me – but something kicked in my solar plexus and I knew you were perfect prey. From across the room I could see you'd registered my charms, your interest allowing you to hold the gaze for a couple of seconds before turning your head away. You thought I was out of your league, no doubt waiting for a younger extrovert City type fresh from the gym. You were wrong. Such men do not interest me, and I do not interest them. I don't smile enough. I have issues. A young man's arrogance is in its infancy and too tenaciously clung to. I'm drawn more passionately to men with regrets; they make far better confessional subjects.

I walked up to you, correctly identified you, and then time stopped.

You seemed irritated that I knew who you were. You wanted to be anonymous – to enjoy the privilege of several million other Londoners. Tough. You sacrificed that when you entered politics.

'Train delays again, eh?' I announced. 'Still, it's not your fault.'

You asked if I was waiting for someone.

'No. I'm on my way to Brighton,' I said, 'but I just can't face the packed trains after there's been a cancellation. I thought I'd wait around for a bit. Read a magazine or something.' I waved a copy of a fine art brochure at you. That surprised you. You expected to see a celebrity gossip rag, didn't you? Wrong again.

'Me too,' you said, looking uncomfortable, unsure of my motives. 'You already know who I am. Can I ask your name?'

'Kirsten Caine.'

We shook hands. So formal an introduction for what would transpire. You went on to talk about the M25, comparing what's the worst mode of transport at this time of the week, and I affected a look of polite boredom although I was amused. You were babbling – a classic masking technique when sexual interest is piqued by a stranger.

I moved in closer, leaned on the bar, and you noticed my shape; my suit jacket had fallen away to reveal my hourglass frame and soft figure-hugging top. You kept darting your eyes to my chest and it was so easy to draw you in, to hypnotise you. When you offered to buy me a drink I thrilled to the sight of you pulling money from your important man's wallet kept in your important man's trousers. At that moment we already had very different ideas about how the evening might progress.

The bar began to fill with braying blokes pumped up for the evening booze-a-thon. I could see they depressed you, wearing suits sharper than yours, with youth on their side, calling their lovers on their mobiles.

'They're all so full of themselves,' you said bitterly. 'And so noisy. In fact, the company of men has begun to bore me.'

You stopped short of elaborating but there was definitely some jealousy there. You went on to declare what you would do differently if you had your time again. You could have made it as a big shot in the 80s, ducked out of politics when your lot was in the wilderness, but it didn't happen. You didn't want to ruin your credibility. You're not exactly what one could call a loser – you're just sore about personal failings. I'd find out soon enough what they were.

'Ever get the feeling you've been cheated?' I asked you, but you didn't get the Johnny punk reference. Poor you – all the time you were stuffing your off-the-pegs in the trouser presses of Travel Inns you could have been having a whale of a time. But you couldn't do that; first with your studies and then all those civil servant briefings and reports and policy documents, it was just rush, rush, rush. And, of course, there were always your ambitions of high office. And all that time something was being neglected, wasn't it? And it's been hurting you to the point that you can now barely concentrate on the job.

I could sense you were extremely cautious. I could have been a journalist. It's happened to you before. A couple of pints too many at some tedious conference and suddenly you're saying something you shouldn't. You've always picked the wrong ones. Women ... you just can't trust 'em. You have to let go sometime, though; you hold yourself as stiff as a board. You're divided up into parts like a clockwork doll and you walk with the shoulders of your suit rather than letting your hips move you forwards. I bet you look crap on the dance floor.

You try to ignore foolish pop stars but I can imagine that just once you have stood in front of the mirror at home and grabbed your crotch, just for the hell of it, trying to imagine what it would be like to be a tattooed sex icon with an audience. Maybe it was after one of those terrible days in the House. You tried to concentrate on your posture but all you could think about was the PM's Q-time – so you gave up. Supper was ready. The missus had cooked something with scallops and fennel.

Five minutes later and we were seated at the anonymous-looking tables, talking about City Hall. The TV monitors were playing MTV. Some R'n'B starlets were popping and pouting. You didn't register it. It was all beneath you, the youth culture of modern life. You asked me stilted questions about my education and of course I lied, as I always do when I meet someone like you. I was erudite, attractive and bright. I, like you, was dressed in a pin-striped suit and the night held promise. Although you should have been heading back to your constituency for Friday surgery, just for once you fancied a bloody change. And who could blame you?

And while you were in this state of trust – almost willing to think of me as an equal in terms of education and class – I pulled from my bag a copy of Georges Bataille's *The Story of the Eye*.

'This is what I'm reading at the moment,' I said, betraying no hint of its content.

You'd never heard of it. I pulled a face that made you

feel dull. Yesterday's man. I talked about surrealism. You said you'd never had time to get into art, but you knew all the main artists. Oh, is that right? You rattled off some names but they were the usual ones people come up with when they really know so little: Dali, Magritte. Yawn. I mentioned Man Ray. He was a photographer; you knew that much. Luis Buñuel had you stumbling for a moment and you glazed over until I talked about the divine Deneuve – the original and only *Belle de Jour*. Something registered. You saw it at a student film night back in the late 70s and were confused by it. French ladies in Citroëns meeting Japanese businessmen in hotels when they didn't even need the money. Insects buzzing in jars. What was it all about?

I shifted closer to you for just a second before I stood up to go to the loo. You looked me in the eyes and I could see the questions forming. You were intrigued, besotted. I was different, strange. I wasn't talking about celebrity, politics or fashion. You wanted news from another world – my world. You were suddenly seized by the desire for authentic experience – but you didn't even know how to ask for it, although in the shadowy corners of your mind you had a premonition of having to beg.

Dear Mr Cabinet Minister. All the social climbing, all the rigmarole and protocol and long-distance travel are nonsense if you can't grab that special thing that is the opposite of death for one fleeting moment. In that bar, last night, all the stars were in alignment and you made the decision to let me be the open sesame. You wanted to reclaim your cock, hard in your pants as a young man, and all the girls you never did 'cos you were under the cosh of your own making. Go back in time. It's the local art-school disco, boyo, end of spring term in 1972, and there are so many people around cooler than you, but just this once you're gonna get lucky. The DJ's playing 'Itchycoo Park' and optimism is everywhere.

When college shuts for summer there can be picnics with hippie girls in cheesecloth and the scent of wet grass. You'll doze in the sunshine and read some Gramsci. The old guard is on the backfoot and you've a head full of revolution. And in those fleeting seconds of your retro memory we looked into each other's psyches, and I knew you were snared for joy.

You remember 1972 very well. You were eighteen and full of vim. *Up Pompeii*, *The Benny Hill Show* and *Casanova* were on the box. You liked it, even though it was low culture. You'd never have admitted it to your friends, but you enjoyed watching all the crumpet run about showing their knockers. And suddenly, in your head, in a bland chain pub in the modern transit zone of Victoria station, over three decades later, you were young again – full of wonder and spunk. The hypnosis had begun. And that's when I drew your attention to a page in *The Story of the Eye* – the scene in the church. Simone is wanking in the confessional; Sir Edmund is faintly bored but loving her death wish. You took the book. You couldn't believe what I had handed you. The character of Sir Edmund made you think of Sir Stephen ... now where had you read that? Didn't a girlfriend once have a book, a strange book, with a Sir Stephen in it? It always gave you a queasy but exciting feeling when you read it. You shuddered. I smiled. Something trembled down below – I wasn't sure if it was desire or fear. I walked away on heels that give my posture authority. You counted the seconds until I returned.

You've not read anything like Bataille before. Suddenly it was all spilling over. You flicked through other pages, eyes alighting on scandalous passages: young girls sitting in saucers of milk; pissing themselves in wardrobes. Can you imagine your wife reading such a thing? Christ, no. She prefers nothing more challenging than a post-colonial memoir – fragrant geishas and magic realism. I came back to the table, still smiling, still looking poised and professional in my suit. I gently took the book from your grasp.

'Why are you showing me this stuff?' you asked. You were suddenly shocked and confused. We'd only just met. We'd been talking about philosophy and art and then suddenly you were reading pornography in a crowded bar.

'This is the real surrealism, not Dali's melting clocks,' I said, leaning closer and stroking your hair. The effect was unnerving. You wanted to give in to it – someone so attractive, showing you tenderness – but you weren't sure if you could trust yourself not to cry. I continued in a gentle voice: 'There's a cyclone coming, Simon. So why don't you enjoy yourself for once. You know, like you did in the seventies.'

You didn't answer, and that last sentence really wound you up. You weren't always like this, grey suit and grey hair. You were an idealist. Your foundations were built on something more solid than most people's hedonism. How could I know what it was like then? Not everyone took drugs. Some people were trying to change the world. You stuffed your head with dialectical materialism and Marxist ideology. All those sit-ins and heady hopes and left-wing debate – it was all over once Maggie came to town. These days you prefer the opera, and that's a bourgeois little thorn in your side. You've turned into your father. So yeah, it looks like you've been cheated.

You felt confused, but increasingly aroused in my presence. I touched you just enough to let you know I was keen on progressing this intimacy. You wanted to read aloud from the book and fuck me to delirium on the seats in front of the young blades. Give those arrogant little shits an eyeful. You can do it. No Viagra required; you've got enough libido to keep it up for a year, haven't you? Oh, God, it's been so long since you've been able to let go.

It came to crunch time. The plates were shifting. You were going to take a risk. Your mouth was dry even though you kept trying to quench your thirst with your pint. You were twisting around on your seat, your penis as hard as iron. You hadn't been so hard in years, not since you used to chase northern birds who wore too much make-up, being grateful for when you could spunk into their candy faces. You liked that, didn't you? You liked them sluttish and dirty with their legs wide open, showing their juicy pink, all ready for you.

These days, you've taken to buying porn that features Asian girls because their long lush hair falls down onto their tits, and that's always so exciting. In me you saw someone fuckable, nicely dressed, who has thick luxuriant hair and shining lips and eyes that have the very Devil in them. You could see that hair falling over your cock; see those shiny lips sliding up and down. You so badly wanted some of that. Your wife keeps her hair short these days and that depresses you.

You told me you couldn't take it any more and I wasn't sure whether you meant the inane music or your own arousal. Just for a fleeting moment I discreetly slipped my hand between your legs and brushed over what was there. I looked you in the eye to register my approval. You breathed out slowly in a hiss and closed your eyes in rapture behind your glasses. Sweet. It's what happens when desire becomes overwhelming. Then it was time. Cometh the hour, and all that.

We left the bar and glided down the escalator that led to the main concourse. Your arousal was so intense you were willing, just once, to miss the bloody train; to go with me and see what happened. But Christ, what were you thinking? You were not even drunk. Would I have slipped something into your drink? One of those sex drugs? Or maybe Ecstasy? In your more random moments you've thought about trying it. You wonder if your step-niece does it. She's at that age. You imagine being sixteen again. Things are a bit different now, eh? The kids aren't reading Marx any more. They want to vote for pop idols, not prime ministers.

Teenage glitter queens were clacking noisily across the concourse in their party shoes, heading out on the town. The girls are all so sleek these days; stardust eyeshadow, permanently moist lips and perfect skin that the light dances over when they laugh. If only young people knew what they had, and how very beautiful they were. You felt sad for a moment but I didn't let you put up any obstacles to what you'd started. There was no time to think, and no turning back. This was not a night for regrets. You'd had a belly full of being on your best behaviour, of trying to do everything right and getting no thanks. Fuck 'em. Just this once: fuck 'em.

I hailed a cab to my place in SW3 – that familiar sound of a diesel engine but this time the taxi wasn't taking you to a hostile press conference or to Television Centre. This time to the unknown. We got out by Bibendum and the Conran Shop. You'd been around here before with Members of the House. Must have been an R in the month because you had oysters. I looked confident and beautifully groomed as we entered the apartment block foyer. I was carrying a polished black-leather Samsonite case like someone in a Bond film called *Fuck and Let's Die*.

I said good evening to Gordon the concierge – unlike the usual breed of inscrutable Africans or Irish men marking time to retirement this guy is youngish, 35-ish, my age-ish. English. He spends so many hours in that chair, so many eccentric old residents to deal with. He's got the measure of me, but he's too polite to ask questions. I've seen his eyes light up when my Japanese friend Miko comes to visit, when the pair of us head out in uniform. Discretion is assured with Gordon. Last night I was the smart new aide to the secretary of state. Of course, she's advising him on budget forecasts for the next select committee meeting.

My manicured nails clicked against the plastic key fob – those square, sharp little claws that would later press into your flesh. I was taking control already. Up to my apartment on the top floor and you found yourself needing another drink to calm your nerves. You worried you might not be able to get it up but you shook away the thought, remembering the stuff in that book. It got you so excited you wanted to read more. You kept asking me about it. What happens to that priest? Why did they have to go to a bullfight? You resolved to buy a copy to find out. The big Waterstone's in Piccadilly would have it.

I unlocked the apartment door and we entered. So you were going to be unfaithful to your wife again. That didn't faze you. You could release some tension, you thought, or, if it didn't work out, you could just leave. It was still early. Still time to catch the last train or find a hotel. But this was not the apartment you were antici- pating; it was gloomy and the décor seemed odd – more like somewhere you'd expect an avant-garde art student to live. You considered the fact that it might not be mine. Maybe it belonged to some guy who was going to jump you. Suddenly it all felt wrong. The walls in the hallway were painted deep red and decorated with prints of Francis Bacon's screaming popes. That could be you in that chair if you don't watch your manners.

You entered the main living room. Curious ethnic artefacts featured prominently, like something out of Freud's museum. There was low-level seating and lava lamps. You hated it. You had a sudden longing for the pale wood and understated décor of your own study. This place needs an airing, you thought. It looks like a hippie hovel, a den of iniquity. Now it's dark.

You couldn't get a handle on me. Had I played you for a sucker? You felt odd, disjointed, a little dizzy. You got the notion I wasn't quite what I seemed: that there was no medical qualification; no racks of sophisticated clothing; no crate of Chablis in the kitchen. Actually, your suspicions were correct about only one of those things; I have impeccable clothes and I always keep a small cellar. I do love the sound of a popping cork. You were tense and I'd put on some very curious music. You looked at the CD case. Some group you had never heard of. So what if it's not like your place, you told yourself. You're not moving in; you're going to be here less than two hours. You shitty little snob, you got that wrong. You've been here fourteen hours now.

I watched you eye the room with the calculated arrogance that comes so naturally to you. I gritted my teeth and told you to make yourself comfortable – take off your shoes and jacket, loosen your tie, relax. I'd mixed two vodka tonics and had calmly taken up position opposite you. You swallowed it too fast. It went down a treat. You remembered a sentence from that scandalous book: 'The paralysed wretch drank with a well-nigh filthy ecstasy at one long gluttonous draft.'

You suddenly burst out laughing. I smiled and fixed you another, then I stood there magnificent and commanding, drumming the glass with my nails as you squirmed slightly on the sofa. You wished I didn't look at you like that. I was not being what you would have called the perfect host, although you couldn't quite put your finger on what was wrong. Conversation had all but ceased. So what was it I wanted from you? You would have expected to be led to the bedroom by now but I looked as if I was waiting for something, watching you too closely for comfort while the sombre soundtrack of Coil's *Love's Secret Domain* accompanied our awkward moment.

You felt something begin to happen in the base of your spine. You tried to speak but all you could do was giggle. It was unnerving as well as exciting. A fluid ripple shot from your groin to your lips. You didn't dare stand up. You reached out for the glass but swiped the air instead. You noticed my Italian leather heels sinking into the carpet just enough to exact a frisson of fear and excitement. You made a lunge at them and then suddenly started planting kisses on my ankles. Just what was going on? I hadn't touched you, yet you were aching for my attentions. Was I some kind of magician? You don't make a habit of letting people – especially women – get the upper hand. And you certainly never let anyone see you out of control. But you were transfixed, yet you couldn't work out why. And just when you thought I was going to prolong the agony even further, I very gently ran my hand through your hair and tugged it slightly.

You complemented my caresses by pressing yourself against my hand like an unneutered cat. You were consumed by strange feelings but you managed to stand up. Everything was looking pin sharp and colourful at that moment. I ran my hands down each side of your body and you shivered for more of my touch; your shirt was made of the finest cotton and the quality didn't go unnoticed.

'Pink. My favourite,' I said.

'What are you doing to me?' you asked, barely audible. 'I feel strange. I feel ... I feel like it's going to be a long night.'

I didn't answer. You looked very confused then, especially as you felt like you wanted to roll around naked on the soft fur rug by the window and be stroked like a pet. It was drawing you in. You wanted sensual rapture. You were unwinding. For the first time in decades you felt the courage to be yourself, despite the unknown quantity that would be my reaction. Christ almighty, there was a thunder brewing. You began to strip off as best you could, shirtsleeves tangled up in your watch, as you ripped at them in frustration, giggling, wanting to be in a natural state.

Off came those terribly expensive, lined trousers (the ones that wifey likes you to wear because you look so slim and smart), and you launched yourself in a dive that was at once sporting and abandoned onto the synthetic weave of the rug. It all changed from there, didn't it? A Cabinet minister rolling around on the carpet, in an altered state ... now that simply has to be worth investigating!

You asked the question, 'What is it? What have you given me?' You hoped with what sense you had left that it wasn't LSD. I wouldn't be that cruel.

'It's MDMA. A dance drug. It won't hurt you,' I said. 'You won't start seeing things or go mad.'

I seemed perfectly sober but you felt like an insect under a microscope. You tried to be indignant but you couldn't raise the anger. You wanted to be outraged; what I had done was a crime, but how would you prove it? You made an attempt to be arrogant but all you felt was immediately fraudulent. You imagined what the chief whip would say if he could see you. Another burst of the giggles erupted. You spluttered your drink all over the carpet. I watched you, waiting for the perfect moment to release the bats from the belfry. Not yet, I was thinking. You had to get over the silly bit first. To let your psyche adjust before you were ready to fully appreciate what was going on.

'How time is slipping underneath our feet: unborn

tomorrow and dead yesterday, why fret about them if today be sweet!'

You looked up, half naked and startled. You blinked behind your spectacles and looked as if you had gone into shock.

'You haven't heard that for a long time, have you?' I asked.

'What's the next bit?' you asked back. 'Something about a caravan.'

'One moment in annihilation's waste, one moment, of the well of life to taste. The stars are setting and the caravan starts for the dawn of nothing, oh, make haste!'

'Yes. Yes. I'd forgotten that. *The Rubáiyát of the Omar Khayyám*. Wonderful. It's about ...'

'Seizing the day?' I offered.

'Yes. But it's so magical and uplifting.'

Now, there are two words you've rarely used in your lifetime.

You rolled your naked chest on the rug and giggled.

'Magical is good,' I say. 'And more than a little of doing what you want now and again.'

It is at this point that I noticed you still had your socks on. Black and conservative. At least they were not decorated with Disney cartoons. If there were any hint of that sort of idiocy I would have had to take a knife to them, or maybe threaten to saw off your foot like the beautiful Japanese sado-girl with her garrotting wire in *Audition*. But it was OK – they were just slightly dowdy; not something that was going to provoke a psychotic reaction. I haven't had one of those for a while.

I changed out of my suit and into something less businesslike but you didn't even notice that I'd been out of the room. You were kept so busy, playing with the plants and staring at the carpet and running your hands over your body like a courtesan in a harem. I allowed myself the luxury of settling down onto the rug with you. I took one of your hands and ran it over my top. Dolce and Gabbana. It's beautiful. Dr Baum, my analyst, sent it to me on my birthday. I admonished him for being 'unprofessional', buying former clients presents, but he remembers so fondly the days I used to curl up on his lap and tell him all my troubles. I will definitely have to tell him about you. He likes to hear every detail of what I do.

It didn't take you long for you to notice I was not wearing a bra over my 34E-cup assets.

'They're a treat, aren't they?' I said.

You cupped them and brought your face to them. You'd never had your hands on anything like them. I could see what this sudden intimate contact was doing to you. You kept saying you must have more of it, then you threw yourself in an uncharacteristically am-dram fashion to the floor and all the desperation began to come out. I had administered a psychic emetic, an expectorant of narcotics, poetry and magic. I began to stroke you and tell you it was OK. I couldn't help but snake my hand to your underwear, though. And it only took the lightest of caresses before you were pushing yourself against my hand. You wanted a little bit of everything at that moment. You were then – as you are now – a writhing bundle of civil servant frustration clawing at the temple doors. It's been a long time coming.

You gave in to desire and kissed me deeply. The suit, the timetables, the reports from your department, the drudgery – it was all gone. But even though I was delighted to see you enjoying yourself so much, I still had to exert my superiority. I do like to give people surprises. While you were in that receptive state, I pulled the Samsonite case towards me. Click click. There was lube there, of course; all I had to do was select the correct size of appendage for the harness I was already wearing.

You hadn't noticed. You probably thought it was some kind of fancy belt. I calmed you and eased you back down onto the rug. You squirmed and writhed so beautifully. You'd had a snog and were feeling more relaxed.

'It's all OK,' I said. 'You're getting in touch with your feminine side, aren't you?'

And, before you knew it, I'd whipped down those paisley-patterned boxer shorts and I was gently but insistently priming you for your debauchery. This is what you'd wanted all along – to have the responsibility taken away. That is the king of all sensations.

I'm very skilled at sodomy. I become male at those moments when I grasp the faux penis and ease it into its designated destination. And I eased into you before you knew what was happening. And the power I had over you was soaking me between the tops of my thighs. A heady bouquet of ripe scents rose from the nexus of the action. All the deodorant and aftershave was evaporating and we were down to sweat and musk and pheromones. Your temperature went up by several degrees. Oh, I must say, I did like the cut of your jib when you were squirming about underneath me. You said no, this is not what you wanted, but I hushed you. You didn't try to stop me physically and your protestations rang false as you began to enjoy the novel sensations. In those moments there was just you, being fucked, having to work at going through the barrier of where 'no' used to be.

As you lifted your head to take a breath from your ignominy, I turned you around to look at a print of Félicien Rops' *The Temptation of St Anthony* that is framed and set on one of my low tables. Suddenly it all made sense. A voluptuous girl on the cross is defiant in the face of a miserable patriarchy emaciated by moaning and denial. It made sense to you because at that moment you were opened up in head and sphincter, a martyr to your cause. Stephen Stylites, but given over to temptation rather than pointless suffering. It reminded you of what you truly wanted, of what you've been missing, of what it is never too late to grasp: that which a man should resolve to change with his dying breath. And as your body built itself up to an explosion that sent your world spinning off its axis, a flash of blinding light cascaded at once in your amygdala, at once in your prostate. In all this darkness there was revelation. The all-seeing eye that is at once both omnipotent and dread filled was looking back at you. Your long-dormant imagination sparked itself into being. You got it. You jetted out your release into the rug and you were shaking and crying out and begging me to kiss you deeply and take away the greyness for ever. You were incandescent with joy. The dark welcomed you at that point, when I became your salvation and nemesis.

It was not the evening you had expected, but it was the start of our mutual irreversible fortunes of lust. And that has to be more exciting than reading the chief whip's directive for the coming week's votes on the train home, doesn't it? For the last fourteen hours I have been working at stoking the fire that has barely smouldered as a tiny ember for the past thirty years. And now the flames are fanned, there will be no going back. I have seen tears, wrath and joy over the course of this long night. It's always intense like this when I have a new subordinate to initiate – and please don't think me blasé about these duties. Each one of my acolytes has been special to me and, if I look a little drained, it is not from the ennui of familiarity; it is merely that I put so much effort into the process. I take my responsibilities seriously. There are changes of clothes and all manner of exacting tests to plan. So here we are at 6 a.m.

and, I must say, you've had rather a night on the tiles, you old tomcat. And it's not over quite yet.

It took a couple of hours for you to wind down from the initial excitement. I even let you phone your wife to tell her you wouldn't be home. It's not every day that a member of the Cabinet is anally assaulted on class-A drugs, so I allowed you some basic rights at least. You were so malleable then, and I took you to my bed and let you rest next to me, but less than an hour ago you awoke with such a need of me that I swiftly had to bring your desire to the appropriate situation. As delicious as it would have been to let you at me in the way you wanted, sloppiness on my part would not have been to my advantage. How are you ever going to effect a transformation with some half-dozing, semi-naked partner that you would see as an equal at best? No, I have to be in control. I have to always make it dynamic.

In the half-light of dawn I have once again dressed for sex and dragged you from your comfort zone. So here I stand, 5 feet 8 inches tall in four-inch-heeled ankle boots. I am wearing a double-zip-fronted black tunic of military appearance that releases to different degrees of exposure: unzipped from the top to reveal my generous breasts; unzipped from the hem to part the tunic at the apex of the thighs. My arms and midriff are snugly covered, however, and give me authority. And my stockinged legs are there to tantalise you, to make you imagine them wrapped around your head while my heels scrape your back. In the throes of passion you wouldn't care that I may tear the flesh. We haven't gone that far yet, but I can tell from your desperate countenance that you could easily bear such discomforts for the thrill of having your face enveloped by my sex. Breakfast call, my darling.

It's a grail you are yet to worship at, and I am

determined to string out the waiting until I am frantic for physical attention. Ladies given to such sensibilities have to suffer the discipline of long-delayed gratification. While you squirm and howl and cry out your pain you are at least receiving contact. Mistresses and dominants must endure long hours of denial: the greatest punishment of all. Don't think we do not yearn for the solid flesh of inflamed manhood; that we don't want to feel the weight of another body on top of our own – to conmingle sweat and breath and know the material reality of skin on skin. Yet we cannot allow ourselves such casual vulnerabilities. We who are not as others dare not chance such intimacies that would threaten to undermine our raison d'être.

Once the veil was lifted then all would be lost. It happened to me once and no good came of it. Once a man is witness to a woman's need of him then all her dominion crumbles. It is *you* who are wanton, not I. Look at you now. You know only your desire and it resembles nothing other than suffering. My exquisite leather boots and belted uniform won't galvinise my flesh against the final void, but how heavenly they feel in passing! Aesthetics *do* matter and, despite your suburban styling, I think you'll agree with me on that one. My fancies, although futile, are sweet and attended to with complete attention. What value can be enjoyed in now!

You are erect and begging for my touch. The room is dim, with fairy lights providing the only illumination. Their glow is kind but I am not. All I grant you is the graze of my boot gently placed at the underside of your penis. But the pitiful sight of your longing is too much to bear. You have been crouched here with your hands tied behind your back wearing nothing but a shirt for some half an hour as I have walked around you demanding confessions, lashing your buttocks with a tawse when I got a particularly juicy reply. Could I be accused of extraordinary rendition? Taking you to an unfamiliar place to perpetrate unusual discomforts? I have been sitting on a chair in front of you, masturbating for the past five minutes. It's no wonder you are almost in tears.

I take your gag off then shuffle the chair nearer to you so that I am supported while I touch your genitals with my stockinged feet. The ankle boots are off and you are grateful for the feel of my Wolford 10 deniers against your cock. I have perfected a way of cupping my feet and moving my lower legs back and forth to perform enough friction for the task. It is good exercise, but my supple legs don't feel any strain. You wouldn't have thought yourself a foot fetishist, but at this moment you are in thrall to my toes, my soles, my heels, my ankles. I let you know very firmly how privileged you are to be allowed this honour. You will buy me a year's supply of Wolford stockings for these few moments of disgrace. And it is only a few moments too. Kneeling as you are, it is difficult to get the required thrusting you seem to like, but you have been so close for so long that if I didn't take control of the proceedings I feared you might have thrown yourself flat on the carpet and made it happen.

You are lost in your need, your eyes closed. It's a good thing I took your glasses off you otherwise they may have flown off your nose with the physical exertions. I may hold you in contempt for what you represent, but at this moment you look beautiful in rapture – it's the great elevator. You cry out and utter a stream of expletives, telling me what even an idiot can predict is about to happen. With my stockings on I get some measure of how it must feel to wear a condom, to be denied the flesh on flesh contact, yet I didn't want to go bare-legged as I would have lost authority. Now you are into the 'oh my Gods' and I brace myself for a curious sensation as you descend into the spasm abyss. I feel and see your moment of warm shameful triumph – pumping and throbbing and dirty sweet. What a revelation for you. You have been grinding at it with your wife in the same way for almost twenty years and now, in the space of fourteen hours, you have reached two body-wracking orgasms without the touch of a hand or cunt. Buggery and foot play, my right honourable friend. Who'd have thought it?

I burn inside from wanting, but it won't be you I take into my body. Not yet. There are others who serve that purpose. You must not know the urgency of my needs or see any evidence of my private life. I must retain a superior being above your level of baseness. I discreetly wipe my feet of your excesses with the towel I put down earlier, to save your knees carpet burns and bruises. Discomfort need only go so far. There are tears falling from your bowed head and, in a moment of gentleness, I lift your chin with the crook of my finger. You lean forwards and kiss me, even thanking me. It's a tremendous turn about of energies: you contrite; me affectionate. I untie your hands and massage your wrists and forearms. I brush back your dishevelled hair in a gesture reminiscent of when I first touched you in the bar; it is damp with sweat. I fetch you a robe from my bedroom and run a hot bath that we will share. We had such illuminating conversation after your first debauching and I know you've got so many more questions. We'll talk later. For now, I think both of us should surrender to the comforts of repose.

2 **Psycho-the-rapist**

From the unobserved vantage point of my window I watched you leave my apartment block early this morning. The leaves of the plane trees lining the street were beginning to turn russet and, since there had been a sharp downpour, the delivery men hurried to make their morning drops at the fish restaurant opposite. Six storeys down you crossed the street to hail a cab in the rain outside the Chanel shop. You cut an insignificant figure in your suit and overcoat in this part of town but still it thrilled me to see you, knowing who you were and what I'd done. I smiled, thinking of you taking questions from your constituents later that day, maybe feeling the aftershocks of my ministrations as an unexpected twinge tickled your anus.

I always feel suffused with a triumphant glow after introducing someone to the uncommon delights. And you were my best yet. Better than I had anticipated and so ripe for subjugation. No regrets, eh, O Grey One? And now you've been awoken, who knows what will transpire or how much you might need me to assuage your longing. Like some vampire lover who has shown you the beauty of the night and initiated you into the dark clan, I have given you everlasting life through intense release. You can't go back now. I've changed your energy, even your DNA. You are my own Mina Harker.

When it dawned on you that I might present you with a bill before you left, I was quick to dispel any notion that this was to be a financial arrangement. You fell into your shame with such enthusiasm that processing a fee at the end of it would have taken the magic away. Anyway, I don't do this for money. I'll explain more when you call needing me again. And you will. A man like you doesn't taste the long-withheld ambrosia only to reject a second helping. He may very well gorge on it to make up for lost time.

You have been waiting a lifetime for this – to know such exquisite explosions – but you dared not volunteer the first step to realising such a thing. That would be tantamount to an admission of something not altogether wholesome dwelling within. Well, Simon Charlesworth, it's time to give the beast some air. Time to have me raining down on your right honourable arse with luscious severity. Do you know the demonic glee I will let loose? To extract confessions of wretchedness and unholy imaginings from you will be the zenith of my deviant life. I do delight in this catharsis, when the foundations of a fool's worldview begin to shake and crumble.

I've known a few like you: civil servants, policy makers, think-tank directors – all ignoring that underneath the management speak and spreadsheet solutions they too know glimpses of the chthonic realm. Yet there is something altogether more desperate about you. There's your age, and the regrets you harbour. You are not loud, bold or beautiful. You do not wear designer glasses or read style magazines. You whisper past us unnoticed in tan trousers, carrying briefcases, wearing overcoats. You are faceless and legion – one of the fifty-something, middle-class, white British males without rhythm who determine public policy and you, Simon, are its prototype. Yet still, underneath this bland exterior lurks the ravening beast of lascivious need. *The wild dog shall flesh his tooth in every innocent.*

You are the product of a faded England, educated in the old way, with the old disciplines that worked so well. You learned then what today so few can master – the ability to delay gratification. And you have been delaying for a very long time, subsuming your desires into regulating and controlling everything you could get your little hands on. Fixing things that weren't broken, legislating against spontaneity, siphoning the vibrancy out of our natural, ad-hoc rhythm and imposing petty rules. Charlesworth, you mealy-mouthed traitor, I will release you into the primal playground of your ancestors and teach you that all men are not born equal.

You operate in a stupor of your own arrogance, not bothering to register even what season it is. The irony is, you have the same urgency of seminal fluid rioting in your testes as your Palaeolithic forebears yet you persist in denying it with your suits and copies of *Marketing Week* and Sudoku challenges. Government man, I will take you back to your body. Back to nature. Certain organs perform certain functions. It's no grounds for indignation or disgust, but rather pleasure – a means of accessing a higher level of consciousness. I will make you crumble into crisis. I will turn your thoughts to the parallel states of degradation and ecstasy that form the extremes of human experience, and you will know both states with humility. All you grey men – all looking for power in the wrong places, not knowing what you have at your core; what we all have. The path to joy recognises no material status. The ecstasy of orgasm is the elevator, the everyday religious experience. The serpent can uncoil. *Kundalini Shakti* can awake at any time from slumber to become King Cobra, up and hissing.

It thrills me to know the details of our extraordinary evening together will stay locked in the pores of your skin. Your embarrassment will be closely guarded and I know it will have rocked you to your core. I can be sure you won't phone your cronies and brag about what happened to you. You didn't feel the necessity to record me undressed on your camera phone, to later show your colleagues in the Commons bar the tart you picked up last night. It wouldn't cross your mind to behave so deplorably. You see, for all your former left-wing ideology, you have still hung on to your manners – values instilled in you by the systems you sought to eradicate. It doesn't take much to get you dropping to your knees and showing deference to your superiors. You like it really. It's good for you. People and countries need boundaries. Take them away and we get the very opposite of utopia – a universal sense of entitlement regardless of circumstance. They never wanted equality for their fellow men, those ravening hordes you sought to liberate ... they wanted Prada and plasma TVs. There is no better way to give you a reminder of the basic principles of human nature than through the thwarting of your own desires. I relish your re-education so completely that the very thought of it sets me atremble.

I sit in the living room curled up in my dressing gown, drinking coffee and listening to Radio 4, thinking about your debauching. I run through a variety of scenarios and humiliations I'd like to bestow upon you, smiling at their ingenuity, imagining the turbulence you will feel. The glee of it all has me quite exhausted, and I return to bed for a couple of hours' more sleep before surfacing around eleven, ready to make a start on the catalogue I have been commissioned to design by Curzon Antiques of Mayfair.

Your grey, narrow mind probably thinks I am dependent on dominating men for money, but again you would be wrong. I trade as a graphic designer. It's true I accept gifts now and then but I do not charge for my skills. It is the love of harrowing the hearts of weak-willed servants like you that drives me to these deeds. I need no other incentive than my desire to exercise a superior discipline by physical means. Every stripe on your backside will be matched by a shrill howl of indignation at your predicament. This, and the inescapable admission of your deserving such savage remonstration for your lily-livered ways. Once you come to know the benefits of confession and admonishment, you may even find renewed vigour and verve in your life. Let's face it, things have been somewhat drab for some time, haven't they? Your lifestyle is not exactly a dazzling kaleido-scope of colourful experience. But that's all set to change now Ms Caine has arrived.

Curzon's catalogue plans lie on my desk. Their rarified world of Ming and lacquer is getting an overhaul, shak-ing off its fusty image and aiming for a new clientele. I have farmed out the photography to my friend Gareth – the subject matter something of a change from the usual rough trade he scrutinises through his lens. Trans-lating the whole thing into French at the same time nicely trebles my fee and keeps my design skills pressed into service. My fluency in three languages already puts me at an advantage working for the international art scene and, being realistic, the sight of me making an entrance in one of my business suits clinched the deal. I do play the top-drawer corporate face so well. I was dressed for this role yesterday, when we met. I'd been to a production meeting at Curzon's London HQ. That's why I'd looked so smart, seduced you so easily.

I walk through contrasting worlds. In the morning I can be taking tea with fine art auctioneers. In the evening I may be mingling with mistresses, dominants, fetish photographers and the acolytes who justify their existence. And at the weekends I can be found in the woodlands of old England, my heart singing under the oak. For only nature can bewitch me and bring me to peace, stimulate my imagination and rejuvenate my heart. Only in nature can I hear the song of something else.

I love the collision of art, eroticism and aesthetics. But then, so did Dad. To him, art was his way of getting in touch with the elemental, the metaphysical. His spirit resonates around me – his art collection, his passion for anthropology, his subversive humour. He never stopped collecting. In between his dark periods he accumulated friends in high places and wowed them all. Framed photos of him are all around this flat: in the hallway, opposite the Bacons, Dad with Princess Margaret, Lichfield and Peter Sellers; in the bathroom, Dad with Brando and James Caan; in the kitchen, Dad with Kubrick.

Dad lived the life he wanted, contributed some of the best set designs known to 70s cinema and he genuinely loved me. The fact he loved his wanton lifestyle more and sent me packing to a Swiss convent when Mum died is something I didn't accept with good grace at the time, but all great artists have their addictions. That he made it to the age of 66 was an achievement. I blame the cocaine he was still taking in the weeks before his heart gave out; he'd never given up the partying, the gallery openings. I haven't changed much in the flat over the two years since he died. His collection is still pretty much where he left it – ethnic art from Oceania and silk screen prints by his old mates from the Slade who went on to be famous. There's even a Hockney here that I could fall back on if times got really tough. You turned your nose up at it, and I loathed you for displaying your ignorance. I can see there's going to be a lot of skin tarnished before you can even hope to understand the creative fire of artistic genius. Have you ever burned with a wild creativity, Simon Charlesworth? Felt the molten heat of talent running through your veins? You think you're important, with your Cabinet position and your house near the south coast, but the vultures are still your future. Being a jumped-up bureaucrat in a suit doesn't grant you eternal life, my honourable friend. You are just one of the millions whose puny little passions are born from a common spring. Life is so much more fun when desire bursts forth from the well of the marvellous in pursuit of the blissful, do you not think?

I hold up a mirror to my subjects and show them what they really are whereas you and your stinking government go to every effort to hide its intentions. Do you think we really believe your fine-spun horse puckey? Let me tell you, your lexicon of fudge and lies will be a flimsy defence against the coming apocalypse, when the whole house of cards comes fluttering down and people like me will head for the woods with a husky and a rifle.

I work until 2 p.m., then reread my latest email from Ian Baum.

> Hey, KK Caine. How's my favourite phallic woman? Your desire to own the penis is an unnatural, infantile pleasure that is bound to result in trauma if you don't learn to accept your own physiology. The vagina is inferior to the penis – and you cannot own the penis. We'll go over this aberrant behaviour on Friday.
> Dr Baum

It's time to take the tube to Belsize Park for my weekly assignation with the man formerly known as my shrink. As usual, I dress as conventionally as possible – a world away from the army-booted and dreadlocked 25-year-old he first analysed back in 1991. I take on the appearance of a forty-year-old woman who is indistinguishable from the countless middle-class female neurotics who inhabit the North London baby belt. To look at me in my Phase Eight dress and Emma Hope shoes you would guess me to be a mother, a well-educated wife, a docile consumer, whose head swirls with the aspirational distractions of *World of Interiors* and *The Moro Cookbook*. My accessories are designer favourites and my demeanour perfectly realised – slightly smug with a smattering of status anxiety. You've seen me a thousand times, waiting at the school gates for little Jocasta and Ruben, or scouring the deli at Waitrose. You think you know me but you really don't. You might see me stepping into the analyst's practice in that leafy NW3 address to weepily address what you assume is my loneliness, and it makes you feel better about yourself for being stable. But the joke's on you. I step into his office to confirm my status as a Sadeian woman and feed his insatiable need for deviancy.

As usual, he greets me with the underplayed shaking of my hand, as if we were meeting for the first time. There is no need to make small talk. We're not lovers that fall upon each other within seconds, grappling with bra straps and shirt buttons like they do in movies. We like to drag out the longing, so we relish formalities, torturing ourselves with games of let's pretend. Let's pretend we're authority figures, bourgeois neurotics, juvenile delinquent and welfare officer, arresting officer with clipboard and handcuffs, personality sex offender and victim turned accomplice. We are aroused by language over touch. This isn't a skin-on-skin affair and I don't think we've even seen each other naked. This is not about bodies.

I settle into his room. I love this room, this garden flat, with its French windows and small leafy courtyard. Around the walls on neat shelves is a collection of works relevant to his profession, which I too have devoured: the Penguin Freuds, the Lacanian reader, the Kristevas and other feminist theorists. There are large illustrated books on subversive art, biographies and extremist political theory. Ian sits as always in his black leather chair, smiling and swivelling gently while I make myself comfortable on his two-seater sofa. It's not the one on which he first laid hands on me, but it's in the same place. I am bursting to tell him what has happened and he is expectant with the need of me. I don't give him your name, but I tell him your profession and I spare no details of the sex. It's the telling I love, especially when I'm in character. Sometimes I think everything I do is done just to entertain Ian Baum. I'm still trapped in the transference that began fifteen years ago because I've never met anyone else who can match his sexual intelligence. Pleasing him pleases me; allows me to play without having to take the lead. I am strong enough to enjoy parodying myself, to indulge our mutual nihilistic humour. No one and nothing is sacred.

I owe him everything I am. He taught me so much. I was a wreck when he found me and he set me on a new direction, introducing me to the dark masters of philosophy. I'd spent twelve years in a Catholic girls' school where micro hierarchies and obsessive rituals prevailed. I'd been on the receiving end of the martinet at the hands of nuns and prefects. I had known the cavernous dread of waiting dry-mouthed with fear outside the punishment room. Had been dragged to the summit of agony for transgressing some ridiculous rule. It was only after my long built-up indignation came out that I was able to find my inner sadist – the convent girl's revenge. At school I had always been put upon. After Ian had his hands on me I could shine as a woman of magnificent grace and cruelty and have dominion over men. I was Dr Baum's Juliette, his Simone, his Ming the Merciless's daughter. It naturally fell into place. I'd been awoken to what was different in me and, once I realised the power I held, I was saved from the void of self-destruction.

While my former classmates went on to marry diplomats and spawn bratty children, I bypassed the maternal instinct to become an amoral bitch goddess with a head full of de Sade and Deleuze. I've learned subterfuge, cunning and a poker face. I ditched my anti-fashion statement and learnt how to blend into any environment. I can wreak havoc more masterfully if you don't see me coming.

Psycho-the-rapist. Break up the word and you've got Ian Baum. Now I'm the dirty little delinquent that gets it all over her. Gets his cock shoved in her face and is made to suck it while being interfered with. The show-off slut to his sexually predatory cop or social worker. And she'll shut up about it and tell no one if she knows what's good for her otherwise she'll be back in the behavioural unit. All it will take is one referral from him, especially as she's got previous. So she says the things he needs to hear. And because 'she' is an inverted younger version of me I never have to act too hard. I just have to remember being stuck in that bloody convent halfway up a mountain going mad for something to happen. Or being on remand for arson and criminal damage the day Ian Baum first came to assess me and, within two minutes of meeting, both knowing our relationship would never be professional.

He wants to know what I was wearing when I snared you; how you'd begged for my attentions and also when I would see you again. That I'd withheld the treasure, allowing you only the foot and not the cunt – the buggery and not the intercourse – brings him to breathless excitement and hilarity. He finds your suffering priceless, particularly that I denied you pleasure through conventional means. What you had been disallowed he prepares to take and, as always, with a force that is genuine but reliant on my acted resistance.

He leaves his chair and presses me up against the back of the sofa, arms pinned down by his strong hands. His penis is already hard in his trousers, his breath hot against my neck. Once aroused he has to act instantly, he cannot delay gratification. It's his weakness. No one is immune – not even the analyst. He whispers obscenities in my ear in what he imagines is your voice. He is only a couple of years younger than you, and he makes a very good job of playing the 53-year-old MP. He is rough, though, and I get my knickers ripped off as he rubs my sex with his fingers, almost to my crisis, before he pulls me down onto the floor, hurriedly disposes of his trousers, footwear and nondescript jumper, and climbs on top of me. He makes himself so tight against me; my legs are together, inside rather than outside his, so I get the friction I need to orgasm without the use of my hands. The sensation is addictive. Although my role in this game goes against the sexuality I'm driven by – which is the need to dominate – I always come hard at this outrage, to the point of almost passing out. I lose myself and become Ian Baum. I too become psycho-the-rapist, complicit in the violation of the unfortunate subject, who should be me but is really nobody.

Oh, the delight in abjection! I effectively disappear, able to mingle my desire within his and surrender to the sweet feeling of shattering degradation. I am not submissive, not even flesh. I become only the desire, the will to power, the sensation itself. I relinquish all need to make any effort bar channelling the voice of the abject. What I wish to do to men of power, he wishes to visit upon women of privilege – the women who resemble his ex-wife. That's why I dress so straight for him – feminine and conventional, as if from the Boden catalogue. He does the physical deed for both of us. It's mutual therapy. Both of us violating bourgeois convention – ignoring medical professionalism; annihilating social protocol.

And in this evaporation I am brought back to my

body through the gathering fires of orgasm. As I lie there on his floor, coming to the point of meltdown, I toy with the idea of driving you to the red mist of losing control – whether with me or someone else. I do not need the extra push but the thought brings me to a moment of triumph such that I fill the room with unintelligible cries as Baum is unstoppable on his way to the blissful event.

We play music and read books for a couple of hours before going out for dinner – very much as equals. He takes me to an old-style Italian behind Hampstead tube station where we do our proper talking of the week snugly tucked into a booth.

'So, of course this fucker is going to want to see you again, isn't he?' he asks, digging in to the olives.

'Can't say. He'll have had a bit of a shock. God knows what he must be thinking. He'll be on his way home now, having to act as normal . . . have a normal domestic time of it over the weekend.'

'He'll be thinking it was the luckiest day of his life! Does he live in London?'

'No,' I say. 'But why do you want to know?'

Ian throws his hands up and says, 'No reason. Just getting an idea of him.'

'He's married,' I say, not giving much away, 'as are most MPs. The good people of Britain don't like a fairy politician, as we know.'

'So . . . Cabinet, back bencher or opposition?'

'I'm not saying,' I insist.

Ian is nosy – it's his nature, and his job. We're alike in that way, both relishing the details of what lies under the stultifying conventions of upper middle-class marriages, but I need to be careful and keep him at arm's length on this one. Once your identity is out of the bag, it's no longer my secret, and this time I don't feel like sharing. I steer the topic of conversation to how status anxiety plays out its tragedy in the neuroses of middle-class women. This is where Ian's old wounds get reopened.

Baum was married with two young children when we first met. They're now at university and still costing him a fortune. I'd idolised him back then and wanted us to be a couple, but of course it couldn't happen. I played a part for him then as I do today. I was the fantasy figure from his teenage years made flesh – his Patty Hearst, his Squeaky Fromme, his little Ulrika Meinhof who could wage revolutionary war with her cunt. I loved the games but, with the romantic delusions of youth, I'd convinced myself there was going to be more. But there was no way Baum was leaving his academic author wife for a 25-year-old Nietzsche-spouting hellcat. He wouldn't even dream of taking me to a North London dinner party. But his arrogance came back to bite him; his wife left him five years ago for a millionaire gynae-cologist and he is forever looking for ways to turn back the clock. To recapture the way things were between us in the early days.

I come back to the concept of the animal in man: just because someone gets a ring on their finger or a suit on their back doesn't mean they've excised the primal forces, the need for cruelty, the eternal unconscious wish to defile the sacred, the will to fail. Ian, like most men, thinks the human superior because he has language. This is where we part company. I'm the pagan to his rationalist. This debate goes on, through the bread and olives and into the pasta. He keeps referring back to you, and a couple of times I'm nearly caught out, almost casually answering a question about where you live, but realising it's a trick the second before I speak. I deflect his interest to the issue of your foot fetishism, which provokes a little more animated conversation. We debate Lacan's theory of lack, and how high heels represent the female 'penis'.

This is the conversation I love and cannot have with anyone else. Ian explains so succinctly all the raging elements of dissatisfaction and hypocrisy in modern life that I find myself transfixed by his intelligence. Yet even he cannot transcend selfishness and anxiety. It is the great sadness and disappointment of our bizarre liaison. As Ian continues to speak of taboos and transgressions, I drift into wanting to assume majesty over you again – you the novelty, the experiment. I must put my feet on you once more. Take you to somewhere you've never been. From that chance meeting in Victoria station I have set in motion a journey to somewhere exclusive: your own psyche, until now unexamined and uncharted territory. Exotic travel for the brave, wouldn't you say? This year, Charlesworth, you may browse through your *Guardian* travel supplement and consider Mauritius, Uruguay or Iceland for a little adventure, but I am going to launch you into the bloody stratosphere as far as 'foreign' goes. I ponder how far I might be able to take the outrages and Ian reckons I can pretty much get away with anything while I am denying you what you want – power over my sex.

'Don't forget what you have,' he says. 'And what you represent. He has to be contrite in your presence because he sees you as somehow pure, being true to your beliefs, while he's a lying sycophant, toadying around his party leader. He's vulnerable. He's looking everywhere for ways to please, to get praise from superiors. And you are his superior, intellectually. Making that dynamic sexual is blowing his mind. What he'll want from you most of all is intimacy. He's crying out for it because he's obviously not getting it at home. You have seen right through his charade. You know he's vulnerable. You're returning him to the anal phase, then indulging the Oedipal phase by scolding him and rewarding him. He cannot hide himself from you as he hides it from his wife. There's your power.'

I feel high with it all. It is unlikely you will ever admit to wanting to place yourself under my sexual control, yet you cannot know the exquisite moments of the power exchange by yourself. You need to hand the responsibility for your orgasm over to me. You would think it contemptuous in another man, that he should go crying for permission to explore his abjection, to not be self-reliant. Yet how would a man of your means find such an outlet for himself? Only by reckless, creative and bizarre masturbatory practices, surely. I think of the trauma you will be undergoing; the foundations of everything you've ever thought about sex being so radically turned on its head. Yet it's nice, isn't it, Charlesworth, to feel so urgent for once? You know you cannot keep suppressing the Great Need for much longer.

'So, I hope to see some of this recorded,' says Ian, looking at me with raised eyebrows and the implication that this is more a matter of when than if.

I immediately feel a rush of irritation. Like I can't do anything without paying a material tribute to him for the permission. He has cultivated huge issues of entitlement when it comes to me. I keep forgetting that these days he has the habit of turning fun to obsession. He's become an avid collector of home-made porn. He especially likes to see footage of people debasing themselves and being debased – male or female, he doesn't mind. We have watched it together: the panty poopers, asphyxiants and animal lovers. Not for arousal but for the eternal fascination with aberrant behaviour. Ian has always said, 'If you can imagine it, someone's doing it.' He's right. And the secret sordid obsessions of ordinary people are the most fascinating of all. But Ian wants control over my secrets, and I feel less and less inclined to give them to him as the months roll by. It's been my weakness – the need to hand over the trophies of battle to my commander. In this, I'm like you, Charlesworth. I too crave praise from the one who blasted open those temple doors.

'Well, I *would* film it,' I say, being evasive, 'but you would recognise him. It's part of my promise to not reveal his identity, not even to you. Client confidentiality and all that.'

'Like I'm going to do anything,' he says. 'Who do you think I'm going to tell? How many secrets do you think I have? Thousands. My clients have admitted all kinds of things to me – and it's stayed with me.'

'Yes, but this guy is not one of your clients. And as far as I know, none of your clients have been in public office.'

'All the more reason why you should tell me.' Baum is chancing his arm.

'I can't.'

'They're all corrupt ... politicians,' he begins. 'They think they can get away with everything. It's one law for them and another for the rest of us. They use our taxes to pay for all kinds of shit. Listen, you can get close to this guy and find out what else is a cover-up. If he's cheating on his wife, there'll be other secrets too.'

'It depends what you classify as cheating. In his eyes, I doubt whether being drugged and buggered would have been his adulterous sex of choice. He's a desperate man. He's fragile. And I'm *not* revealing his identity, so please stop fishing for it.'

Ian shrugs in a manner that implies I'm the one being unreasonable, but the truth is he can't bear me withholding details. He wants to get his psychoanalytic mind wrapped around your desperation, hear more details of your need for me; have me lead you down a path of degradation that will satisfy his need for vicarious, vicious amusements. But I want this one all to myself. I've been stupid. Revealing your status is a red rag to Ian Baum and, for all my conviction that you will become addicted to the thrill of me, I have no real way of knowing whether I will see you again. You have my card and my mobile number. I will have to wait for it to burn a hole in your pocket.

We are tucking into our pasta when he asks me if I would like to go on holiday with him at Christmas – a time of year we both detest. He's brought this up a few times and I've always skirted the issue. Since his divorce he wants someone to accompany him on those city breaks he loves so much. It's a nice idea in principle, but I know it would ruin what we have. I couldn't bear to have the inevitable mundanity of holiday preparation and his stilted attempts at the local language intrude upon our extraordinary relationship. I fear I would go off him. I would be too judgmental of what he wore, of walking down some leafy boulevard for dinner with a man shorter than I am and shabbily dressed. I need him to be just who he is and continue our fun just as it is, secreted in London's leafy, anonymous, suburban streets. But I sense an anxiety of loneliness encroaching upon him. He has drunk a whole bottle of wine to my two glasses.

I've made the usual suggestions about meeting women online but he isn't interested. It's me he wants. Now I'm a woman of independent means and to all intents and purposes a respectable citizen, I've become desirable. The thing is, I'll never be in love him with again and, for all his marvellous intellectual wit, I wouldn't want to wake up with him. I don't want to hear him snore or watch his underpants drying on the radiator. I rarely sleep with the people I have sex with and no one has my heart. It's just the way I am.

3 In Every Dream Home a Heartache

I left your apartment block at 8 a.m. and was back in my constituency just after eleven. If running surgery after having slept only two hours was purgatory, it was nothing compared to the numbing realisation that Lorna's brother Robert and his wife Sarah and the kids were coming over for dinner that evening. I was beat, a shadow of myself. After getting through a day of surgery issues, all I wanted to do was curl up and sleep the whole weekend. The last of my energy had gone into a meeting about car boot sale licences that dragged on until half past four. And for my sins I then had to find a reserve supply of stamina for my in-laws.

I've gone through a riot of concerns since Thursday and have barely been conscious of what I'm doing. I have tried to put the whole thing behind me as a lapse of reason – one mad night that won't be repeated, that saw me vulnerable, stupid even. I've castigated myself for being so foolish, although of course I would never have consented had I not been slipped that Mickey Finn. I was coerced. And into anal sex, no less! I should have been furious with you about that. After I'd sobered up, I'd expressed to you my deep abhorrence of drugs and the people who sell them, yet for a reason I cannot fathom I couldn't bring myself to cause a scene about it. I'd never in a million years have sought out class A drugs – or anal sex, for that matter – but the circumstances were unusual to say the least and, I have to admit, neither of these unique experiences was altogether unpleasant. I am almost proud of myself. But no one must ever know. Lorna would divorce me without question and I know she wouldn't hesitate to share the details with Sarah.

Initially I told myself that the routine of work on Monday would erase any remaining traces of the incident. I would go back to the pressing business at the House. However, when I arrived home and was faced with the numbing routine of domestic familiarity, Thursday's events made everything more starkly apparent. It wasn't as easy to put them out of mind as I had thought. Something had changed. The smell of wood polish, washing and one of Lorna's signature marinades greeted me in the hall and I felt a tide of contradictions welling up: I like this, it's comforting; I loathe this, it's stifling. I was spent and, embarrassingly, my anus was sore. Yet to my shame and surprise it smarted almost pleasurably, similar to the aches I've enjoyed as medals of exertion earned at the gym.

How could I think about anything else but you and what had happened? I was foolish to even think my mind would blot it out so easily. I bathed for an hour, soaking my pale, middle-aged body in the steaming water to rid myself of any physical traces of the deed, but it didn't stop me feeling slightly wretched kissing sixteen-year-old Amy and eleven-year-old Josh as they turned up with Sarah and Robert. Here's Uncle Simon the sodomite, the pervert, the drug abuser. But the great balm of the guilty is that no one can tell what you have done or are thinking merely by looking. The tendency of my class is to think the best of one's relatives. Robert didn't suddenly down cutlery and exclaim over the starters: 'Christ, what the bloody hell have you had up your arse?' There was no pillory set up for me after pudding, and Sarah didn't huddle her children close to her and yell at me not to come near them.

Most comforting is that Lorna doesn't seem to suspect anything, and for that I'm grateful. I couldn't have faced a scene – not in the state I arrived home in. As always she'd been too wrapped up in her own self-imposed commitments: her mother, her job, the shopping. It helped that I had managed to call her on Thursday night about 10 p.m. after the effects of that drug had worn off. Told her I was staying in the London flat, that it had been a late one at the department, that I couldn't face the commute. It's a story she hears with regularity, although I always make it home on Thursdays for surgery on Fridays so I was expecting an even frostier shoulder than usual. But, busy in our large kitchen, she barely had a word to say. In my pathetic struggle to cover up my misdeeds I overcompensated, offering to help with dinner preparation – something I never do. I stood there gormless, looking at the workings of the solid Bakelite-brown timepiece that hangs from stout chains attached to the kitchen ceiling. It's a talking piece, that clock. Everyone who comes into this kitchen for the first time mentions it. It was due to be thrown into a skip before Lorna rescued it from the postmistress when the local post office closed down. God, wasn't I just the villain of the piece over that issue! If I've learned one thing in politics, it's that people never appreciate progress.

Lorna told me I looked awful, although she didn't offer any physical comfort, of course. All dinner preparations had been taken care of. The bream was braising in the Aga with the roast veg. The table was already laid. The only thing left to do was open the wine. I mumbled my dismay at no longer having the stamina for those late-night votes and was ushered out of the kitchen and upstairs to bathe and change. When Lorna is entertaining, one does well by staying out of the way. I trudged upstairs with a sense of impending doom knowing that, once I emerged and came back down, it would have to be as a cheery host.

I soaked for as long as I could, idly toying with myself and drifting into reveries of futures possible and regrets of pasts absolute. For the first time since I can remember, I had new sexual memories. I replayed everything I could recall from the previous night: the elation on leaving the bar with you, the shock of your apartment and its curious décor, the drug taking effect on my body, you quoting from *The Rubáiyát of Omar Kayyám*, and the scandalous acts you performed on me. How does a woman become interested in such outlandish behaviour, if it's not for money? Being in the House, one hears whispers about other MPs' sexual predilections but I've always found such gossip facile. This sort of activity is for perverts and pitiful lonely bastards. Yet through no searching or effort on my part I have come into contact with what I suppose is a dominatrix. You must be known to some of the shadow Cabinet. Not least because it's likely to have been a set-up, although you swore it wasn't. No money has changed hands. To be honest, I'm confused.

The thought of being outed as a sexual freak makes me feel ill. It would ruin everything, everything, and it would be a lie. I don't know what went on last night but I'm sure as hell not about to repeat it. Maybe my opposite number in the House is up to mischief. I've seen his scrubbed Etonian face sneering at me and I wouldn't put it past him to pull a stunt like this. That's the trouble with our lot – indulgences are regarded as unseemly, yet the opposition is famous for them, comfortable with them, even. Sexual tittle-tattle is not part of our history. It's not what brings down our governments. So we've cultivated an almost puritan ethic to disassociate ourselves from the opposition.

I matured under the political rhetoric of the early 80s,

when sex was discussed only in terms of rights; where earnest young women in stripy tights and cardigans stood on picket lines pretending they didn't want a good seeing-to from the best-looking of the striking miners. And earnest young politicians like me trying to make a name for themselves couldn't hold a candle of credibility to the sweat-soaked brawn of Orgreave. When I think back to those times I'm embarrassed for myself. I allowed my ears to ring with the slogans of militant feminism. The women had the moral high ground and I was terrified of being thought chauvinist. I'd have been shouted down and excommunicated from the party if I expressed the way I really felt. I missed out. A working-class bloke could have got away with it but I was supposed to know better, be 'above all that'. But I've missed 'all that', haven't I? Lorna has been my only long-lasting relationship. And I have to admit, at this rather late juncture in my life, that I want to make up for lost time.

Maybe you could be the answer. You're attractive, composed, sophisticated. I tried to imagine what people might make up your circles and I felt a stab of curiosity and apprehension. How would I converse with them? Who might they be? Crazy artists? London's trendy set? Of course, I need to be assured you are discreet, because I ache to get at you properly. Have real sex with you. Surely you don't just wear those contraptions and fuck men in the arse, do you? I mean, it was all right at the time, and it's something I'm strangely glad to have experienced, but surely that was a one-off. It's been a long time since any female has shown interest in me sexually. Maybe you misunderstood what I was expecting. Things I wouldn't have dared to ask for were just done to me without a thought as to whether I'd like them or not. Maybe that's what you thought I'd want, because all the MPs you've dealt with have wanted that.

I wonder who they might be. Surely you must know people I know? I need to find out. Most of all I need to make sure I'm not about to see myself in a Sunday tabloid. You assured me that was a ridiculous suggestion but surely you can see my point?

I told you we could maybe see each other again. I admit I'd like to have the chance to tell you what I want, and to speak to you properly. I have your card. Even the thought of that is exciting. Yes, an affair is what I could use. Not kinky stuff, just an affair. Some wining and dining and a few extras. I don't think I want to leave Lorna; she's an ideal wife in so many ways. I just want someone I can explore this . . . other side with.

At the possibility of our spending another night together, I realised I had come to full erection. So the doorbell ringing sent a cold shock to my system. It was time to perform – sacrifice an evening that could have been spent refreshing myself for one of dead time in conversation with relatives. I don't mind Sarah, she's always perfectly charming, but Robert really is the end, wittering on about his DIY and his cars like some over-grown schoolboy. He's all doughy, he's got a head like an overblown football and he makes me nervous. He moves with alarming ill co-ordination: an arm flung suddenly to the top of the bookshelf; a leg kicked out under the table. He's a bumbling lunk who has never had to worry about anything because his mother – my mother-in-law – has mollycoddled him from birth and still dotes on him. If I were Lorna I'd have felt usurped by this cuckoo to the point of homicidal rage, but the worst Lorna has ever said is that he had it easy, or that 'Mum always wanted boys'.

Over dinner, at the large dining table in the through lounge, my mind kept drifting. I'd not been paying attention to the latest installment on Robert's garden hose saga and Lorna gave me a sharp nudge to at least engage with him as the same species. She's very particular about dinner party discourse, is Lorna. God forbid I should be anything other than avuncular with a bream on my plate and my brother-in-law in my face. 'A hundred foot it says on the box, but do you think I can stretch it the length of the garden?' Frankly, Robert, I couldn't raise the required interest if my life depended on it. I've never been one for B&Q antics. We usually get a bloke in to deal with that stuff. I'm helping to run the bloody country, for Christ's sake.

The women, as always, were perpetual in their conversation, not silent for longer than ten seconds throughout the dinner, comparing respective farmer's markets, waistlines and schools. Both Lorna and Sarah tried to get me to join in. Yes, the organic chutney was fucking wonderful. No, I'm not keen on trust schools. That had Robert out of his pram, barking on about the wonderful funding that some of the actively Christian schools were receiving. For crying out loud, he was even going on about how they were instilling family values.

He was spouting opinionated drivel, as usual. We operate a no-politics rule at home for obvious reasons and Lorna stepped in to quash it by busying about with the serving of pudding, complete with some ubiquitous declaration about it being naughty and highly calorific. After the women had exhausted the disingenuous mutual self-loathing that always seems to accompany dessert, they switched to discussing their book clubs. I momentarily thought of fetching my new copy of *The Story of the Eye* from upstairs and contributing to the conversation. The sense of how inappropriate that would be, especially in front of Amy and Josh, raised my temperature in a flash. Instead I forced some chat about the forthcoming Grand Slam with Robert, plus how his triathlon training was going, which took up all of five minutes.

He soon gave up getting any animated interest out of me and instead took to playing Sarah's fool, as he often does when he bores of adult discourse. It's as if he may be asked something too grown-up and scary and won't be able to answer; that his cover will be blown and the truth will be out – that he's never really left Mummy's skirts. That he doesn't actually have an adult opinion and he's substituted one domestic Madonna who mopped up his mess for another. He's still big bouncing baby Robert, except now he gets excited about performance cars, the latest gadgets and rugby. He was making puppy dog eyes at Sarah because he'd bolted down his chocolate pudding and was expecting some of hers. He even began pawing at her and keening, presuming this infantile display was endearing. His own son Josh has far more dignity, and would never make such a spectacle of himself, although he was at the stage of conversing in monosyllables with his attention focused solely on his PSP.

I wanted to see Sarah push Robert's bloated balding head off her shoulder and slap his face for insolence. See his petulance vanquished. But then I remembered in bold relief my own pitiless self thrown half-naked on your rug, sobbing, with my arse on fire, and I stopped short of showing my usual disdain for his fawning antics and managed a weak smile. Was I really as bad as him, though? Like some kind of performing pet or overgrown baby? I cogitated on what it means to be a man these days, now we are no longer required for grunt duty.

My existential quest was thrown into discomfort as I felt a pair of eyes on me. Of the entire company present, Amy unnerved me the most. She was regarding me with curiosity, sensing something strange about my actions, noticing me deep in thought. Did she know something? Every time my eyes flashed to hers, I felt myself filling with guilt, attempting some action that would cover up my crushing self-awareness – pouring more wine or clearing the plates. I've never been comfortable with children, and especially not teenagers. They're far from gullible. Moreover, they seem to know the truth about everything, can spot when adults are lying and won't accept anything less than transparency. They hold all the cards, and they own the future, the young bastards. They've staked their claim on territory that will very soon be falling from my grasp, reminding me that time is running out.

Yet it wasn't her youth that discomforted me as much as her probing stare. For a moment it reminded me of yours as you'd watched me shed my clothes and inhibitions. Amy, like you, sensed my vulnerability, knowing that I wasn't Uncle Simon the Cabinet minister, but ageing Simon Charlesworth, the fraudulent weasel who was about to sacrifice his dignity for the taste of some exotic other reality – one that was a million miles from a suburban middle-class dinner. There was no point being defensive. Even if she had an inkling I was playing away, deceiving her Aunt Lorna, she would be entertained by the intrigue, I'm sure. She's a bright girl. A girl who will one day inhabit a truly exotic world, I don't doubt, with her flair for fashion design. At this moment in our lives, curious though it is, we have parallel ambitions – we both yearn to escape our routine and know something of the wild life.

She caught my gaze and silently sought to share her opinion. She looked at her step-father making an idiot of himself, raised her eyes to the ceiling in desperation of his weakness, then looked straight back at me with an imperious smile. Sarah's daughter from her previous marriage, she had inherited all of Sarah's good looks and acquired none of Robert's gaucherie. I mirrored her action, unseen by anyone else, happy to fuel her disdain.

A gesture of exasperation in the face of a relative's antics can be brought about by endearment, but not in this instance. I could detect traces of actual loathing for her step-father. There was some real venom there. Since Thursday I have been awoken to the cruel beauty in woman. And, appalling although it is to admit, for a few seconds I allowed myself to imagine being bared before her, under the scrutiny of her heavily made-up eyes and under the crush of her young thighs. Is it possible to be outraged by one's own thoughts? I felt wickedly amused by the inappropriate thought of Amy doing to me what you had done the night before.

Lorna and Sarah moved to the sofa and continued chatting about exercise and diets, as usual. Robert blundered in where he could and fussed about making coffee, something I usually take charge of. Instead, I took myself to that exotic place, sharing with Amy a moment of exquisite conspiracy and allowing myself the indulgence of thinking the unthinkable.

Later, in bed, I wanted to fuck, but Lorna was pleading fatigue. I took her rejection as an insult. It's not about how busy one's day has been; desire will break through no matter how tired you are if the need is there. And my need has suddenly become so urgent. I pestered her slightly and tried persuasion, running my hands up and down her legs and playing with her hair. I even thought about pulling the puppy dog trick that seemed to work for Robert but dismissed it immediately. Still I got nowhere. I called her a corpse and that caused a fractious exchange. So we 'had words' instead of having sex. I went to turn off the side light, but insult to injury was to follow when Lorna insisted it stay on so she could read her novel. I turned away from her in a mild rage and seethed with the abject loneliness of a man denied physical contact with the woman who shares his bed.

My irritation battled with my desire for long enough to effect exhaustion. I eventually fell into the sleep of the dead, preceded by memories of your feet in my back. It's been a long time since I've gone to sleep with a hard-on.

It's Saturday afternoon and I have locked myself in the bathroom to touch myself and think about you. Lorna was up by the time I awoke so I lay there in a stew wondering whether or not to call you. I should, of course, consign it to experience, to put all my energies into my job, not least my constituency. The timetable for the Community Services' Empowerment Project has to be presented to the council meeting in three weeks' time. I've got the private finance in the bag, but I need to meet the managers of each of the borough's social services departments before we can move forwards. I've got to sound enthusiastic about the targets. Upstairs want to see representation from disabled and ethnic groups, but getting that lot involved at any level is an uphill struggle. I suppose that'll mean another fifty thousand quid will be spent on marketing materials – leaflets showing the beaming faces of happy diversity. Not only this, but there's the ongoing feud over the ring road. The new development out to the east of the borough is not going as smoothly as I'd anticipated. Some old wood needs to be flattened and the tree-huggers are already up in arms. It's a thousand years old apparently. Well, it's had a good innings then, hasn't it? I'm sorting out a plan that'll bring jobs and services to an underdeveloped area. Still, it's all on hold while the protesters' lawyers root around for some old treaty of protection. I've already had a word in the right ear at the council's legal office. Make that piece of moribund legislation conveniently go missing, I told them, and it'll be bonuses all round.

But does this stuff have to fill my entire existence? Can't I have a little reward as a man, in my marriage, in my private life? Sometimes I think it would be easier to just see a prostitute. Year in, year out, I've been on sexual rationing with Lorna and I can't stand it much longer. I've exhausted myself with trying to predict her moods. Everything has to be absolutely fucking perfect before she'll get her knickers off. Come to think of it, I haven't seen her breasts for about six months. It's no good trying it on if there's a dinner party planned for the following week because her mind won't be on anything but meal plans. Tuesday nights are no good as the recycling van comes Wednesday morning and she has to think about whether she's washed the tin cans. Sometimes, it's as if she resents me even being in the house. I'm like some obstacle to her domestic perfection.

Oh Kirsten, just once more I want to feel your feet on me. I've never had a woman's feet on me before yet, since it happened in the early hours of Friday morning, I haven't been able to get the sensation out of my mind: that rasping contact of your stockings against my shaft; the sharp prod of your ankle boot on my balls. I've always liked women in high shoes, but how could I have told anyone about it? It would have been round the Commons in a matter of hours, and I couldn't have asked Lorna – there's nothing in her wardrobe that even comes near what I'd like. I know exactly what she would think if I told her of my penchant. It would be sympto-matic of a midlife crisis. But now I've had the feet of a beautiful woman on me it's like coming home. Coming home. That's a laugh. I come home to familiarity and boredom and Lorna not wanting it 'cos she's too tired and sensitive or is at a crucial moment in one of her bloody novels. Some Iranian woman is sobbing her heart out over her martyred brothers; the smell of the bakery in her home town has brought all the memories back.

No, it's not conducive to getting in the mood, is it, Lorna? So what am *I* supposed to do?

I tell you what I'm doing, and Lorna would have a fit if she could see. I've taken a pair of her tights and I've put my hand into where the foot should be. I'm pumping myself with a 15-denier fist and the feel of the nylon against the smooth head is exquisite and it's not going to take long. I've got a picture locked into my mind of your heels sinking into that carpet, that Italian leather so snug around your perfect feet. I want more. I want your heels in me, all over my body in sharp little points. I love the sound of heels on a smooth marble floor. It sounds like . . . Mistress. I would fall down and lick them if you would let me. I remember your scent and remember your touch and I picture you in a variety of tantalising footwear. In ankle boots, in knee-high boots, in classy pumps with an ankle strap, in lace-up thigh-high boots that take ten minutes to get off. I imagine these shoes being worn with different costumes – short baby-doll nighties, not that you'd ever wear something like that, but I like to dream.

Yes, that's it. You, in a tarty baby-doll nightie and high-heeled boots, walking around me, with your long dark hair unpinned and falling down your back. Your legs are long, muscled, tanned and bare and they could crush me if you got upset. You have not allowed me to touch myself until your say-so and I'm about ready to let you do anything if I'll be given my way eventually. I'm to be allowed to masturbate against your boots – against their curious but delicious fake snakeskin texture – and I'm so grateful that I'm sobbing with relief. You allow me to unzip my trousers and I take myself in hand. You watch me, fascinated, as I masturbate for you. I'm still fully dressed in my suit and it makes the subordination more humbling. Here I am in the uniform of my profession – the suit and tie – and even dressed for power I am feeble in your presence. Of course, my position aids this humiliation. I am then prostrate on the floor, crawling around your feet, licking the calves of your boots, my hands running all over them. I rub my penis against the leather and over the instep of your foot until I'm nearly there. Then you make me beg: 'Please, Miss K, please may I be allowed to come over your boots? I am nothing but a putrid servant who cannot control himself. I look up and see your face. You shine with knowledge, intelligence and something else. Something I've sought all my life to know intimately. Miss K, I am going to spurt it out all over you. Please let me do it.' And the thought of this vision is so intense that I can almost feel your touch, feel the leather.

I'm in a rapture. My cock is hard to bursting. All I know is that I have to have more of it. With the nylon-clad fist I work really hard, and with the other hand I rub my balls. My thighs are tightening, the sinews stretched. And with an almighty shudder it's upon me. To hell with the consequences! As I jet out into Lorna's tights I know my new-found love of these unusual pleasures is not going to stop there. And it may be the rush of blood to my head, pounding in my ears, but I'm sure I hear your voice, laughing.

Recovering from my exertions after a refreshing nap, I awake with a clear head and renewed attention to what happened on Thursday night. Lorna has gone out shopping; we passed each other on the landing as I emerged from the bathroom and we barely spoke two sentences to each other. I don't even care if she guessed what I'd been doing. I have to have an outlet for these feelings. They've always been there, although I've kept them locked away in a safe to which I've purposely lost the combination. You blew the doors off when you gave me that drug and now my secrets are flying about with the risk that others might see them.

I'm sitting in my study, looking out of the window, across the fields, thinking about everything but what I'm supposed to have my attention on. My anus has returned to normal and I wonder if I will want – or even crave – that sensation again. Somehow, repulsive though it is to admit it, I know already that I will. I have never known such a feeling. It was an invasion of fearful magnitude that provoked such intense release. This must be what the prostate gland is for, although I wouldn't want it from another man – that's the part of the idea which repulses me – but what you did was skilful rather than repugnant. I felt your bare breasts grazing my back and smelled your perfume as you were doing it. It was a wholly heterosexual experience, but also almost a religious one.

For your boldness I actually admire you, even though your lifestyle scares me. I feel as if I walked into a film set that night, that it was not me but some other character I witnessed writhing on your floor, allowing you to do what you did. Good grief, I would not have even had the courage to pick up a stranger in a bar, let alone take them home and unleash all that illegal, bizarre behaviour. A simple fuck would have done the job. But maybe that attitude is a symptom of what's been going wrong. Maybe other people's sex lives are a lot more interesting than my own. Is everybody doing this kinky stuff?

I get the feeling you wouldn't be in the least bit perturbed if you knew I was in the bathroom jerking off into a pair of tights. You would see it as a primal passion or something. I've been giving a lot of thought to the things you said that night as we lay next to each other after the event. I listened with rapt attention because

I've never heard anyone speak like that before. These are new ideas to me. And what of Lorna? Where's her primal passion? What riots in her imagination? How have we shared twenty years and grown further apart? You're right, I do feel cheated. After spending that amount of time together I should be able to delight in adult fun with her, but these days, at our age, it's almost grounds for divorce. She just wants to attend bloody craft fairs and bring an endless supply of rustic lifestyle decoration to an already ludicrously anachronistic kitchen. We live in the bloody home counties, for Christ's sake, not a show cottage in Hardy country. She's fallen victim to the same delusions as her peers – local women in their forties who romanticise the past through Laura Ashley-tinted glasses. They don't want to know about the consumption, illiteracy and rickets that blighted the scullery maid and the sweep; they want to think of flower sellers in pretty hats, striped butchers' aprons and pot pourri petticoats. I loathe the naivety.

In Lorna's saccharine history there's no room for the horny-handed son of the soil, whipping down her knickers and giving her one in the woodshed. In those days, when blokes wanted a portion, they took it, especially from their wives. And by God I bet it felt good to have the right to do so! I can't go on like this – being denied my essential needs. Lorna, you are driving me to seek the attentions of another woman. A woman I must see again.

Left alone in the house is almost like being left alone with you. With nothing to distract me, you occupy all my thoughts. I fondle my mobile in my pocket and ponder on whether or not to call you. It's a foregone conclusion, but it doesn't make it any easier. I take your beautifully designed card out of my wallet and rub my thumb over the pink spot varnish of the logo. Your initial – K – sits in the corner. There is a mobile number and an email address. The unmistakably illicit look of the card makes me sweat just from holding it. Am I really going to phone a woman of dubious morals for 'services' like some clichéd old Tory from a public school?

I cannot reconcile the fact that the woman I lay next to and with whom I shared such stimulating conversation must be a prostitute, no matter how refined the costume or well groomed she may be. I am vulnerable to scandal, and the thought of it terrifies me. The semi-rural tranquility in which I live with Lorna is well protected, but I can all too easily imagine things taking a wrong turn. I have to be so careful from hereon in, should this thing develop. There's the small London flat we could use. It is so wonderfully anonymous. Yet of course I am extremely wary of inviting you there. Suppose there was a scene?

There is a question mark hanging over the legality of your status. I need to be sure you are the woman you purport to be – discreet, professional and independent. I want to believe you are not closely associated with the unthinkable coterie of criminal elements that populate the trade you are part of – prostitution and drugs, obviously. Those two words echo through my brain and scold me as I walk around the house, deep in thought, but I also remember the scent of your body, your fantastic breasts and the sight of you brazenly masturbating. I settle in the living room and sit holding the card for some ten minutes, imagining a host of scenarios both arousing and ghastly. Finally, I am propelled into action by the thought of the alternative – of not calling you. Of wiping the whole incident from memory and continuing life as normal. But the nagging futility of that makes me instantly melancholy. Surely I can at least dip a toe in the water of this other life. Transfer my enthusiasm for predictability and safety to more enervating activities.

I stand up and regard myself in the large mirror over the fireplace. I am not yet an old man. I'm only just over fifty. That's not old these days. And if I feel lust rising in my veins then I absolutely should be able to enjoy the pleasure I'm owed; that is natural. You said something about this, when we were lying in your bed in the early hours of that morning, that to deny desire is to give in to the mundane. I haven't been able to get that out of my head, because the mundane has been my domestic life for longer than I care to admit.

The clock sounds louder than usual, possibly more audible due to the silence in this house. I've rarely been so still, so frozen by indecision. I'm often compelled to turn up the radio louder than Lorna likes, especially if there is a particularly invigorating concerto on Radio 3. I cannot bear the oppressive emptiness of a space crying out for human action. I suddenly want to run around the house screaming and yelling like a five-year-old child. Simon with his toy tractor, coming to mow down Robert and his smug family values. I bet Sarah doesn't refuse him his needs. Why should that stupid cunt get a regular portion and I have to suffer? He's younger, but I'm surely more attractive. Women don't fancy him. They might want to mother him, but surely nothing else. You wouldn't want him; wouldn't stroke his hair, like you did me. He's barely got any left.

I feel such emptiness, puzzlement and silence booming inside me. Is it just ambition and the will to power? Isn't there a great need, as well, for something to which I can give complete attention, like Robert's stupid triathlon? Thursday night was the first time I can remember when I gave myself over to something bigger than myself. When I effectively lost control – an unthinkable condition – and placed myself in the hands of another person. I cannot imagine doing that with Lorna. What would she do? Look bored until it was over? And in any case I wouldn't trust her with my pleasure. You were perfect, giving me your total attention so I could lose myself in the moment. This is what I need. I look at my face, pale and expressionless in the centre of the reflection of the living room. I have melded into my environment, with its cosy cushions and inoffensive landscape paintings and I am indistinguishable from all it represents: safety, dependability, boredom. Fifty-three years of being diligent have brought me to this point – the moment when I dial the phone number of a dominatrix prostitute.

I'm instantly taken aback by how warm and friendly your voice is. I'd expected an imperious tone, or at least that you'd be distant, but you sound genuinely concerned about me. You laugh as I tell you that I arrived home for dinner still sore, and it is the genuine laugh of an exuberant woman I want to be near to. I'm still half expecting the details of that night to appear in the papers, so I am very careful not to elaborate further. I want to trust you but I'd be a fool to do so in my position. Surprisingly, you're the one that keeps the conversation businesslike and we arrange an innocent enough assignation – the Tate Modern on Bankside at 7 p.m. this coming Wednesday. This fits in perfectly with my plans. I'm giving a talk at the London College of Political Sciences that day on business ethics in public/private partnerships. It's only a short walk along the river.

As I close my phone I begin counting the hours until I will see you. I feel the sudden onset of pure excitement, as if I'm not in complete control of what is happening to me. It is as if I have had a shot of adrenaline. This middle-aged body is at once revitalised, as its middle-aged brain relishes having sexual secrets. For the first time in my life I may be able to explore, without recrimination, the adult side of erotic life. I ponder on the word 'erotic' and my loins tingle with the promise of what our next meeting may hold. After what you called my 'appalling lack of knowledge of the history of subversion', you plan to educate me in art. I thought my knowledge of the arts was commensurate with someone of my age and profession but apparently you want me to 'think more deeply' about it. This all sounds pretty innocuous, and not at all what I'd expected from someone who presumably works in the sex industry, but it bodes well. I'll start reading that book. At least you didn't expect to be taken to some nightclub frequented by footballers and tabloid hacks. I am more than ready for you, Kirsten, and looking forward to the unknown quantity of Wednesday. I am keen to make an independent assessment of your status and hopefully embark on a very adult affair. This time, however, I intend to remain completely sober.

4 **The Return of the Repressed**

I prefer to get around unhindered by the hell of other people, so my transport of choice most days is my feet. I enjoy walking around London at dawn, and in the afternoon – anytime when the rush hour isn't in full pelt. I donned trainers to walk to the Millennium Bridge up through King's Road, Pimlico and down along Millbank. I passed your HQ, where I imagined you going about your ministerial day, getting hard at inopportune moments in the excitement of this evening. Now I have changed into my evening shoes, thrown my trainers in my bag, and am standing on the bridge watching the steam rise out of the Turbine Room, knowing that you are already waiting for me as it is five minutes past seven.

You'd strung out your indecision as to whether or not to call me until Saturday afternoon. I'd spent the morning at my fitness centre, swimming forty lengths, before continuing work on the catalogue, interrupted by emails and texts from Ian Baum, pestering me for more information about you. I didn't give it to him, and I would have been annoyed but for his opinionated reminders of the corruptible and detestable qualities of authority figures like you, which of course he is right about. I was just finishing a section on Japanese miniatures when my mobile rang, displaying a number not stored in my directory. I experienced a throb of triumph hearing that you wanted to meet again. I'd begun to have slight doubts: that logic would override your desire, that you would have tried to forget what had happened and put me out of your mind, but the pull was too strong. And that pleased me.

I emailed Ian to let him know you had called and he laughed like an excited child when I told him we had another date. I am prepared to give just enough to keep him happy. He's got to be weaned off me, though. And weaned off the carrion I provide. I love the sex we have – there's nothing else like it – but in my darkest moments I imagine he will take me somewhere I don't want to go. He's getting more and more reckless whereas I want more subtlety and distance.

I watch the river for a while. The skyline provides that familiar, impressive collision of architectural styles, reigned over by the great classical dome of St Paul's and the fabulously audacious Gherkin. The cup and the sword. The chalice and the lance. This vista that has seen fire and pestilence looks more dramatic now than at any point in its history, and is possibly the world's best urban riverscape. Yet it is misleading. I would go as far as to say it's a con. A trompe l'œil. The riot of blue and purple lights from the South Bank and all the postmodern gimcrackery makes London look more exciting than it actually is. Staring at it puts you in a state of suspension; you can believe you are part of some exciting future. But if you so much as walk away from it to a bus stop, the veneer of exciting modern London dissipates and the drab reality of the prevailing culture insinuates into every pore. One is immediately faced with a tiresome journey home in the company of the gormless and the barely literate, bellowing inanities into their mobiles. There's the lack of anything healthy to eat in a five-mile radius under £20, and the very high chance of having your bike stolen, your car clamped, or your sensibilities assaulted by some piece of moronic marketing: 'Imagine! Monthly bills on your mobile!' Part of some exciting future? I don't think so. I realise the riverscape for what it is – a testament to the success of the Church, the monarchy and big business, prettily illuminated and reflected, but with a millennium's effluvia darkly slithering below.

Bronze Age armour was thrown into this water when the Thames was called Isis and battle-weary ancient Britons made offerings to their elemental gods and goddesses. Helmets, shields, breastguards: they all went in as thanks for triumph. I would throw in everything I owned if I thought it would save us from the corruption and dereliction that will engulf this city in a final conflagration. I often wonder if the endgame will happen in my lifetime, and which party will be in power when it does.

I approach the long sloping descent to the Tate entrance and immediately spot you in your suit, holding your briefcase. Again it is your insignificance that defines you among the foreign tourists and young couples with backpacks. I too stand out against them. To look at me you would think I was fresh from an ambassador's reception: my hair is wound in a neat dark coil at the nape of my neck, and I have on a Chanel suit and signature bag that one of Gareth's fashion bunnies swiped from a show. You will be confused yet beguiled by my appearance, unnerved by what it might be masking. You can't trust anyone these days. It has been almost a week since I first met you, and I feel a frisson of excitement at being able to get my hands on you once more. My perfect prey needs to feed; he aches for my stinging touch.

'Kirsten.' You say my name aloud and I turn to you, smiling. I offer you my hand and you squeeze it too hard. You are hungry for contact. We greet each other formally with a kiss on each cheek. You blurt out some anodyne comments about your journey and the weather and the talk you gave this afternoon. I tell you I'm glad you went down well in your lecture, although I add that party politics is inherently corrupt and all political leaders seem hell-bent on turning Britain into a corporate toilet. You look bemused at my vitriolic outburst but I remain aloof.

You ask if we can get a meal later, seeming daunted by an evening of art history, but I allay your concerns by telling you I have a table booked for 8.30 at my favourite Japanese restaurant in SW3. We both know the reason you are here, yet it is impossible for you to start talking freely about your needs and what you have been going through since last week. I will calm you, help you relax. I want to hear your story. It's always a little difficult getting over nerves, fearing exposure, and I'll do my best to ease things along as gently as possible – for the first hour at least. As we take the long slow escalator to the third floor where the surrealist collection resides, I stand one stair up from you and can feel your gaze burning into the backs of my legs. I can sense already that you want to touch them, to pursue your desire free from obstacles. How on earth are you going to play the worldly minister when I know so intimately what you have begged for? I turn so that I am side-on from you, my arms resting on the rubber handrail.

'So ... how have you been feeling?' I begin. 'No more tears I hope.'

You look away from me, then up at the ceiling, as if in exasperation. I know you're not about to tell me right away how it's been, but I do know. I do feel for you. I know you've lain in your bed, curled foetal in the dark in the early hours, blinking at the moon and hurting. How you've barely eaten and thought of nothing else. I went through all that. Instead you open with a classic paranoid stream of denial.

'Look,' you begin, in a harsh whisper, 'I'm not stupid. I know the names of plenty of others in the Commons who pay for people like you. I'm not like that. I just want to get that clear. I'm not interested in that sort of thing.'

Oh really? I'm waiting for the 'but'. You sound like all those women who say they're not lesbians but ... You're prepared to admit to only so much, to desiring only the approved repositories of collective lust: the film stars, the pop divas, the unthreatening fem-bots. You daren't admit that strange triggers fired you to ecstasy.

'Does the minister protest too much?' I jest. 'You don't have to justify yourself to me. I enjoyed what we did on Thursday. It's nothing to wind yourself into a pretzel about. You're mistaking me for some other type of sexual professional. And, before you ask, I'm not some goldigger looking to make a fast buck from selling her story. I find such vulgarity an appalling betrayal of trust. I like my privacy too, you know.'

'Well, that's another thing. I can't take risks, whatever I may or may not like, sexually. Can't you understand that? I've a huge public profile.'

'And a huge penis.'

You stare me, agog, and trip up as the escalator reaches the first floor. I bet it's a while since you heard that.

'Stop worrying,' I say, with a flourish of my hand as I smoothly stride to the next escalator. Good, you are almost jogging to keep up. 'I do this because I enjoy it, because I'm very good at it, and because I fully understand its place within aesthetics, literature and art. No other reason.'

You crease the side of your mouth but I wouldn't call it a smile.

'I don't know about literature and art but I've heard other members of the House talk about people like you. About dominatrixes. I can't believe I'm even saying the word. Look, I know what you do. I probably even know some of your clients!'

'For a start, the plural is *dominatrices*, and I don't have clients; I have friends, lovers, acquaintances.'

'Why did you target me, then? How did you know I was going to be in that bar in Victoria station? It seems obvious to me.'

'Our meeting was fortuitous,' I reply 'but I didn't "target" you. It was pure coincidence. I'm often passing through Victoria station and that's a bar I frequent. It's a good place to meet interesting professional men. I like hearing their troubles. I know ways of making them feel better about themselves.'

'So you prowl bars in railway stations to pick up depressed men?'

I smiled. 'I like the Gothic undertones. Yes, I suppose I do "prowl", but my prowling is all part of a larger experiment I conduct alone. I like to observe, and listen. To see the foolishness people invest their time and emotions in.'

'So, it's not to earn money, then? For drugs or anything?'

I throw back my head and laugh. 'Simon Charlesworth,' I say aloud, to your obvious discomfort. 'I can answer an emphatic no to that question.'

You are puzzled and nervous, but we have arrived on the third floor. In order to ease you into the history of surrealism I begin by asking you who talks to you in your dreams but it's not a conversation you want right now. You want to quiz me for ten minutes while you extract every detail you can about my lifestyle.

You want statistics and facts, it goes with the territory, but I know that in the space of a few hours this habit will be turned around and you will be captivated. I'm simply too good for a 53-year-old bored midlifer to resist. I stand imperious next to you while you fire questions at me that achieve little but verification of how vulnerable you are. But that's why I'm drawn to you. You're a pushover. You're having trouble matching me to your preconceived ideas. I can't blame you – I'm not the usual rubber-clad priestess of the night that snatches MPs from a whisky-sodden settle in St James's.

It's my standard of education that baffles you the most. You suspect I have a drug problem, that I'm involved with gangsters. With pimps. That chaos will encroach onto your home life, your work life; that the whole thing must stop now if I'm associated with anyone like that. I laugh again and stroke your hair. You like that. Maybe some of your colleagues have come unstuck this way. I know the sort of women you are concerned to avoid. They dress as imperial mistresses but are weak underneath, slaves to their mobiles or dealers, wearing too little, too flashily, to be class acts. They want money and status and things. You cannot envisage any other type of woman inhabiting the exotic realm of extreme sexuality but they do exist. I exist. And I want invisibility and freedom and less. I am still stroking your hair as you tell me all your rational fears, and it would be so easy to insinuate my leg between your legs and kiss you passionately. You bleat a bit about the drugs.

'I bet you've felt worse after a few pints,' I say.

'Actually, you are right about that,' you admit after a pause. 'Although I was dog tired the next day I didn't have what you could call a hangover. I was so caught up with, you know, with what happened, I didn't realise it at the time, but yes, I have felt worse after three pints of bitter in the Commons bar.'

You smile. And that's a joy to see.

'Please trust me,' I say, linking my arm in yours. 'I am about to encourage your subconscious mind to burst through your persona and it will be so much fun. Now let's go see the guys who did it first with art.'

You frown at me quizzically, but before you can ask me to explain what I mean I lead you to the rooms. They are busy, as ever.

'So, tell me about these surrealists, then,' you say.

I begin my spiel and you stand still like a good little public servant as I deliver a potted history with a flourish.

'The surrealists were important because they blew away the cobwebs of the previous old order that brought us the futility and horror of the First World War. It's easy for us to be blasé now, but at the time they were radical. As Dadaists they raged against injustice and war using absurd humour. Then they turned their attentions to the personal, inner life. They poked fun at sexual guilt and explored our polymorphous perversity. Actually, Freud came up with that one but the surrealists underwrote his revolutionary findings with art that was dynamic, shocking and loaded.'

'I like that idea,' you say, repeating it quietly to yourself, 'polymorphous perversity. Not sure what it means though.'

'It was denied by common culture back then, of course, and it's still denied today.'

'Can you explain?'

You are so polite, and really trying to follow me.

'The fact that desire takes bizarre turns, that curious thoughts enable us to orgasm. Our public lives teem with repressed unconscious wishes because our imaginations are allowed to go only so far. We deny what we truly think by not airing it. We daren't. We'd be judged too harshly as each has to castigate that which is taboo. Yet the stronger the denial, the more urgent the wish. And the bigger the problem. The ad industry plays on this.'

'I thought advertising used women's bodies to sell everything?'

You seemed proud of that statement, no doubt repeating it parrot-fashion from one of your *Guardian*-reading female colleagues, thinking I'd be impressed. You underestimate me. You probably even think I'm some kind of liberal humanist. Woefully off the mark there, dear Simon.

'The challenge facing the subversive is to reintroduce the over-civilised human to nature. To return him to a more primitive reality. What the surrealists were able to do so easily, some eighty years back, was to lampoon the bourgeoisie. They ridiculed the po-faced elite and invoked a carnival.'

'But art itself is elitist,' you throw in. 'Most people were working in factories or down the pit in the nineteen-thirties. I don't think Salvador Dali did much for them.'

Oh, so you are remembering your socialist roots. Little bit of the old militant rhetoric coming out there.

'Yes, but the effect trickled down,' I say. 'Look at the Marx Brothers. They were surrealist. Straight from the id. It was always the petty officials who were the butt of their jokes, those who tried to prevent riotous fun. Think about it. Think what happens when we deny ourselves the opportunity for riotous fun.'

You are taking all this in. Somewhere in that noggin the truth is ringing loud and urgent.

'The main thing is that the surrealists were the first artists to address the concept of uncertainty in man,' I continue, 'to look at his raging libido and the return of what's repressed. Before them you have to go back to De Sade for the nearest lucid and fully honest exploration of man's darkest instincts.'

You never liked art much, even at school. It didn't have enough numbers in it for your liking. After all my talk you manage an 'OK' and we arrive at the three-dimensional work – Oppenheim's furry cup and saucer and Eileen Agar's wonderful *Angel of Anarchy*. That giant female head wrapped in opulent fabrics and feathers is as good and sinister as anything Man Ray put together.

'These are two rare examples of female work,' I tell you. 'Surrealism, dominated by men, was as much focused on aesthetics as the Pre-Raphaelites, yet they didn't go in for naturalism or the religious allegory of the latter, of course. They concentrated their quest on the search for marvellous – most usually found in female beauty, for its ability to throw a chap into an erotic convulsion.'

'Are these works all about sex, then?' you ask.

'Mostly. But not necessarily about fucking, and that's important, if not a little bit relevant.'

I watch a shadow cross your face, memories of eroticism without fucking.

'They represent a form of erotic delirium but point to its source as being multifaceted, even random, and all the better for the element of surprise. The chance encounter.'

'But you just said they concentrated on female beauty. I cannot see much of that here. I mean, look at that.'

You point to a collection of photographs of Hans Bellmer's *Poupées* – some of my favourite works.

'Eroticism linked to the uncanny always causes a scandal, especially when it draws you to a place where meaning collapses. Bellmer brings the dark male unconscious to material realisation. And still, this more extreme expression was only the natural development of nineteenth-century European fairy stories made adult.'

I turn to you, and lay my hands on your chest.

'Fairy stories are dark as well, remember. Strange how there are no new ones.'

You stare at me from behind your glasses, dumbfounded, wondering what relevance this has to your life or anything you are involved with. We'll find out soon enough.

'Think of the Brothers Grimm,' I continue. 'All those dark forests. There were far worse things than wolves that could give you a fright.'

'So, are you telling me that fairy stories are sexual too?'

'European fairy stories, absolutely!' I say emphatically. 'They are mostly about lost innocence and body horror, the shock of puberty and what lurks unseen in the night. The uncanny by any other word.'

'I suppose there is always an element of wickedness in fairy stories, isn't there?'

'Ice queens, wicked witches, haughty princesses, beautiful vengeful women you would be foolish to upset.'

You stand bemused, mouth agape. How do you equate it all – the drugs, the sodomy, the art, the unexpected? I know it's terribly confusing, but it will make sense soon enough. You gather your thoughts for a few moments and wander to different exhibits.

'But is surrealist art only about, what was it you said ... erotic delirium?' you ask.

I stand back and regard you. To think I've got you asking such a question! I could giggle with glee as maniacally as a mischievous sprite in a heathen legend.

'Erotic delirium is the ideal state. Since God died – roughly about eighteen-ninety-nine – we can't rely on unproven patriarchal deities to deliver our pleasure.'

'I've never been a Christian.'

'I was sent to a convent boarding school from the age of six. I learned a lot about guilt.'

You follow behind me, as I draw your attention to some André Masson sketches. I point out that he illustrated the original edition of *The Story of the Eye*.

'Do you know, I used to think the nuns could see through walls and skulls.'

'Skulls?'

'I mean, I thought they would know what was actually going on inside my head. I would be punished often enough for such piffling misdemeanors to know there was more to their malevolence than God's law. I'm sure God didn't care if I stacked the lacrosse sticks untidily, but the nuns did. It didn't stop me having fantasies about the priest, though. It may have been decades since the surrealists were poking fun at the clergy, but my first communion was pure Max Ernst.'

You look at me speechless, and it's almost endearing that your expression is approaching something like erotic delirium itself.

'It was an ecstatic experience,' I continue. 'And an irrational one. When I was punished I was in rapture to the majesty of the Lord and all the saints. I loved my welts. I dedicated them to the Virgin Mary. The little girl dreamed of taking the veil.'

'I never knew anything like that,' you mumble. 'Sadists, those nuns. It was just C of E in our house,' you say. 'Just weddings and funerals, you know.'

'So you didn't know much of the uncanny when you were a child, then?'

I am probing now. Asking you to think back to when you were the young Simon, lost in his world of *Look and Learn* and Airfix decals.

'Well, there were a few ghost stories, but nothing really. I was able to recite "The Rime of the Ancient Mariner".'

'Didn't you have moments when you knew adults were discussing something forbidden?' I asked you.

'Were you not ushered up to bed so you didn't see any rude stuff on the TV? I remember seeing it at my nan's house when I'd come back to England for the holidays. She'd go to bed early and I'd get to see all kinds of things. I couldn't believe it.'

You smile. 'By the time the rude stuff came on TV I was already in my mid-teens.'

'So, the perfect time, really.'

'I guess so. I can only remember being concerned about strikes and union rights. Bringing down the Heath government.'

'How dull. Wasn't this the time of glam rock?'

'Yeah, but that was for girls. Blokes liked prog rock. And life was anything but glamorous then, I can tell you.'

'What did you like? And don't tell me you never had time for music.'

'Pink Floyd, Crosby, Stills and Nash, Grateful Dead, Camel. Actually, I preferred American bands. Little Feat, Gram Parsons, Neil Young.'

'I see.'

I try to picture you spinning the West Coast sound in your student digs, PPE reading piled up in a frosty northern hovel. Three-day weeks, appalling food, transit vans and large milk bottles. To think my dad was going backstage at Crosby, Stills and Nash gigs and partying with them while you were scowling over books on Trotsky and listening to them for light relief.

'So, have you always had a sexual interest in women's feet?' I throw in loudly, as we stroll past the Yves Tanguys.

A woman swivels her head round to look at you, then whispers something to her husband, who also turns to get a glimpse at who the pervert might be. You fumble around for words, but nothing intelligible comes out. You shrug and mutter and turn a little pink in the face.

That's got you bang to rights, you old dog. You step closer to me and whisper urgently: 'Look, I don't know what that was about. The shoes, I mean. I've not done that before. Ever. Or any of the stuff we did. That was a one-off. It was crazy stuff. I told you.'

'So why did you phone me, then, if it was so scary?' I ask, a trace of triumph evident in my voice.

'I don't know. Look ... can we leave?' You glance around and seem agitated. 'I'd like to talk to you, *properly*. I can't concentrate on this ... art lesson. Not today, because my head is full of what happened last week. It's taken as much energy as I could muster to pull together enough notes for today's speech. Have you got any idea what it's like being in the public eye?'

'Indeed I have. I've performed on stage at the Rubber Ball.'

'The what? Look, whatever that is, it's nothing like addressing the mayor's delegates and the heads of industry that are funding major transport links for the coming five decades. This is my job, Kirsten. I'm the bloody secretary of state for public policy, for Christ's sake. Do you think I've got time to learn about articulated dummies and sewing machines wrapped in blankets?'

You are in quite a flap. You need to be reminded of who holds the most important key here.

'There is always time for an articulated dummy,' I say, smirking at your flustered outburst. 'Or some sushi? Or would you rather go see some of the other rooms? The Brancusis are always worth a squint.'

'No,' you say. 'No more art. Not just now. Look, I'm sorry. The truth is I tried to forget about you and what happened but ... but I couldn't. I guess I'd like to talk to you properly. My head's a whirl with all this art. It's a great building but let's go somewhere more intimate.'

We walk out of the exhibition room and into the concourse where the escalators run through the middle of the building. I guide you to a quiet alcove with a soft seat angled for that perfect river view, now it's dark. It's your first confessional. And how sweet will be the unburdening. I try not to picture you dressed in a lace veil and Communion satin but the idea tickles me all the same – so very Max Ernst. I make a mental note to apply enforced feminisation at some point, should I get the opportunity. I then listen to some of your tedious professional insecurities – the bit where you bemoan your lot.

'I carry a lot of responsibility,' you whine. 'I'm where I wanted to be but it's such a fucking nest of vipers I can't get anything done the way I want it. There are people after my job, out to undermine me. I've got plans for progress but there are so many traps being laid for me.'

I nod my head, trying to not look bored.

'There are great opportunities coming to London at the moment. And there'll be a lot of changes, especially with all the huge development about to take place for the Olympics. Everybody's fighting over who will have the land once the event is over. And that's before you've even taken the opposition into account. This is from our own. It's so frustrating. I have to be on my guard every waking moment.'

You look me in the eyes to express the severity of your dilemma.

'But what about the moments when you are not awake?' I ask smoothly. 'Or when you are suspended between the two – say, in the hypnogogic state?'

'There, you see, I just don't understand what you're talking about. You cannot possibly know what I have to deal with.'

You are in a flounce of your own importance and I'll

make you regret that undermining statement. I know everything you're dealing with.

'You don't understand, or you don't want to understand?' I ask, turning it back on you. 'What about those moments when the unconscious bursts through? When you dream something so vividly it is in the room with you? It seems to me you need a little time out from the stresses of your work. You are overdue an assessment of your self.'

You sigh and lean back on your hands. Your groin is prominently thrust towards the window and I want to make a grab for it. Instead I look you up and down and try to conceal my true intentions.

'I haven't been able to think of much else since the other night,' you go on. 'My wife is frigid and doesn't want anything to do with me except as a status symbol, so she can be the minister's first lady, spending his wages on nonsense we don't need.'

'You just need to think about things differently,' I say. 'Get a little perspective. Face up to the fact that frustration's got the better of you. It's not a big deal. It can be sorted out. I can help you do that.'

I resist letting loose with what I really think you need – a lesson in submission at Ms Caine's training academy, whimpering in a harness.

'Look, what I was thinking ... I mean ... I find you very attractive. And you look stunning tonight.'

'Oh, nice of you to notice,' I interject.

'I'm sorry. I should have said that the moment we met. I'm falling down on my manners. It's just that I've got so much on my mind.'

'Oh, don't worry. I'll give you a little reminder later so you won't do that again.'

You swallow and blink. 'So, can we continue this?' you ask, ever linear, logical, needing to progress, feeling the urgency in your loins.

'What? The exhibition or our friendship?' I ask, some-what facetiously.

'Our friendship, of course.'

'You mean, now that you have realised I am not a prostitute?'

You display regret at the conclusions you jumped to.

'Actually, I've got an apartment. It's in Bayswater. I'm there usually three nights a week. I'm there tonight.'

Well, well. You sly old hound. The offer of free sex is too much to turn down, isn't it? Away from your 'frigid' wife and fancying something a bit naughty? Think you can get away with it, Charlesworth? Think I'll give up on the weird stuff and soon you'll be calling the shots in bed as we share some diplomatic immunity?

'It would be fantastic if you visited me there,' you continue, too nervous to look me in the eye. 'You could come there tonight. That is ... I mean, if you find me as attractive as I find you.'

How easily you step into the right foot holes. I need to go easy on you for now, though. You are vulnerable. Exasperated by your responsibilities. You want uncom-plicated sex with a sophisticated, perfumed, Chanel-dressed woman. I shan't scare you with missives from the dark underground.

'Speak to me about the other night. What did you feel?' I ask, laying a hand on your leg.

'You know already that it was like nothing I've ever experienced.' You look out over the river. 'You're trying to embarrass me.'

Your leg quivers. You are so, so desperate for what I can give you.

'I'm not, Simon, honestly. I'm asking you to go over it with me, so you can fully and consciously process what happened. Speak to me about the sexual element of your experience.'

'You sound like a psychiatrist.'

'Then expect to experience some deep probing,' I joke. 'Come on, let's get some food. We can talk over sushi.'

I stand up and you follow me as we leave the gallery for the restaurant, taking a cab to King's Road. It is over several exquisite portions of sushi nori and black cod that an arrangement of sorts is drawn up. You know nothing of adult role play, or what it's like to be open about having an unconventional sexuality. You don't have that privilege. You're a slave to conventions, protocol, governmental responsibilities. You have wrapped yourself in a mantle of deceit, pretending you're respectable but underneath you are raging and desperate.

I order sake from Miko, my partner in perversity and our waitress for the evening, and teach you that, with this drink, one pours for one's companion. The sake is warm and helps the conversation flow. You are dizzy already from surrealist art and being near me. You are of course eager to know more about me. I deflect any questions that probe too personally.

'I want to know more about how you felt the other night,' I persist. 'Your debauching.'

'You make it sound very sordid.'

'You have to rethink these negative judgments,' I say. 'Last Thursday was not sordid. You experienced a moment of transition. A revelation almost. Let's go beyond your concept of sordid and think about ... epiphany.'

You lean in to me and, in hushed tones, utter, 'Yes, it was revelatory, but did it have to be so debased? I mean, up the, you know ...'

'I see. A taboo zone for a man of your standing, of course.'

'It has nothing to do with my career. It's just the thought of it. It's unnatural.'

I show frustration with your narrow-mindedness.

'You need to think more creatively, Simon. I think

you'll find that humans have been "unnatural" for countless millennia. Wet cunts and hard-ons were with us at the beginnings of time. And anal sex, come to that.'

You shrug and squirm at my candour. Sorry if what I'm saying is alarming for a gentleman politician.

'Who came up with the idea that genitals can only be allowed to connect with other genitals of the opposite sex once their owners were married?' I continue. 'Cave dwellers in prehistoric times used dildos, you know. And tenth-century Hindus built temples of erotic love about the same time as Christians were stoning women to death for being in league with the Devil.'

'I didn't know. Thanks for the history lesson. Look, it's all very well for you to be so happy-go-lucky about the whole business, but that was my first time experiencing something like that.'

'But it won't be your last, eh?' I quip.

You sit back in your seat for a few seconds, thinking.

'This is your chance to explore something of your inner life. Am I right in thinking your sexual life has been sheltered, unadventurous?'

You nod your head, resigned that you cannot lie to me.

'Are there things you've always wanted to do and have never done, sexually?'

'Yes. So many. So many. And I've never met anyone like you before,' you offer, almost romantically.

I ignore this classic, older man's gambit, and I don't go fishing for compliments, which puzzles you.

'I imagine you have to spend your entire life putting on a face.'

'Day in, day out, at the Commons, at home . . .'

'Our time on Earth is fleeting. We are capable of so much exploration, yet so many of us go constantly in dread of our natural impulses, our natural curiosity. There's no time to experiment with divinity or disgrace.'

You stare at me blankly, then continue talking shop. It's still too early for you to open up completely. You prop yourself up by changing the subject, chatting about your job.

'I'm driven by what I do. The party's achieved so much. I'm helping to run the country. I don't have time for philosophy.'

'No time to seek the annihilation of the rational individual in a violent, transcendental act of communion? Sorry, you're not following me. I'll try to make it easier. Have you ever taken a shit outdoors?' I ask.

'What kind of a question is that?'

'An honest one. Answer me. Have you ever taken a shit out of doors?'

'I can't remember.'

'So yes, then. And I bet you really stared at it, didn't you, in that private moment? Just you and your turd, alone together.'

'This is a fine conversation for dinner!' you exclaim, suddenly becoming all Northern and righteous.

'Think about that sense of transgression,' I say. 'Some awful thing that should remain hidden has come outside. Try to imagine a sexual equivalent – the private erotic side of you being allowed to express itself, but with diplomatic immunity from recrimination. That's what you experienced the other night. And that's why you didn't rush to leave once it was all over. You can't tell me you're not changed by it, in a good way.'

I watch you reeling at the images I have planted in your mind. Turds. Diplomats. The private you.

'I don't know,' you say, stroking your glass. 'No ... I did like it. It did feel kind of therapeutic. I guess this is all a form of therapy, isn't it? Albeit a very weird one. I was planning to seek marriage counselling. I was going to try to get Lorna to consider it.'

'You have problems there, what with her being "frigid", of course,' I say, disdainfully. 'Perhaps you should get her to spend time alone with her turd too.'

You ignore my facetiousness.

'Plenty of women her age go off sex. It's not uncommon, is it? But I'm not going off it. My feelings are getting stronger.'

Lorna's not frigid. She's probably sick of you being so secretive and swaggering about in your suit but she's too timid to seize the nettle and take control of the situation because she thinks she has no power. I bet you've had the same routine in the bedroom for years and she's just put up with it. No woman should have to suffer such ennui. And I bet you don't talk to her, don't ask her what she wants or ever discuss your desires. You just want to get your end away with the lights off while your mind reels with something more piquant. And now she's withholding the goods the demons are rising and the fabric is crumbling.

I often deal with the fallout of marriages gone cold. Mistakes made by women who don't give due thought to what they're getting into when they get swept along with the confetti and flowers. They forget the gristle and goo that lies underneath. All men are dirty dogs who need to be kept in check. To be regularly purged and made to confess, with the appropriate punishment meted out. It's as much her fault as yours that the marriage is foundering.

'That's why you need to keep a diary,' I say. 'We'll find out why your feelings are getting stronger. We'll explore all your dirty little secrets. I want you to start tonight. Put in it everything you've ever wanted to write about your desires, not just what you thought that day, but a lifetime's sexual longing.'

'I don't know. It's too risky. I can't write that sort of stuff. Not in my position.'

'Who's going to know it's you? Use a different handwriting. It's safer than email.'

'Well, OK, I'll think about it. It's not something I've done before.'

'It'll be strictly between us. Think of me as your sex psychiatrist. We can play a game. I can be your lady confessor.'

'Lady confessor ... gosh, I rather like the sound of that,' you say, loosening up a little. You excuse yourself to go to the loo, where of course you will be handling your genitals, as all men do all hours of the day and night. You're warming up, relaxing. That's good.

Miko comes to the table, bringing our food.

'That's him,' I say. 'What do you think?'

'English salary man.'

'Kind of. Should be an easy job for you, if you think you can bear it.'

'I get a better look when he comes back. He looks nice and polite though. Easy.'

This stunning young fashion-student-cum-waitress stands by the table as you rejoin us. She asks you if you want anything else to drink and you order a Sapporo beer. I watch her closely as she assesses what kind of rope she might like to use on you; how she can truss you like a chicken in seconds and terrorise you with that voice of hers. When she leaves the table I begin to question you further.

'Tell me about your libido, Simon.'

I work my way through the nori rolls, expertly dipping each roll into the wasabi and soy sauce with my chopsticks, my mouth watering before each taste sensation. You are using a fork and your fingers but I decide not to reprimand you so early on for this gauche display. Easy does it. I want to concentrate on your confession.

'The moment I'm out of the office it's the first thing I think about. I've even started thinking about it at work. But I don't want to be like some lecherous middle-aged man.'

I snort, because that's exactly what you are.

'It's everything I'm against, socially, politically, but I've started ... buying porn. Lorna would probably divorce me if she knew. She was in the Women Against Pornography group at the GLC in the eighties. I keep it hidden at the flat or tucked under old boxes in our garage. I especially love women with long dark hair like yours.'

'I'll let you touch it later, if you beg hard enough,' I say. 'But you'll need to go through a period of adjustment first. You are far too arrogant to be allowed such generosity so soon. You need to learn that access to divinity is found through worship.'

'You speak about sex in a very strange way. Is this sado-masochism? Is that what I'm getting myself into?'

'You tell me, Simon. What do you think?'

'I don't know what to think.'

'There are no dungeons, no dressing in rubber or leather. Just our imaginations. Tell me, is that sado-masochism?'

'It was that thing with the feet,' you say. 'I couldn't forget it. I loved it.'

'Ah, yes. The feet. Your fetish. You evaded my earlier question. You won't be able to evade me if you want to take things further. There *will* be questions asked in the house.'

'Look, what I need to know is, is money involved in all this? Tell me.'

'Money ... yes, I suppose you would be curious about money. OK, how about this? You pick up the bill wherever we dine, drink or stay – a hotel or whatever. And pay for petrol and taxis. You may please me with presents, too, like you would with any other woman. And if I remember, you are already in debt to me for a consignment of Wolford ten-denier stockings. But I'm not going to charge for the things we get up to. I'm not like those dominatrices your colleagues have known.'

'Why not charge?'

'This is between us, as individuals. This is not something I do to earn money.'

'What *do* you do, then? Something in the arts, I'm assuming.'

'Yes, something in the arts.'

'And you're a dominatrix part-time? How strange you are.'

'Stop trying to pigeon-hole me, Charlesworth.' I wag a perfectly manicured finger at you. 'You need know nothing of my personal details. This will not be an affair how you envisage it. It's not a romance. Consequently, things like deep kissing and intercourse are not to be expected. From time to time I may allow you either, but they are not to form the greater substance of this arrangement. You'll need to earn such rewards.'

Your face falls.

'However,' I continue, 'you will be allowed to unburden this great weight you are carrying. You can share your secrets with me, whatever they are. We will play games of mistress and servant.'

'And what might that mean? Kirsten, I need to know what I'm getting into here. Can't you imagine what my life is like? All this stuff goes against everything I'm supposed to be. Can I ask for what I want? God, this is all so weird.'

'You can ask for anything. You may or may not get it. But it's because your life is so high profile that you need to escape to a secret world. And I've got plenty of places I can take you. You don't have to worry about initiating sex. Forget the usual male/female dynamics. Forget the stress of having to do all that. I will make all the moves.'

'What, whipping and stuff?'

'You don't have to worry. I'm not going to hospitalise you.'

'Well, that's a bloody relief!'

'Without suffering you cannot possibly expect to achieve anything. And it's not all whipping and caning. Punishment need not involve the reddening of flesh.'

'Christ, all I want is normal sex.'

'Then off you go. Go and have your "normal sex".'

'I want more than that, though,' you complain, almost indignant. 'I want sex and conversation. With someone intelligent like you.'

I continue to dip the exquisite black cod into the soy sauce.

'So many women are so caught up with ... non-sense,' you continue. 'Meaningless drivel, obsessing about diets and shopping.'

'Yes, it is so very dull, isn't it? Look, if anything is too much for you, seriously, if you cannot take whatever I'm dishing out, you can use a safe word.'

I go on to explain the procedure and the word 'Tony' is set.

'These are some of the lovely things we can do together: you can worship my shoes, my legs or even my breasts. If and only on the condition that you honour me and show me respect.'

'Oh my God, your breasts. I've only felt them so very briefly.'

'You will learn worship. And I will learn your secrets. You must write down everything you want, everything that comes to mind and email me. Of course, there's a lot you won't be sure about because you won't have yet had the experience.'

'I can tell you now what I want. It's easy. I want to fuck. I want to feel some woman's tight fucking pussy around my penis and I want to have my hands all over her breasts and arse as I spunk into her. OK?'

You look up from your outburst to see Miko standing by our table staring at you with those big 'Hello Kitty' eyes and you immediately curl into your corner, shocked she may have heard. She collects our empty plates and asks if we want anything else. You sit back into your seat, face beetroot red.

'No, thank you,' I say, 'but I think the gentleman might.'

You get flustered, wave your hands around and ask for the bill.

'You're good-mannered on the surface, aren't you?' I say. 'But a nasty dirty little boy underneath. A classic rioting mass of contradictions. And stop looking so fucking guilty. Anyone would think you'd murdered a child's pet.'

You smile. 'Do you know what a relief it is to be able to tell a woman such things and not have her storm out of the room offended?' you say.

'I have been told this is something of a relief for men in high office.'

'I want to hear the sound of high heels on marble floors or gravel. That sound ... it haunts me. I want to see you walking around in boots and a short dress. Really short, like, just under your buttocks.'

'I can tell you've thought about this, haven't you?' I say haughtily.

'I want to tell you what I did last week. Just before I phoned you, I thought about you walking around me in boots and letting me touch you and rub myself against you.'

'This can actually happen, you know, if you are prepared to do penance. I don't have boots on tonight though.'

'No, but you have high heels on, and I like them just as much. Anyway, I was thinking about you like this and I was so excited. This is all new to me. How is it that after all these years I've suddenly realised I love women in high heels and boots?'

'Maybe you remember something from a long time back. Did Lorna ever wear them?'

'God, no. It's been sensible shoes all the way. She does have some boots but they're just boring. I don't know where it comes from.'

'It's unlikely that you would develop a fetish so late in life. They're pretty much fixed by puberty.'

'That's a long time ago!'

'Indeed. But what aroused you then may be coming back. There is a link here to the exhibition. I think it could be the return of the repressed.'

'So, it's been unconscious, and whatever happened to me last week brought it out?'

'It's very likely. But I can see you're already getting excited. I bet you're already getting hard. I'd be so enraged if you embarrassed me, and you wouldn't want to suffer my wrath.'

I am already setting the tone for how this evening's scene will progress. We swallow the last of our Sapporos, you pay the bill and we make to leave. You are prepared to risk me coming to your place. It's all ready, you say. I can't wait to see your place. I have a few sneaky lifesavers in my bag: a change of underwear, a pair of handcuffs, a small penis lash and a butt plug – equipment that will serve the same purpose as a fully equipped dungeon. The main item I carry around is my questioning mind and my sensitivity to what men like you need. In my ultimate fantasy I want nothing less than you thrown into a pit and mauled by brutes. Your shirt ripped off your back and the crack of the birch across your flesh. I want you in the stocks and left to the mercy of whatever bandits may happen upon you. But easy does it ... a lady in a Chanel suit does not, of course, hold such savage desires.

5 You Make My Day, I Make Your Hole Weak

I accept your offer of a visit to Bayswater. I don't plan to stay the night. It's ten minutes in a cab from there to my place. I can give you a couple of hours of delirious joy and then leave. I'm having fun with this – making you squirm and confess, squirm and confess.

We pull up round the back of Hyde Park, between Paddington station and Lancaster Gate. Your apartment is set back from the road in a row of Georgian-style properties. There's a transitory anonymity about the location that I like. It's a zone where nobody dare ask your business and the creeping suffocation of residential living doesn't get a foothold. No one's about to make you join their neighbourhood bloody watch committee and nose around what you get up to. I know a few doms that have premises in the area. The real Whiplash types who are dexterous with a suspension harness and experts in isolation torture. They're all fine ladies with transvestite maids and impressive kit. I admire them, but I couldn't do it day in, day out. I would lose my touch. It would become too much like work. This is all pleasure to me.

You unlock three security bolts and we are in your flat. The design is pure 1970s split-level styling and I imagine a good amount of grooving went on in this pad back then. The entire wall behind one sofa is completely mirrored. There's a work desk and a low table, a TV and a couple of bookshelves and earthenware vases with decorative twigs in. The kitchen is small and functional and the first thing I do is open the fridge. I love looking in other people's fridges. There's some Philadelphia cheese, some bacon, a pint of milk, some cans of Coke and a couple of bottles of mediocre wine. The surfaces are spotless and the cooker doesn't look as if it's been used in months.

You open one of the bottles of wine and we settle into the living room. You sit next to me on the sofa, which feels a little too domestic for me. I stand up and draw down the wooden blinds so any prying guests that may be staying at the hotels surrounding us don't get an eyeful.

'Time to get back to the feet, Simon,' I tell you, and enjoy watching your nervous reaction.

'Ah, yes,' you say. 'The return of the repressed. It was when you ... you know, when you started rubbing your feet on me, last week, at your place. I just want to tell you that was the most turned on I've ever been. I would have done anything.'

'Do you like women in high heels?' I ask, still standing up and walking a few paces around the room.

'Yes,' you croak and I thrill at how I am embarrassing you into a confession you have never made to anyone.

'Not very politically correct, is it, to be drooling over images of women in clothes that hinder their movement?'

You don't answer, but look away from me, unable to admit the reasoning behind the truth.

'Well, it's time for you to know that a high-heeled woman can also be a dominant woman – not hindered at all. Would you like to touch my feet, Simon?'

'Yes, please. I want to touch you. I want contact with a woman. Not just your feet but *you*. I want to feel *you*.'

I smirk. 'Yes, I'm sure you do,' I say.

You take off your suit jacket and loosen your tie. I

must admit I do like this part – the steamed-up civil servant getting all hot under the collar and me being privy to his chastening. You put down your glass and stand up to embrace me. I almost squeal with disgust but instead I step swiftly aside and you look confused. You just haven't learned, have you? It's not going to be like this. I'm not some materialist little puppet you can impress with your status and expect to maul whenever you like because I've let you buy me dinner. You'll need some time to adjust to how different the rules are with me. I order you to drop to your knees.

'This is where we began, last week, do you remember? You fell to your knees and began stroking and kissing my feet.'

'Yes, yes, of course I remember,' you say.

You are beginning to get the hang of the game. You ask me if it's OK to touch my leg. I grant you access to everything below the knee and that sees you becoming very animated. You like having something to do. There are hands wrapping around calves, over ankles, over shoes. Being a dirty boy, you roll over onto your back and try to sneak a look up my skirt. Oh dear. I stand one foot on your chest, the heel grinding into your ribs. You look almost elated.

'You think you can be clever and get more than you are entitled to,' I say, 'but I will teach you that you cannot rush at me like some panting adolescent and expect to get what you want. I know your tricks. You think you can have access to the most private part of me. Well, let me tell you, you are a long way off earning that reward.'

'I saw it before,' you begin meekly. 'I know you had knickers on, but when you were doing that to me with your feet last time you were sitting on a chair and touching yourself. Please, please, can I see it again? I want to kneel down and bring my face close to you, between your legs. You let me do it last time. I want to lick you. I can do it.'

'Urgh!' I exclaim and dig the spike of the heel into your flesh. 'What makes you think I would allow that dog's tongue of yours to go anywhere near me? When I want pleasure, I will do it myself.'

Actually, that's a lie, because soon you are going to learn how to bring me to climax just the way I like it. But it's good to string you along. Suddenly you seem to capitulate into playing like a natural.

'I am your plaything. Treat me like a dog. I know I'm not worthy of touching your, what shall I call it, Miss Caine? I do not wish to offend you.'

'You will call it by its original Anglo-Saxon name,' I reply.

'You mean, the C-word?'

'Yes, the C-word. But it is always to be called "beautiful" or "glorious" if it is applied to me. Say it.'

'I want to touch your beautiful cunt,' you beg, and I can tell you are not used to using this word in front of women. It still holds a power for you, and the taboo is exciting. You were well brought up, taught manners; taught to keep your foul little-boys' dirty talk in the men's room. I'll exploit your embarrassment for all it's worth. I quickly think of Miko and what she'll do to you once she gets her hands on you. She's not hampered by British reserve. She'll make you her own prisoner of war for a day. I look down at you and you are hard against your fly zip. You are thrusting against the material and obscene in your gestures. All from having my feet on you.

'I cannot allow you to touch it,' I say with a regretful tone. 'But I may allow you to *look* at my beautiful cunt.'

I release the pressure off your body and take a couple of steps forwards so I am standing over your head. You slide both hands up my legs.

'It's dark,' you say. 'I can't see anything.'

'Are you complaining, you four-eyed fuck?' I enquire, with a sharp tone.

'No, Madame K, no. I would never complain with you in my presence. Just let me see it, please, I beg of you. Imagine how I feel.'

Oh, I do, Simon. I do. I imagine so well because I am feeling something like it myself. There is nothing I would rather do than take hold of you and plunge it into me right now; grind down on top of you and take you to paradise. But that would burst the bubble far too soon. I have plans for you that involve so much more torture and I unleash a stream of invective that you have invited.

'"Imagine how I feel."' I tease, echoing your whiny voice. I unzip my skirt and step out of it. You are left with the vision of my legs, towering athletically over you, clad in dark-brown stockings with an old-style suspender belt holding them up. Over the top of the suspenders are knickers, black with white edging. They cover the entirety of my buttocks and are made of sheer material. There's a little of the 1950s about them. They're not vulgar like the thongs of underclass sluts. They're what you would call 'fully formed', and they've got you in a right old froth.

You can smell my arousal. My body cannot lie. And I am seized with the need to be a bad girl. Even though you are a pale specimen in your fifties I am more aroused than if I were with some muscled young stud. It's always been this way. I can only know full arousal with a man who is desperate for me. And you are so desperate. You lie there, your thoughts given only to focusing on my legs. I tread on your white shirt, pressing down on your upper arm then using the heel of my shoe to graze your nipples. Your face is immobile, expressionless – either in fear or concentration. I'm going to give you such a time of it. I squat over you and you groan your appreciation. What you crave so ardently is now pressing down on your face. I muffle you with my thighs either side of your head. I can feel you are touching yourself but if you think you're going to spurt a horrible mess all over the place, then you are in for a shock. You cannot resist it; you want a bit of everything and, in a matter of thirty seconds, I feel both hands come up to grab my arse.

'No!' I shriek and stand up. 'Did I give you permission for that?'

'No, but ... surely ... surely ...'

'You're rubbing your nasty penis and you expect to touch me with the same hands! Your penis hands! You are forgetting who I am. You touch yourself only when I say!' I yell. 'All you have known about women from your previous pathetic encounters, forget it. You have not met anyone like me before. Therefore, you do not treat me like your bovine Labour Party frumps. You are way ahead of yourself and this is why you have to learn humility and punishment.'

'Do I have to?' you whine. 'You can't be serious. Can't we just do it?'

I laugh at your arrogance. It's the laugh of the cruel countess. The evil witch-queen of the forest.

' "Just do it"? Sounds like some fucking corporate slogan. I'll tell you what we'll "just do", Simon Charlesworth. We'll have those trousers off and you on your fucking knees! Now!'

Oh dear. Your face has gone all grey and worried. You turn around and kneel up. Your erection is bulging urgently. You take a large gulp of wine, unfasten the belt, then the top button.

'Stop!' I order. 'I want to see this in slow motion. I want to see what kind of a state you have got yourself in, thinking such things about me.'

I sit back onto the sofa while you fumble about. I still have my Chanel jacket and blouse on. My hair is still in the chignon, but has loosened.

'I want you to unzip yourself slowly,' I tell you. 'Ease that zip down as if you were a stripper. Very, very slowly. Think about your audience.'

There's nothing I love more than to see the male in an aroused state, indulging in wanton display. It is fools and the poorly educated who go at it without preamble, who strip bare and pump themselves into a fast frenzy, conscious only of their goal. Such a thing should be savoured. And clothes enhance, rather than hinder, the process. There'll be no nakedness in this quarter. Exposure, yes, but not nudity.

I watch intently as you tug on the zip.

'Learn to move your hips, Charlesworth,' I order. 'Imagine you have a hula hoop. Yes, like that, but slowly. Grind yourself as you ease it down.'

You attempt a little hip movement but I can see it doesn't come naturally. You are so ill-co-ordinated. I try not to laugh.

'Bigger circles. Have you never done yoga?'

'No.'

'Never mind. Just watch me.'

I give you an elaborate display, mimicking the action of someone undoing a zip while gyrating. You take to this and then, a millimetre at a time, I see your cock appear, outlined against your briefs. You have already been oozing into your underpants. I rest one manicured finger on the tip of it and you immediately push against it.

'Please,' you croak.

'You can say please all you like. This is my show, my rules,' I remind you.

You put your hand into your pants and rearrange

yourself. But the hand lingers there and you start to pump your penis, slowly, working it inside your briefs. Your eyelids have half-closed and again I am fascinated by the vision of the Cabinet minister given over to complete arousal.

'You are allowed two minutes,' I say, looking at the carriage clock on the desk. 'Two minutes of your filthy self-pleasure. But first, something you must do for me.'

I stand up in front of you and order you to slowly peel my knickers down with your teeth. You shout out your appreciation and it tickles me to feel you struggling to get purchase on the silky material. You make quite a meal out of easing them over my bottom. I feel your disappointment as a sigh of hot breath under my buttocks as you know you are not allowed to linger. I do, however, let you rub your face against my legs for perhaps too many seconds longer than would a sterner mistress. All the time you are trying to take liberties. When I step out of the knickers you look at them like a small dog expecting something to be thrown for him to retrieve.

'Well...' I say.

'What?'

You are so feeble I am exasperated. 'I don't want to see untidiness. Pick them up.' You go to reach for them and I quickly snap at you. 'With your teeth, you fool!'

You crouch down so your head is on the floor and then sit up with them hanging loosely from your mouth. It takes a steely determination not to burst out laughing. I allow myself a small smile and reach forwards, snatch them, and then roll the sheer material into a ball.

'We know where these are going, don't we?' I say. 'Open wide.'

You look mortified but still you obey, as I stuff the rolled-up panties into your lying mouth.

'That's better. Can't mislead anyone now, can you? Not about to fudge any figures and reports before the select committee with those in your face?'

I speak to you as if I were addressing a three-year-old, and I can see traces of indignation begin to appear and you issue muffled acknowledgments through your gag. I won't overdo it. It could interfere with your arousal.

I sit back onto the sofa and demand my display of masturbation. You once again have your hand on yourself, emboldened by my raising a leg and pushing my foot against your shoulder as you stare avidly between my legs. Well, you would, wouldn't you? Your trousers aren't even off yet. They have merely slid down your legs. What a lewd boy you are. Your eyes strain for the optimum view, and your breath whistles from each side of the gag as you chop up and down. You must have got your superior attitude from having such an admirable size on you. Did you take a ribbing about it at school? I wonder. It's such a beauty, so wasted on a snivelling little politician. I know some boys who would get down on their knees and drool to take what you've got in their mouths. Reminded of your arrogance I slide my bag towards me and whip out the handcuffs. You can see what's coming and a horrified expression crosses your face. You even spit the gag out – a punishable offence.

'No, please. What do I have to do to get some pleasure here?' you plead.

'Your two minutes are up, Charlesworth. Too bad you couldn't reach completion.'

I stand up and dangle the cuffs from one finger. They clink heavily. The real deal. Not some flimsy high-street sex-shop version. They're genuine SFPD. Got them from one of my gay friends. Believe me, the former owner used them for humiliation a lot more excessive than I'm about to perpetrate on you, so you should consider yourself lucky. Lucky I don't bundle you up, make you wear my panties and deliver you to some of the Anvil boys. You're getting off lightly considering what could transpire if I played out some of the scenes I've witnessed as inspiration.

'Hands behind you!' I shriek.

You try disobedience and you struggle, but I'm unsure if you mean it, or are easing along the play. Now, this really is what I like – using force. I am behind you and, in a flash, I have your arms pulled together and your wrists clamped. It's gratifying to press myself up close to you while you are still in your shirt and tie. My bare cunt is so near to you but there's not a chance of your touching it. I lean in and whisper in your ear, in as sinister a voice as I can muster:

'Don't even think of trying to escape. Do you think I'm going to let you just kneel there and wank yourself stupid staring at me as if I were some slut in a porno mag? You are going to be invigorated and you'll thank me for it every step of the way. Your insubordination is shocking. Who said you could lose the gag? It's going back. It is.'

You are bound and kneeling. You can't go very far. You would be hobbled by your trousers if you tried to stand up. I stand with my stockinged legs right in front of your face and you strain for contact as I dangle the knickers in front of you. You look so crestfallen and I have a sudden charitable idea, considering the liberties I am about to take at the other end of your body. I will allow you some joy in your plight. I pull the panties over your head, gusset inwards and giggle at the sight it makes. It's like putting an Easter bonnet on a pet dog; pathetic but at once endearing also. Your eyes are partially covered but you can just about see me pull a small multi-fringed lash from my bag and run it through my fingers. The handle is pewter, beautifully crafted in the shape of a penis – heavy, but not as thick as yours. The short leather fronds are thin and whippy but the overall effect in action is more refreshing than painful. You stay kneeling, frozen with anticipation and then, for a few delicious moments, there is contact, as I ease your briefs fully down and reveal the mighty gristle. Your hard penis sticks rude and red in the air. I begin my ministrations.

'You are going to confess your private thoughts, Charlesworth,' I begin. I order you to shuffle forwards, so you are nearer the sofa and I can sit down once more. I stretch out my legs so the shoes are placed near to your knees. So close, so close to what you need.

'What have you been thinking about at home in your lovely domestic idyll when wifey isn't there, hmm?'

'I've been thinking about you, Miss Caine. About your shoes.'

'You have been doing more than that. What exactly were you thinking?'

Before you have time to come up with an answer I have brought the little lash down onto your penis.

You gasp, but do not add any squealing to your cries.

'Very good. You see, it's not so bad. You had better give me details.'

'I got hard thinking about you wearing boots. Zip-up boots made of shiny material with high heels.'

I nudge the underside of your testicles with my toes.

'Yes. I think I've got some of those.'

'Please, can you take me in your hand. Or rub your feet on me, please, Mistress.'

'I'm considering it,' I say, taking some much-needed sips of wine. 'And what did you do, when you got hard?'

'I went into the bathroom, where I usually go to get some peace from Lorna, and I masturbated.'

I lean forwards and lash at you from above and from underneath your equipment as if I were a conductor using a baton. I could put you out of your sexual misery at any time with the use of my hand or mouth, but I am so enjoying seeing you squirm; the Cabinet minister at the end of his tether.

'You have absolutely no control,' I say. 'If you think I'm going to let you have your way and let you get what you want easily, you are wrong. You need to be worked over, boy!'

I take the lash to you again, watching your penis twitch in response as you wince, imploring me to get to grips with your flesh. Not yet, my darling little minister, I still have something else in my bag of tricks and I produce it with a smile. Like the penis lash, it is made of beautifully fashioned pewter. It's only small, and there's nothing to be scared of.

'What's that?' you ask, unable to see clearly with my pants on your head, before begging for something to drink.

I pull aside your musky headwear and allow you a few sips from your glass before I lash you once more for manners.

'Thank you.'

'That's better. It's going inside, Charlesworth. Where the sun doesn't shine.'

'Oh, Christ. Can't you just finish me off in a normal way?' you plead.

'Oh, this will finish you off all right, but we're not doing "normal" tonight. Good things are sometimes worth making an effort for. Have you not found that, in your parliamentary life? Or do you prefer to cut corners and weasel the votes your way?'

'But it's not fair,' you moan.

'I know,' I say with mock tenderness, 'but think what fun your mistress is having!'

I walk around you and make an observation. You have to lean forwards for me to gain access. The best way will be over the sofa, so you have something soft to brace against. I anticipate a violent emission at some point in the near future, so I fetch a tea towel from your kitchen, and cover the plush velvet of the seat. See, I think of everything.

I pull up the panty-mask to remove your glasses then gently lay my hand in the small of your back, tipping you over so your backside is exposed and ready for violation. Tonight won't be the night that I take a birch to you, but your meaty man's arse will be such a perfect target when I do. There's a good handful of buttock there. Although you don't have a spare tyre or flab, you are slightly thick around your lower portions, like any man of your age. But I'm pleased to note there is good definition to your arms. You are a regular at the gym. There are few things worse than weedy arms in a man over forty. Only skinny young rock stars can get away with that.

I hold the butt plug near to your face. 'Kiss it,' I say. 'Learn to know what is sacred.'

'I'm not kissing that!' you protest.

'Oh dear. This is all so new to you, isn't it?' I say.

'Well, of course it is,' you grumble, muffled by the cushion.

I go on to explain how disrespect for my instruments is disrespect to me, and how this is all for your own good. This is done with my hand tightly screwed into your hair. I could slap you about so hard if you really displeased me. On the second attempt of holding the plug to your mouth you manage to purse your lying little lips.

'That's right. Pucker up. The more obstreperous you are, the rougher I will be.'

That does it. From here on in you are contrition itself.

I trickle lube over the top of the metal and work it up and down, warming it with my hands so it won't be such a shock to Sammy Sphincter. Then, my favourite moment. First date, second date and again I'm having your arse. In he goes. Your face is a picture, all squashed on the seat. Surprise surprise. You gasp then hold your breath.

'Remember to breathe,' I say. 'Breathe into the discomfort. Relax. I know what I'm doing. If you're good now, then I will reward you beyond your dreams.'

I nudge the plug slightly back and forth and run my free hand down your back, stroking you. You become accustomed to the sensation, even pushing back on it in the correct rhythm. I reach under you and then begin to caress your balls. You groan and beg for attention where it matters most. I can really work you now, make you promise anything, say anything. I want to hear your worship.

'You are so impatient, but you are behaving well, letting me do this. If you want my hand on you, then you must repeat after me: "Madame K, you can fuck me in the arse any time you like."'

You comply. 'Madame K, I am only fit for cleaning your shoes. You are a goddess among women and I am so lucky to be fucked by you.'

Again, you repeat my words and earn the grip of my manicured hand firmly around your penis, the nails digging into the gristle.

'Oh, thank you, Madame K, thank you. Please take me all the way, please.'

I run a fingertip over the head and smooth the copious lubrication of your pre-come down the length of your shaft. I must admit, I do like to get hold of a nice meaty weapon like this. The thought of this hardening in your smart suit has me so wet I am aching to feed it into myself, but I can't, I can't. Instead I move myself round to the side of you, so I can access the plug and your penis. I take off my shoes – those fetish objects of supernatural power – and rub my stockinged feet up and down your legs. You begin to angle yourself back and forth, maximising the time I have my hand around you.

'I am doing this as a special treat, Charlesworth.'

'I know, miss, I know.'

'What will you promise me if I take it to the top?'

'I will buy you something you want. Something beautiful. Some lingerie, the finest.'

'Yes, I'd like that. I insist you take me to my favourite store very soon. But I want to hear you say something.'

'What? Please, anything.'

You are gibbering now.

'I want to hear you say "I'm Miss Caine's dog and I'm going to spurt my filthy load."'

Such disgraceful statements from such a well-bred lady.

I make you repeat it three times as I work you, every now and then pressing the plug into diligent service.

'Oh, Christ, I'm nearly there,' you pant. 'Can I have the panties back, please? It's the smell of you. It's like nothing else.'

It's the most genuine thing you've probably said all year, so I reward you for your honesty.

'Yes, yes, thank you. I'm just your dog.'

You push yourself against the seat in a frenzy, muttering obscenities until there is one that's louder and more discernible.

'I'm a filthy fucking dog, just ready to fuck your cunt, you bitch, you fucking bitch.'

Oh dear. You couldn't resist that, could you? You went way over the top. And I feel the warmth spreading as you arch your back and spurt come all over my hand and into the towel. There's loads of it, you dirty bastard. You, with your spectacles and briefcase and ministerial privilege, what a mess you are! You gasp and guffaw into the seat, trying to catch your breath. I wish I had stuffed my foot in your mouth, and I tell you as much for the cheek of taking my name in vain, but you are still laughing the relief of the long oppressed.

I get up immediately to find the bathroom. I am so aroused I can barely walk straight. I shut myself in and text Gareth. I need to party to oblivion to get this out of my system. I look at myself in the mirror. I let my hair down and it falls in a heavy curtain around my shoulders. I wash my hands and tidy my make-up. He texts back. The boys are there. Miko is coming round later. They're filming tonight and I might want to get my hands on their new young star – some bisexual Euro boy who will do anything for £100. They know the score. It's all done without emotion and no questions asked.

I return to the room and you are actually passed out with the plug still in you, my knickers on your face and your hands still shackled. I smile and gently release you from your bonds and discomfort.

'All over,' I say.

You look at me blearily.

'You're beautiful,' you say, sounding woozy and grateful, 'with your hair down like that. I thought I was going to get your hair on me, you know, down there.'

'Maybe next time, Simon. I have to go now.'

You sit up, pull the panties from your face and massage your hands, expressing shock and disappointment that I won't be staying the night.

'Why not? Am I so bloody awful you can't sleep with me? Am I too old or something?'

Oh dear. You've taken a wound to your ego.

'It's not that at all,' I say, businesslike.

'What is it, then? Why are you so ... aloof? You don't have to play this part all the time, you know. I'd like to spend time with you. Not just sexual time, but we can talk about anything. I'd like to get to know you.'

I know if I stayed, like most men you would practically ignore me tomorrow morning on your way to the Commons. And I would not be able to tolerate that. Believe me, you wouldn't want me causing a scene at your grace and favour apartment.

'Oh, you will,' I say. 'But "sleeping together" is not part of the deal.'

'Kirsten Caine, you are magnificent,' you say. 'I've never known anything like it. I want more. I know you do too. More proper sex.'

'You can dream of it. For the meantime, we keep this businesslike.'

'Christ. I'm sick of businesslike,' you moan.

I collect my stuff together but, before I leave your apartment, I sit with you for a couple of minutes, finishing my glass of wine. You have zipped up your trousers, although you still look fantastically dishevelled. There's something of the louche young man you never allowed yourself to be coming through, even though your greying hair contradicts this vision.

'I forgot to tell you ... I got that book, you know,' you say brightly, trying to impress teacher. *'The Story of the Eye.'*

'Good! Read it by Monday,' I insist. 'And the essay by Sontag – 'The Pornographic Imagination'. Email me, telling me what you think. I'm checking my mails all through the day. And remember I want that diary.'

You are eager, like a young dog, newly trained. 'Remind me again.'

'In it you will write all your sexual thoughts and fantasies and memories; everything about your sexuality that you can think of, no matter how dirty or shocking. I want you to hand it to me the next time we meet. It will be for your benefit, believe me.'

'So there might be a reward next time? I won't have to suffer getting it in the ... you know ... again?'

'Not if it's honest enough. I want to be entertained by it. Try to shock me.'

I leave you with that thought as I pull myself into elegance once more, putting my skirt back on. You wave my knickers at me.

'What about these?' you ask.

'Keep them. They're yours now. But you're buying me replacements.'

'I'd like that,' you say. 'God, I don't want the scent of these to fade.' You raise them to your face and inhale.

Before I leave I squat down and caress your hair. You grab my wrist and I sense for a second something needy in your touch. For a couple of moments I feel sorry for you, and I almost capitulate to kiss you, but I give you no more than a smile. You are so perfect for my pleasures and I want to keep you craving more. But Ian Baum won't know this. I shall tell him the evening petered out, that you put a stop to things going any further. I'll blame you as a coward.

I head for the night – for the Bayswater Road and a cab to take me to Gareth's studio. I didn't wash myself and I am ripe with the musk of a woman in the prime of her sexual maturity. Once I am out of the building I feel overawed by the intensity of that scene. I cannot get the sensation of cuffing you out of my system. Of wrestling your hands behind your back and taking you from behind. It is a sensation that is going to be as addictive as the games I play with Baum, but somehow more real because the torment I inflict on you comes from the vast starry interior of my soul, the hunger for total mastery over your desires.

The chill night air manages to cool my arousal a little, for which I'm thankful. Once in the cab I think about everything that's happening. Why I want you addicted to my scent and craving me every minute of the day. Why I got so turned on doing what I did to you, given that you're just an ageing bureaucrat with a lot to answer for. My only answer is that it makes me feel so fucking alive. I want your confessions and your devotion as, in turn, I will invent unusual punishments for you. I've not felt so drunk on power with any other of my initiates. It must be because you yourself hold power, are semi-famous. Yet surely I cannot be that shallow!

I get another text from Gareth – game on with 'Euroboy'. We have the same taste in boys, Gareth and I, and have shared the same disappointment that so few of them turn out to be the artistically inclined, Wildean young dandies we dream of. I used to pine for slips of boys, for their lean young bodies and their sexual stamina, but I can now admit their personalities are generally a disappointment. They're too eager and easily distracted by females their own age, or by cars, or boring gadgets. Young heterosexual men are too lacking in appreciation once the deed is done. They are predictably conservative and fall far too shy of playing the slut. One only has to look at art history for proof of the dearth of submissive male beauty.

A true debauchee should reflect lovingly on his corruption; it should inform his every waking moment, the way he speaks and moves. His sense of aesthetics should scatter sparks of light into the darkness of mundane culture. He should burn with eroticism, not strive to bring futile notions of morality to it. Alas, he is all too rare.

6 **Fire Horse Child**

Being painfully stylish and fashionable, Gareth lives just off Portobello Road and his studio is downstairs from his flat. I arrive to find the place buzzing and a gay porn shoot in process. Gareth is directing as well as operating the camera. His assistant Jon is on sound and some fashion student is doing make-up and continuity. The set is lit, there are empty champagne bottles around the place and mirrors with traces of cocaine in evidence. Not props. I know Gareth too well for that.

'Hi, Kirsten, love,' says Gareth, taking a few moments to light a cigarette and usher me in around the large silver film-equipment cases. I slide into the open-plan room behind the camera, so I can get a good view of the action when it starts. Gareth slinks over and gives me a rundown on the plot, such as it is.

'*Deutsche* boy Jürgen – that's him with the cheek-bones – has picked up straight Polish boy Witek in a club and brought him back to his place for a first-timer.'

'So, it's another Euroboy shoot then,' I say.

'Little bit of tension there, you know,' Gareth continues. 'But there's a surprise ... you wait and see what Witek's got down there. Darling, you are going to want to –' he leans over and whispers in my ear '– get this one on tape for Dr Freud. He's enormous! So, Jürgen can't wait to get Witek in his mouth of course, cos he's a dirty slut. And there's a bit of role reversal as Jürgen ends up being topped.'

'And what's this masterpiece called?' I ask with a sarcastic smile.

'New in Town.'

'Original. So, who's my boy for later, then?'

'Who do you think?' said Gareth, taking a drag on his cigarette.

I look at the two fledgling porn stars in situ on the sofa. They're both wearing shiny football shirts – FC Bayern München for Jürgen and the Polish national team for Witek. I'd not previously considered the appeal of football fetishism but it was starting to make sense. All boys together.

'Don't you think Jürgen's Teutonic face is just perfect?' Gareth asks rhetorically. 'Leni would have loved him.'

I scrutinise both actors, who are smoking and looking slightly wired. They must have hoovered a nose-full before I arrived.

'Just look at that face. Anyway, we're going for the big scene now so settle yourself down.'

'Is he going to be ready again, so soon after the shoot?' I ask.

'I tell you, he's a boy wonder. No worries there, but he doesn't get to come in this scene anyway. We'll clear Jürgen and the others out, and your session will be just you, Witek and me. A closed set.'

'OK then, everybody, places, please,' Gareth shouts and moves in to take up the camera. The boys have read their script, such as it is, and begin to go to their roles. Except it isn't as predictable as I'd expected. Witek, playing the 'straight' role, has been lured to Jürgen's flat on the pretence of watching a satellite-TV football match with some beers. After a few close-ups of Jürgen stroking himself through his jeans, unseen by his guest, he leaves the room to then come back wearing only the shiny team shorts. Cue plenty of close-ups of Jürgen's chest and muscled but slender back. Reaction from Witek, whose sense of sick realisation dawns and he makes to leave. But Jürgen's not taking no for an answer from his 'straight' pick-up.

'We're going for one take,' Gareth shouts. 'Just go for it. Don't forget your lines, Jürgen.'

As everyone falls silent and we wait for the technical crew to get everything absolutely perfect, my gaze falls upon the contents of Gareth's DVD collection. Only he would have the entire box set of *On the Buses* sharing a shelf with Leni Riefenstahl's *Triumph of the Will*. And the thought of the characters from *Are You Being Served* jumping into their neighbour's mise en scène in *Les Diaboliques* is positively sacrilegious. I amuse myself wondering what Simone Signoret would do with Mr Humphreys. Still, more present scandals are about to unfold. Jürgen has wrestled Witek to the floor and they begin fighting, Jürgen telling his unwilling guest what he's going to get rammed up him. If the actors had been male and female I would have found the situation slightly distasteful but, as it is, the sight of this homo-sexual brutality has my arousal levels shooting back up. If only you knew what I was doing now you'd have a seizure. I bet you're polishing off the rest of that wine, sinking into a hot bath with your mind a fizzing cocktail of questions. You'd never guess that I'd have gone to an even more depraved scenario than the one I'd just visited on you.

He's given the dominant speaking part to the German, whose standard of English is much better than Witek's. And as he falls into his role of dominance, the German accent is perfect for the action. He wrestles the Polish boy onto his stomach and straddles him, then pulls his trousers and shorts down over his arse. Jürgen's cock is sticking up hard and threatening and, with his hand on the back of Witek's neck, he forces himself into his anus.

The air fills with profanities as Witek takes it manfully. Gareth works his way around them, changing position and getting in close. He gives a direction and Jürgen pulls out, allowing Witek to turn over. Jürgen is filmed masturbating, and there are some lovingly long takes of him pumping his cock up and down, with Witek capitulating and joining in. Witek strips off his shirt and is made to go down on Jürgen before collapsing back onto the floor in a tussle of sporting rough-and-ready eroticism, taking the soccer celebrations a bit too far, before Jürgen goes for the money shot all over Witek's chest.

By this time I am at fever pitch, although I am stationary, dry-mouthed and silent. I am aching for what the young Polish boy is promised to give me. He is enormous. And he hasn't reached orgasm. Jürgen is collapsed back on the sofa, and has lit a cigarette with a couldn't-care-less expression plastered across his face.

Gareth tells everyone else to leave the room and go into the back studio while he films the next piece as a closed set. Witek knows what's in store for him and he looks me straight in the eye, rubbing his huge cock in his shiny football shorts. This gets me so hot that I gulp down half a litre of water in anticipation of getting my hands on him. I can feel that my sex has swollen and is craving attention. The second the surplus film crew leaves I throw off my jacket and walk over to Witek and feel a shiver of predatory joy as I grab hold of his meaty young buttocks through the slinky material. The heat from the film lights is intense and he's perspiring from the exertions of being manhandled by Jürgen. He's still semi-hard, smelling of sweat and manful exertions and I experience the thrill of violating this sports-mad young buck. His eyebrows have rude-boy slices shaved into them and his hair is asymmetrical, spiked at the side and dyed platinum blond over his natural dark colour. A fake diamond stud is lodged in his earlobe. He looks like housing-estate trash with an angelic face. Thirty years ago he would have been toiling in a shipyard in Gdansk but today he's selling his body for the services of sexual satisfaction.

It feels wrong – and that's why I like it. He's being corrupted by the dissolute privilege of late capitalism. I transplant the dynamics of the scene to a point way back in history, to ancient Rome at its most decadent, just before the Empire fell. The imperious empress is allowed invasive intimacy on a noble savage captured in the Teutoburg Forest. He's about to become gladiatorial fodder, but she's allowed first blood before that glory. Today's servant immediately has his hands on my arse and over my breasts – privileges I usually grant only to Ian Baum. I suddenly remember I was supposed to call him, to let him know what transpired with 'MP X' but I banish it from my mind – I really can't be bothered.

In the meantime I push a stocking-clad leg between Witek's bare legs and feel the hard gristle of his prize packet nudging against my pelvis. He begins speaking what I assume is Polish dirty talk as he roughly plays with my nipples then lifts my skirt to have his hands on me. He is no young gentleman. He immediately brings his hands around the front of me, hiking up my skirt and delving into the moisture of my sex. He starts fingering me in a movement that reminds me of my first fumblings with boys. He is over eager, too rough and crude, and at any other time I would have him on his knees and begging forgiveness. But at this point I need it and I am a little ashamed of myself. I cannot accept that Simon Charlesworth MP has brought me to this extreme state of arousal. Would I have been this turned-on by the sight of the gay porn shoot alone? I cannot know – all I do know is that everything is heightened to a sexual intensity. Every man's lust is a subject of fascination for me. They all serve me in some way. And here is this young Polish man, Witek, all the while fondling himself, growing harder and being bolder, trying to kiss me, telling me in heavily accented English that he is going to fuck me.

Gareth is pulling some creative moves, walking around us and using the camera at oblique angles. By the time he cuts it the movie it will be a work of art, rather than the sleazy event it really is – a forty-year-old woman paying an Eastern European boy for his cock. I'm the one to get down on her knees now and, much as I love the feel of those shiny shorts, I pull them down his thighs to reveal the naked truth. It bounces out like a heavy spring and I instantly have my hands around it, and then my face, rubbing the blunt musky end of it across my lips. I am becoming even wetter, shameless, experiencing jolts of electrical desire shooting through my core. I form my mouth around him and begin to suck. My jaw is aching after an instant because of the girth of him, but I keep up the movement for a few minutes, stopping only to rip my top and bra off so my bare breasts can rub over him. I imagine how grateful you would be, Simon, if I were to allow you such a pleasure. Or even to force you to watch me give another man head, especially with my hair down.

I allow Witek to take the lead from here. He pulls me down onto the sofa and rids himself of the shorts completely. Shame. He's now naked and I have on only skirt and hold-ups. He arranges me so my bottom is pulled to the edge of the sofa. My skirt is then pushed up and he kneels in front of me, hands between my legs to caress me there. The expletives continue, as does his handling of himself. It amuses and delights me to see this young blade of no more than nineteen pulling himself off on his knees before me. I can't resist a little role play and I begin ordering him to make me come, to use his impressive size on me to its full advantage.

Gareth focuses right in on the action and I play for the camera, placing my fingers into the wetness, then making Witek lick them. Despite the fact he knows he's being paid for a performance, he's as impatient to get his penis into me as I am to have it there. I take hold of his cock and begin to move it up and down over my sensitive spot. It won't take long, not charged as I am with the power of making this young man perform for me.

He gets the gist of what I want and begins to go at it with the speed of a vibrator. The sensation is perfect, building me to the moment it will all explode. The look of him, his soft, almost hairless body with that rude blessing between his legs, is exquisite. I now imagine myself to be some ancient deity – a queen of Egyptian sex rites, forcing the better endowed of her slaves to bring her to completion. He's skilled in the art of holding back, has learned to be patient for his porn shoots. He probably knows that if he lunges into me before I am ready I would strangle him for impudence. I think this exercise is something I can torture you with; being older you could be dragged out for even longer. You don't have so cute a face, but your sense of awe would far exceed that of a young buck like Witek. And you would beg so desperately, too, whereas he's probably thinking about hair designs to stave off a premature crisis. At the thought of making you suffer, the molten fires begin to gather. I look Witek straight in the eye and then concentrate on the movement of his hand, manipulating himself to bring me to the moment. He's a dirty boy.

I throw my head back on the sofa, thrusting my pelvis forwards and arching my back. I cry out and feel it boiling over. And then the little shit pulls back, teasing me, kneeling upright with his cock a ramrod, making a gesture with his hands that says, 'Come on, then.' Much as it infuriates me, I shuffle forwards, demeaning myself in a movement that illustrates how desperate I am, and grab him around the hips, digging my nails in. With a deft touch to ensure I'm ready, he then, easy as you please, slides into me as I grind myself close up to his pubic bone to finish what he has started and built up so cleverly – the skilful, dirty little fucker.

So I am there; finally, I am having my long-awaited orgasm, being pounded by the Polish wunderkind who couldn't care less who I am and with whom I don't have to make tedious conversation. I cry out and feel the knots unravel as I ride the waves of surrender. Gareth is exclaiming, 'Beautiful, beautiful!' I know he'll do something fancy with the effects in the edit, make it solarised and psychedelic.

When my throes subside, Witek pulls out for a couple of seconds to roll on a condom. I could leave it there if I was really cruel, say, 'Thanks, you can finish yourself off now,' but I feel like seeing the session through to its end. It is also fulfilling a much-needed emptiness. I'm receiving the live flesh of a young man and giving myself over to watching him, like a voyeur at my own expense.

The profanities come thick and fast as I see Witek's pierced nipples begin to harden and gooseflesh spread over his toned little chest. I sneak a hand down between his legs and cup his contracting balls in my hand as he lets fire into me. And, in the second he knows his reward, his expression seems wholly heterosexual, arrogant and even macho. I let him run with it. I've got a fantastic treat out of it and I am not about to quiz him on his true sexuality. In the heat of the moment I no doubt objectified him more. I throb with joy at the thought of what debasements I am storing up for you. Oh, the delights of depravity!

We had a late one at Gareth's. I indulged myself watching the footage over and over on the small camera screen. It was a real boost to see how well I transferred to film. I know all too well how this material flesh will one day wrinkle and wither, so I shall blaze and triumph with the use of it in its prime. My heavy but high breasts, my long shining dark hair, my full lips and expressive eyes full of wickedness and joy. I was on a high from the transgression of it all, manhandling the football boy. After we'd showered and changed and recovered from our exertions, a small party ensued, fuelled by the usual fizzy liveners as we all looked at the stunning prints Gareth was preparing for a forthcoming exhibition. The boys posed and preened and talked about their hair as they smoked endless cigarettes. The chat was enthusiastic, if a little inane, about fashion and celebrity gossip, but I liked their dandy attitude. Occasionally Witek and I caught ourselves looking into each other's eyes with a mixture of curiosity and lust, but no more would come of it, we both knew that. It was about slaking a need and, for him, earning enough for a great night out.

Around midnight Miko showed up, having finished her shift at the restaurant. She was eager to see the results of the shoot Gareth had done of her the previous week, her doll-like yet sinister countenance brought out beautifully by her new military outfit. On a blonde model from Essex it would have looked trashy, but on Miko it was sensational. She was born to wear it, like some imperial female commander of an elite Japanese regiment. Her head is a collision of sailor girls, rope burns and modernist art. But most of all she loves the

British youth culture of forty years past. She's lost in nostalgia and pines for a London we're both too young to have known. She went wild when she first saw Dad's flat and heard about his art-school life in the 60s – at the height of mod style. She's always scouring Portobello Road for antique clothes, bursting with joy when she finds a Mary Quant or an Ossie Clark.

The thought of this sweet little girl of 5 feet 2 inches with such a deadly imagination being unleashed on you is too good to resist and, fuelled by Gareth's generosity with his intoxicants, we discussed ideas for putting you through your paces the following week. What treats we have in store for you. If you thought tonight was unorthodox, just wait until I unleash Miss Caine's dragon quirt!

I got home in the early hours. Gordon was in the chair, silently untroubled except by the security monitors he was obliged to glance at every few minutes. A classic green-shaded lamp illuminated the novel he was reading. I was still high from the antics at Gareth's, and we struck up an easy conversation about the good and bad points of living in London. After a couple of rants about transport, he handed me a sealed envelope.

'Some guy called for you earlier. Left you this.'

I flipped it over. Ian Baum's writing. A wave of fury rushed up to my already flushed face but I didn't let on I was annoyed.

'He hung about a while, strolling around the foyer, and then dashed off. He was acting kind of strange. I think he was a bit pissed, actually.'

'That figures,' I said. 'Never mind. And thanks for fielding for me.'

'Hey. It's what I'm paid to do. Just wish I didn't have to wear this goddamn uniform. I mean, look at that hem.'

The cut wasn't brilliant. And the bellboy piping was a nasty touch. Gordon deserved better. He was checking me out and, I could tell, was keen to know what the hell it was I did, but a concierge does not probe for information from the residents. He worked here when Dad owned the flat, and he chose this impromptu chat as a time to ask about him.

'He was a flamboyant guy, your dad. Great clothes. Always polite but cool. Something of the wild child about him, even though he must have been his sixties.'

'Sixty-six when he died. Yeah, he was wild all right. Never stopped being wild. It was all part of his thing. He hated conformity. He saw London erupt with excitement. Was the right age at the right time. Art school in swinging London, then the theatre, then the film industry.'

'Oh God, London in the mid-sixties. Just think, you must have had the world at your feet if you had a bit of talent. Not like today when everyone's a fucking artist. Did he work on any films I might have heard of?'

'*Performance*.'

'Shit. That's the ultimate London film!'

'He always said Cammell's vision came from the dark angels.'

'Of course ... Donald Cammell. I always think it's Roeg's movie but it was more complicated than that, wasn't it?'

Gordon began quoting from the movie that I must have seen 25 times. We debated the ending, when Turner gets taken as Chas, driven off to his fate with the big man. We talked about the scene with the bullet, heading for Turner's brain, instead somehow embedding itself in Chas's but, of course, it would ultimately end up in Cammell's some 26 years later. That film. That time. The end of naive optimism and the beginning of drug-fuelled hedonism. I was only three when the film was being made, but the sense of the 1970s getting underway forms my first memories.

I suddenly felt exhausted. It had been a long evening. I wanted to retreat to my zone, put on the *Performance* soundtrack and kick back.

'So if Jack the Lad comes back, shall I tell him that Mr Flowers wants a word?'

'You do that.'

I left Gordon grinning. I hadn't meant to show off, but I find it so difficult to talk about Dad without getting a little hyperbolic. I took the lift upstairs, wondering whether or not to open Ian's note. I decided against it. Whatever it was could wait until morning. Why he couldn't just text me I don't know. When I got in I poured myself a glass of wine and felt compelled to get out the photo box. Ours weren't ordinary snaps. Dad took family photos that could have graced the cover of *Life* magazine. On the top of the pile was my favourite – a black-and-white print of me dressed up as a cowgirl with Dad wearing buckskin pants and a shirt that he always said he'd nicked from Jimi Hendrix. You could almost smell the incense.

Dad told me he started thinking and dressing differently almost as soon as he was on the crew of that film. There was a collision of weirdness, poetry and violence around it that must have been infectious because he never really shook off the Dionysian chaos that Cammell told him was overseeing the production. Working on the movie drove him quite crazy, changed his chemistry, and the dark angels flew him on raven wings to the bottle and the needle. For three years after the film was finished he never strayed more than two miles from Powis Square. And neither did Donna and I. Apart from excursions to the seaside and days out with my grandparents, I spent my pre-school years in a fug of hippie havoc.

There must be a hundred photos of me, nearly always dressed up in my mother Donna's clothes. I'd dress up and dance my arrhythmic little girl dances to the music that always seemed to be playing every hour of the day and night in that mad living room. Mostly the Stones, but also American freak-out bands like The Fugs and the Mothers of Invention. I would jump off the enormous pile of cushions in the corner of the room and drive the adults crazy. They were always dozing on the floor. They didn't want me landing on their stomachs, hashing their mellow. *Pleased to meet you, hope you guess my name.*

It was a house of Indian fabrics, joss sticks, broken clocks, naked adults covered in Day-Glo paint, closed windows, perpetual night-time, and strangers crashed out on the living-room floor. There were exotic pets that inevitably died, a stereo in every room, table lamps with batiks thrown over them, the smell of weed, an impossibly filthy kitchen that no one ate in and a huge poster of the 1920s 'vamp' Theda Bara on the wall of the purple-and-green-painted hallway. I also remember the black-painted bathroom, a constant fear of 'the fuzz', copies of *International Times* on the coffee table, junk paraphernalia and Dad's sketchbooks. Such was my toddlerhood.

When he did manage to haul his ass out of W11 it was the shock of Mum's OD that did it. Drowned in the bath with a gut full of Mandrax. The party was over. I was packed off to convent school in Switzerland and Dad fled to California. He couldn't live with the rage and heartbreak Donna's parents brought down on him for killing their little girl. She was always Donna. I never called her Mum. I barely got the chance to know her. She was just a girl, not even thirty when she died. I remember her through smells. The scent of summer and the henna she applied to her waist-length hair, it crusting to a solid mass on the top of her head as she nodded off on an opiated cloud. The plastic smell of the Play-Doh and the paints she used to get out for me as I sat at my little easel in the garden. The grass was allowed to grow waist high and I used to run unseen in what to me was a jungle.

Dad always called me his fire horse child. I was born in 1966, the year of the rarest archetype of Chinese astrology. We're supposed to be catalysts for extraordinary events, wildly creative and impossible to discipline. So he must have known what putting me in that nineteenth-century institution would do. Still, he didn't put up too much of a fight about it when Donna's parents took over. He was in no fit state to look after a child and wanted an easy escape. Gordon talking about Dad picked at that solemn place within me that echoes when I get flashes of his essence – and then I have to accept that that essence is no longer tangible. The sense of loss is still raw but his obsessions live on.

I woke up hungover yet determined to break the back of the Curzon job. The rain was lashing down and I wondered if I could manage to get through a whole day without once stepping outside. It was nearly one o' clock so I thought I'd treat myself with some down-to-earth comforts. I could ring downstairs and have the porter bring me up a paper, make fresh coffee, muffins and watch the lunchtime news. The living room still had photos spread all over the floor from the previous night's nostalgia. I bent down to scoop them up when I found the unopened note from Baum. I ripped into it.

KC – I was in the area so I thought I'd drop by. I hope you had lots of fun tonight. Sorry I was so nosy last time we met. Don't be angry with me. I didn't mean to pester you about what you're doing. I just want you to know how I feel about you. I wanted to handwrite this, as it feels more real. Do you remember when you used to lie with me on my sofa during the first months of your post-prison therapy, curled up with your head against my shoulder? You used to say you felt so safe with me. I want you to feel safe with me again. What we do stays with us. You can trust me. Come on holiday with me. Missing you. Hope Friday is still on.

Ian.

I sighed and felt annoyed. What *was* I going to do about this Friday? Visiting him at his office would be a bad idea. It would be better to have a little distance, meet in a public place. I was just running through the choice of Hampstead pubs to suggest when the BBC London news came on. And there you were. I frantically tried to record it, but I didn't have a spare videotape to hand so I gave up the search and perched on the edge of my sofa, eyes glued to the screen, my voice repeating inane ejaculations of surprise. I wanted to share my shock with someone: that this man – this government minister – had not 24 hours ago been at my mercy, but there was no one. Seeing you there in your suit, being important, was a pure rush of adrenaline. Suddenly I was wide awake and trembling. There was that face which only yesterday I had squashed onto a sofa wearing my knickers for a mask. There it was addressing the people of London about investment and sponsorship. It was a perfect moment of irony. The public face of reason masking the private experience of irrational desire.

The things I held in store for you excited me to distraction. I could find some brief pleasure fooling around with Gareth's models or playing the uptight woman for Ian Baum, but I craved someone I could lay bare, spread open and debase. I needed again to see the very moment of your stiffening, the instant you are given over to your scandalous needs. I need to seize upon that vulnerability to bend you to my will. The deeds I triumph in are an aberration to you. Enjoy the last few days of your attention being consumed by worldly matters because your psyche is already changing. The exquisite conditions I am visiting on you will make your need rapacious, insatiable. You will want to become like me – a libertine at large – yet your occupation manacles you to convention. It is indeed a dilemma, my grey darling, but one we can surely overcome together.

7 Dog in the Manger

Today was a bore. I had to do a live broadcast on the lunchtime news outside City Hall about the Capital Link scheme. The opposition – peace be upon them – have whipped up fears about the project running over budget and out of time. I wouldn't care, but it's their lot who underinvested in transport for over a decade, and now they're jockeying for the righteous position. I think I got away with it, talking up the 'ripple effect' and the legacy the project will leave for the capital's children. It was only the lunchtime reporters, anyway – poodles rather than Dobermanns. I fell back on the default panacea – talking jobs and new shopping opportunities in areas where stations are redeveloped.

Jason yet again proved to be worth his weight in gold. Sharp lad. Got me the spanking-clean artists' impressions ahead of schedule of a Bluewater-cum-marina-style development that'll tart up Tower Hamlets. Had a lovely graphic of the obligatory clean futuristic train cutting through the design. We can use the new rail initiative as a lever to turf the shabby houseboat hippies off the canals too. Get some serious mooring fees in once the area is redeveloped. Attract blue-chip investment and see the waterways fulfilling their potential as a guaranteed revenue stream. See a 'new, dynamic, vibrant, sustainable community' stretching from the Thames Gateway to the City. What did we ever do before we recruited advertising copywriters?

The plans are looking top notch for the proposed luxury housing development around the East London basin: ergonomic glass architecture, a mezzanine paved area with fountains and designer lighting, a private gymnasium and 24-hour security. They'll be queuing up for them. The next step has to be the reclamation of some of those water-logged playing fields. It's an ideal place for a prestige car showroom, or even one of the super casinos. That would be a nice lump sum up front and healthy rents with no risk of defaulting like you get with small businesses.

I was nervous beforehand, but I think the broadcast went well. The PM's got his eye on me over this. He can't afford any more negative PR over public policy. Health and education have been disastrous, so the river redevelopment is feather-in-the-cap stuff. If this all goes to plan and restores public faith in Private Finance Initiatives it'll see me sitting pretty for the next Cabinet reshuffle. I've got my eye on Health. That's prime for corporate sponsorship.

I wondered if you had tuned in to the midday news. I hoped you wouldn't have seen it in company and been compelled to divulge the details to God knows who. Yet again you have denied me full access and it's driving me mad, Kirsten Caine. I'm beginning to think I should just forget this whole thing and find a normal woman. Or give up the idea of straying from home and just accept my lot. Surely I can woo you, though, make you come around to my way of thinking. It cannot be right that you deny your own pleasure. What are you doing to find satisfaction? Do you use dildos and vibrators on yourself? I wish I knew. I wish I could see it.

I sit reading Jason's new report on potential snags to the East London redevelopment scheme that might arise from the protest quarter. It seems a bunch of them has occupied a café in Hackney that went in a compulsory purchase order. The whole street is crying out to be dragged into the twenty-first century. There are at least two prestige loft-dwelling initiatives happening there, and the building contractors are on a tight schedule. They've opened up the café without a licence and have started serving vegetarian food. What do they think this is? The 1970s? Similar bunch to the scruffs that are kiboshing the ring-road plans in my constituency. We can get them on criminal trespass, of course, or maybe threaten to do them under the terror laws if they're seen filming or interfering with the building work. Of course the charges won't stick, but it should be enough to frighten them off. Everyone knows how long that lot can hold up progress. I can't afford to have these kinds of obstacles happening so early in the scheme.

But my thoughts are straying. I want to spend more time making entries into my diary. I started writing it after you left last night and I already feel the benefits of letting loose some of my private ideas. Kirsten, you are right, it is like a purging. I'd purchased a small hardback notebook for financial doodlings but now it's given over to what I'm calling Project X. I'm conscious of always having it near to me, as if it were essential medication, but it feels as dangerous as dynamite and as addictive as caffeine. Surely I can risk a few moments thinking about the personal side of my life. It can't all be trains and buildings. I pull the book from my bag. I've got to let some more thoughts out – things I've never committed to paper. Fuck it. OK, here it is, ready or not.

7 September
Have been reading old copies of *Forum* magazine that I'd hidden in the garage a few years' back. Lorna thinks I've thrown them out but I kept the ones with the letters that never fail to make me hard and spunk all over myself as I wank off thinking about them. I sneak in the garage and then take them to the bathroom. I enjoy this rediscovery. It takes my mind off the pressure of

work. I like the stories about girls dressing up really tartily. I imagine them to be beautiful Asian angels with long black hair. Even the small ads for phone lines can get me instantly hard. What I really want to hear is women speaking dirty. I think about the women who are always at those meetings at City Hall getting off their high horses and reading out some of those small ads. I want to hear them say it: 'I need to suck your cock and fill my aching hole. Fill me with your spunk while I come for you.' Or even the really extreme ones: 'I'm going to piss my panties in front of everyone.' Imagine that in front of the mayor and his righteous cronies. Oh, it's so wrong, but it drives me insane. Maybe I can get you to say these things. I imagine it's not really your thing, but maybe if I pay you . . .

Writing is getting me hard. I think about you wearing boots again. I reach down and adjust myself and cannot resist a little stroke. I'm feeling reckless. I undo my fly and pull it out under the desk. No one can see; the desk has a back panel that would shield me even if the worst happened and someone was to come in. Maybe I should go to the loos, but I'm so hard already that I'd be pressed to conceal my state. Imagine if I ran into the PM in the corridor, or one of the birds from the Standards in Public Life Committee! I take myself in hand, that's it, pump it a few times. Imagine those slutty women licking their lips and showing it to me. I want a genuine dirty one who's going to love it. Some exotic Asian babe who wants a mouthful of cock. I concentrate on the sensation, getting faster now with my fist until I'm whispering obscenities to myself. Every time I try to write in the diary I turn myself on. I can't write lucidly without getting hard. How do you control yourself? You don't even seem to need that release. It's plain bizarre. One day I'm going to make you show me, and I'm going to make you fucking orgasm for me, you uptight bitch. You fucking beautiful bitch. I want to see your perfect face being spunked into. And it's going to be me, Simon Charlesworth, secretary of state for public policy, shooting a fat wad in your face.

At this, all hell brakes loose and I feel the volcano erupt in my loins, shoot up the shaft and spill over into my hand. I can't catch all of it, and some of it jets onto the carpet under my desk. I shouldn't laugh, but I do, I sit there with my fly undone and with the evidence of my depravity already soaking into the blue hessian weave. Keeping this diary is actually making me even more insatiable for it. And for the kind of sex I'm not going to get out of Lorna in a thousand years. I have to fuck you, Kirsten. I have to know what it's like to feel myself release inside of you. No more of this gay nonsense. Not now I've really started to think about what I want. You are the one who's doing this to me and I'm determined to have you.

I've not gone 24 hours from seeing you and I'm already craving you again. Not for what you've now done to me twice, but your presence, your personality. I wonder what you are doing today and who you are with. I should have asked you more questions about your own life, but how can I even believe you'd tell me the truth. What was all that surrealist stuff about? Fairy stories and dummies? Am I supposed to deduce something from this? Is it some kind of metaphor for my life? Do you think I'm a dummy? Who's paying you to afford a life of leisure in that South Kensington apartment? That must be a fair few quid a month in rent. A grand at least, I'd say. That's not earned by being in arts administration. And you've decorated it like some dingy hippie joint. There's got to be more going on than meets the eye.

Why didn't you stay last night? Most women would have jumped at the chance. Is there someone you had to rush back to? It's all very well for you to say there's no pimp and you're not a prostitute but what exactly am I getting myself into here? Surely you're doing this for money. It simply doesn't add up that you'd bother to spend your time picking up businessmen for altruistic purposes. Hearing them unburden their troubles, indeed. I don't buy it, and I feel rattled by the situation. By you. Yet I've never known such a sexually exciting woman. You're not the type I usually fantasise about, yet I feel an almost magnetic pull to you. I love to hear you speak. I want to have known you for years. I want you to be a friend, my confidante.

It annoys me that I don't have anyone to confide in. It's one of the drawbacks of my position. I have political allies, of course, fantastic advisors like Jason, but there's no one with whom I can share my deep personal thoughts. That's something I used to do with Lorna, but I can't talk honestly to a woman who shuns me in bed. And how could I talk to her about you? Her frigidity has ruined everything. I no longer have any anchors.

It's the bloody conference in two weeks' time and I'm determined I'll fuck you before then. I need a bit of a boost, something to kick-start the old confidence. I'm going to show them I've got private backing for the party's public policies. Politicians are winning votes for youth rather than experience these days. I need to make a stand as real man with something to say – not a boy with some fancy talk. I've got my second voice-coach appointment this weekend. It's definitely helping. I'm learning the give and take of communication, rather than just spraying opinions about the room as if from an aerosol can. I'm slowing down the delivery, making eye contact, learning how to move my head to affect a point of sincerity. It's costing an arm and a leg, but it's worth it. I'm investing in myself, says the voice coach, but she would, wouldn't she?

I know what the old guard would think, the Dennis Skinners and the like. They'd say it was for poofs, and they'd be half-right. But we've all got to play the hand we're dealt the best way we can. I've lost support through mumbling speeches in the past and I'll not do it again. I'm going out to consolidate my position and shine on the podium. It's not just the party I'll be addressing, it's everyone who tunes in. The whole bloody thing is going to be broadcast. It's a fool who ignores the proliferation of media technology.

There'll be the usual ministerial groupies around, but I'll do my best to avoid them. No one forgives indiscretions these days. It's all got to be squeaky clean. So many more women about, that's why. I've shared a few pointless moments with other members' secretaries in my time. Lorna never found out, or, at least, if she suspected anything she never said. Soulless occasions, they were. Women who'd be charming at the bar then once they'd come back to my room they'd lie there passively, magnifying whatever anxieties they had about sex by engaging in anonymous coupling that would prove to them all men were bastards. All I can remember of these incidents are dark rooms in conference hotels. Nothing more demonstrative in the heat of passion than a bit lip or a pair of hands softly resting on my lower back as I pointlessly chugged away. And it was always me on top. I was never lucky enough to meet one who would jump on top of me, look like she was enjoying it or even say what she wanted. I couldn't say if I'd made them come. I doubt it. And they would never tell me if they had. All in all, my dalliances away from home have been exasperating and depressing. A contest of wills, almost: my will to climax, theirs to not allow an inkling of pleasure to register.

But now I've met you, Kirsten, and I can't stand the agony my desire is bringing me. I'm spending half the day with a hard-on, and half the weekend jerking off. I've got to get this thing resolved. I'll take you to dinner. To a hotel. Wherever you want to go. I don't care about the cost. This time I'm going to assert myself and make myself irresistible to you. I'll use my voice-coaching technique on you. With this renewed sense of potential success I feel cheered. I'm hastened to tidy myself. To wipe myself, do up my trousers and visit the bathroom. I'll text you and arrange our next date. I have been daydreaming the impossible notion that you might call me. I have lost many minutes today imagining weekends in Paris, evenings in swish hotels and nights at the ballet or opera. You would make such a fetching companion. Well, maybe that will come. Surely you want my cock in you. I don't understand how you can just walk away unsatisfied from an intimate situation. You don't seem too bothered about the very thing you initiated in the first place. Who do you have sex with? God, I wish I knew.

It's a week since that first night we shared and I managed to make my way home safely without deviation, hesitation or, God forbid, repetition. I stood on the concourse with my eyes fixed on the travel information boards, determined not to be tempted to revisit the scene of the crime. I feared with an almost supernatural terror that, if I did go back to that bar, I'd meet you and relive the entire scene of our first meeting again. It would be like *Groundhog Day*. The train was on time for once, and I wound down the week with a couple of beers in the buffet car, catching up on the arts reviews I'd saved from the paper. I usually only bother to look at the classical music or opera, but this time I read up on the film and contemporary music section so I'd have something to impress you with next time I saw you.

The Times wasn't the only reading material I had on my person. Before entering the station I'd popped into the adult bookstore that still nestles in a somewhat dingy corner of the arcade facing the station and spent £25 on X-rated materials. I stood there, anonymous in the company of other men about my age, my heart beating fast, throat rasping with nervous excitement as I browsed the dizzying array of porn on display. It was warm in there. You could feel the anxiety of the other customers, all like me – looking shifty but bloody glad to have somewhere where they're not under the scrutiny of women. A bored-looking middle-aged bloke sat at the counter, reading the *Racing Post*.

There were magazines catering to every legal fancy, a good deal of them focusing on SM and bondage. I browsed through *Hustler Taboo*, but it was all too American. I've never even entertained the thought of having sex with an American. There were some anodyne publications with titles like *Bend Over Boyfriend*, which featured cheeky-looking girls with flame-red hair and those ridiculous facial piercings. That put me off.

I scooped up a couple of Asian hardcore magazines and a dominatrix directory that I would scour for evidence of you, before folding their wrapper carefully over them and stowing them away neatly in my case. The cashier didn't even look up as he served me, for which I was thankful. I hurried out into the stream of Thursday evening commuters heading home, the knowledge of my sordid acquisitions burning into my brain. I need the traditional stuff. I'm an ordinary man. That weird book you told me to read isn't exactly my cup of tea.

I couldn't wait to unwrap them. I looked forward to getting into the bathroom with them, spending some time relieving the sexual frustration that was becoming an overwhelming presence. I picked up my car from the station car park and, as dusk was shrouding me in the shadows, I couldn't resist a peek at one or two pages, concealed in between my newspaper, just in case anyone should come right up to the window. The pink flashes of pussy looked so nice against the rich caramel skin of those young birds. Oh fuck. Just the sight of one pouting slit got me hard again as I adjusted myself in the driver's seat and ignited the engine. I felt a mixture of indignation, arousal and the thrill of having secret pleasures. It was a bizarre combination. I resolved even more to vent my desires on you. Get that luscious hair of yours wound around my cock and fill your mouth with it, hard, and do it down your throat.

But I shouldn't have to wait until then. I was long overdue some conjugal rights. I drove home hard and made a strong entry through the front door, calling out my arrival. I'm fed up creeping about like six-foot-tall grey rat in my own home. Lorna was sitting in the living room reading a health magazine. The house smelled wonderful and the aroma of something being casseroled tweaked my stomach into reminding me how hungry I was for a proper cooked meal. I've barely eaten since last week.

'Hey,' I said, throwing my mac over one of the chairs and then shrugging off my suit jacket.

She threw me a weak greeting and continued reading a feature on probiotic cultures in bowel health. We've never been a couple that fawns over each other, but there used to be at least an interest in each other's days. Now the communication is clipped and strained.

'Trains were good tonight,' I said, standing before her with my hands on my hips.

'Thought you were home early. Chicken tagine for supper, OK?'

'It smells delicious. I can't wait.'

At least she was still taking an interest in feeding me. I plonked down on the sofa next to her, the promise of dinner not yet managing to eradicate my sexual spur. I turned my body towards her, loosening my tie, and focused my gaze on her legs. She's got good legs, has Lorna. In the summer they tan to a delicious digestive-biscuit colour with fine blonde hairs dusting her thighs and forearms. If only she would grow her hair a little longer. Not go for that short layered look. I think I would even prefer the ageing Essex girl look – manicured nails, blonde highlights and too much make-up. At least those women look like they still enjoy a turn in the sack. Lorna just looks prissy.

'What are you looking all expectant for?' she asked me. 'It won't be ready for at least an hour.'

'That's fine,' I said. 'Perfect. Time for a little ... you know...' I trailed off, unable to come out with what I wanted, what I needed, so inured am I to feeling ashamed of my needs.

'What *now*? It's half-six.'

'And what's the problem with it being half-six?'

'The news is on at seven.'

'I think you could give Jon Snow a miss just for one evening,' I suggested, reaching out to lay a hand on her thigh. 'I've had a busy week. Did you see me on the lunchtime news?'

'It was on at Mum's but I couldn't concentrate on it properly. You know how she is.'

Nice one, Lorna. Thinking about your geriatric mother is just right for the mood. I shook it from my mind and edged closer to her. I stroked her arm but it had no effect other than to make her sigh and put down her magazine in exasperation.

I took hold of her wrist and placed her hand on my own thigh.

'Please,' I rasped as her hand lay there, limp and undemonstrative.

'What?' she asked obviously irritated.

'Lorna, what do you think?' I said, exasperated. 'What do think a man might like to share with his wife in their marriage?'

'I suppose you mean sex.'

'There's no need to make it sound so onerous.'

'Simon, for me personally it is, to be honest.'

It was my turn to look affronted. 'I know you're not exactly the raging nympho of the county but I mean, we could, you know. It's been ages.'

'If you call twelve weeks ago ages. And stop using words like "nympho". It makes you sound ridiculous.'

'Was it that recent? I've been getting the cold shoulder since the beginning of the year. In fact, it's been a gradual decline since I got the promotion. I thought you liked it that I'm in the Cabinet. Do you not find it exciting?'

'This has nothing to do with your job,' she said.

'Then what does it have to do with? Am I unattractive all of a sudden? Got a toyboy stashed away, have you, who does the garden while I'm at the Commons? Or are you having an affair with the local garden-centre manager? You spend enough fucking time in there.'

'Don't be ridiculous.'

'Well, try to see it from my point of view.'

'I've tried, Simon, and I can't. I just don't feel that way. I'm sick of being pressured to feel like I'm supposed to look some kind of ... porn star. This culture makes me sick. It's everywhere.'

I stared at her with the realisation that the chance of a little pre-supper nookie was drifting into the realm of the highly unlikely.

'Do you know, I can't even buy a pair of trousers that

does up around the waist any more. I think I bought the last pair in nineteen-ninety-eight.'

'What the fuck has that got to do with our sex life?' I plead, exasperated.

'Everything's got to be "sexy".' She made annoying quote marks with her fingers. 'Everything's low-slung and designed for teenagers. Skinny crop tops and hipster jeans and ridiculous thongs.'

'Lorna, I don't expect you to look twenty years old. Or wear the stuff you're talking about. I just want you to be my wife in the bedroom as well as the kitchen.'

I knew I'd said the wrong thing as soon as it left my mouth. She stood up, fuming, raising her voice. I'd touched a nerve.

'I don't want you pawing at me all the time,' she said, a wavering tone of hysteria entering her voice.

'I'm not,' I replied. 'I've just got ... needs. I'm a man.'

'You do paw at me. Every bloody morning I wake up with a gun in my back, feeling obliged to have to deal with that ... *thing*, before I can get on with the day.'

'Oh, I'm glad you feel obliged,' I put in, sarcastically. 'But I don't see you acting on your obligation. And, anyway, don't you feel good that I still desire you? You should be glad I get a hard-on in the morning ... that I'm not bloody impotent. Surely you would be even more pissed off if I never tried to have sex with you. Then you'd been crying that I don't find you attractive any more. I can't win!'

'There are other ways of showing appreciation,' she went on, 'in a more civilised way.'

'Uncivilised now, am I? Christ!'

'Yes. Yes, you are.' She'd raised her voice again. 'I know what you've been doing in the garage, reading that pornography. It's ridiculous.'

'You mean those old *Forum* magazines?' I snorted in

derision, dismissing the issue as nothing. 'We used to read them together, if you remember.'

'That was a long time ago, Simon. And I wasn't too happy about it at the time, either, *if you remember*. I've moved on and you haven't. It's immature. Quite honestly, don't you think there's more important stuff to be thinking about than orgasms?'

'Like what? Like what?' I had started to shout.

Right then an orgasm was what I wanted more than anything – shot out at the speed of light from the end of my cock into my wife's cunt. I stood up, furious at her display of righteousness. I made a grab for her, pulling her towards me. I took a firm hold of her buttocks and began kissing her neck.

'Stop it!' she fussed, trying to push me away, but I was determined not to give up.

'Suppose I don't want to stop?' I asked, breathing into her ear. 'Suppose we do things my way tonight and just this once I stop making allowances for you? Suppose you lighten up for five fucking minutes and stop all these stupid excuses why we can't make love?'

'This isn't making love.' She tried to push me away but I clutched her firmly, harder than I'd ever clutched her. I thought of you wrestling my arms behind my back in my London apartment. Now I wanted to do the same to Lorna.

'We've gone past that, *darling*,' I spat, the tussle chafing me to a half-hard state.

'So, what's it going to be then, rape?' she whined.

'You're so fucking extreme, Lorna.'

Just for once I decided to forgo all the political correctness, all the walking on eggshells lest something I say remotely inferred sexual desire from the male point of view. I was furious with her. I wanted to shock her. I thought of what you would do in a similar situation and I felt a sudden surge rush through me, as if you were there, egging me on to transgress the boundaries.

'Yeah, if needs be,' I persisted, grabbing at her trousers.

'No. I don't want to,' she wailed.

'Well I *do*. Why should you always be the one who gets their own way?'

We struggled and I walked her backwards to the sofa and pushed her so she fell onto it. That chintzy, flowery sofa with those big tapestry cushions of country scenes. I leapt on top of her, the urgency filling my balls with sperm and my cock with blood. I thought about the cavemen you'd talked of, accessing primal drives. I thought of the first night I met you, and how I'd wanted to fuck you in that bar. I wanted to know that power, know the thrill of pushing things further when reason tells you to retreat. I'd had enough of reason. I recalled how you had teased me with your long legs, not letting me touch you. It was as if everything I'd paid lip service to over the course of my career was rearing up to mock me. During the most virile years of my life I'd repressed what was naturally seeking an outlet. Now it was fighting back, as a torrent of inappropriate thoughts and actions. I wanted to find out what would happen if I went with my primal desires for once. I wasn't going weasel out of this with apologies, to retreat upstairs and wank myself stupid. I was going to see it through to its conclusion.

Lorna struggled and tried to push me off, but I was not prepared to suffer any more humiliation. I was determined to see the reassertion of dominance in my own home.

'You're going to let me do this,' I hissed, 'because neither of us wants the alternative.'

'You can't do this. You can't turn into this fucking monster.'

'I'm not a fucking monster, I'm just a man who needs his wife – in the old-fashioned way that man has needed woman since time began. Don't you understand?'

'No,' she whined, 'I don't, but if it's that fucking important for you to get your dick inside me then, OK, let's do it. Let's fuck no better than animals, cos that's what you are. You're just an animal. The more important you've become, the worse you've got. More base and disgusting.'

Lorna complained bitterly but gave up trying to fight me off and, disgruntled yet resigned, she shuffled off her trousers, peeled off her socks in exaggerated indignation and threw them across the room as if she wanted to shatter them.

'Well then,' she declared, mockingly. 'There. Are you aroused yet?'

'Yes, I'm aroused, but no thanks to you. I'm aroused because of natural need.'

I wasn't going to hang around debating the issue. I wanted to get in there before she changed her mind. I kicked my shoes off, amazed that she'd capitulated. It was far from an ideal situation but it was the best I was going to get for God knows how long. I stood up briefly to whip my trousers off and then got back on top of her. I felt between her legs and she was hot and damp.

'Oh, this is so romantic, Simon, darling,' she taunted, venom and sarcasm mixing to a poisonous brew.

'What's this, then?' I asked. 'You're wet. I thought you didn't want it?'

'A physiological reaction doesn't necessarily mean psychological consent,' she grumbled.

'Oh, stop being so clever. You just try to enjoy it, darling,' I said, leaning on my side to take my penis into my hand. It was red and stiff.

I caught a look at her and she was affecting an expression of exaggerated boredom. For that I hated her, but I was still grateful even though I knew she'd play the martyr over this for at least a month. I thought about my diary, about the porn mag I'd bought, of the picture I'd looked at of some attractive young woman with her plump sex pouting at me. I concentrated hard on it as I got up close to where I wanted to be. I pumped myself a couple of times, pulled Lorna's knickers aside and then I was at the gates.

'Oh fucking hell,' I said as I slid in, finally feeling the constriction of moist female flesh around me. 'You want it, do you? You're gonna fucking get it. Oh yes, oh yes.'

My eyes were closed. I could not bear to catch sight of Lorna's bored face and, of course, she didn't join in my dirty talk. I manoeuvred my hips so I was buried up to the hilt. I imagined what it will be like when I finally come to do this to you. Oh my God. I buried my mouth against her neck, pumping into her, my breath becoming ragged, my tongue loosening up to say all manner of wild things.

'I'm going to fucking do it in you. Yeah, do you like that? Feel my fucking cock in you. Big, isn't it? Big and hard. It's gonna spurt inside you. Fill your cunt with my spunk. Or do you want it in your face. Want me to jizz all over your face, you fucking whore.'

I barely knew what I was saying. It was coming out like a stream of sexual consciousness, as if I were speaking in tongues. But Lorna began swearing at me then, trying to push me off again, yelling at me to stop saying that stuff, crying 'How dare you call me a whore!' But it all got confused in my mind. I imagined her anger to be your haughtiness, as if you'd caught me doing something I shouldn't, but secretly wanting the power of a man inside you. I pressed my weight down on Lorna's shoulders. I was going nowhere, and neither was she.

'You fucking bastard,' she spat at me. 'I'll never forgive you for this.'

'No?' I asked. 'Is that right? How about some of this then?'

As she squirmed underneath me and tried to get away, she only fuelled my need to dominate – not her, but you. I was turning the tables on the woman who had fucked me in the arse. Twice. Who had made a fool of me for whatever reason for a second time. Well, it was time to get even. I pictured you lying back on the sofa, getting it from me. Getting a right good seeing-to. Something all you women want, isn't it? I couldn't see straight. A boiling mass of sensation was building between my legs and I pressed down and pumped home.

'Yes, yes, I'm coming,' I panted. 'I'm doing it now, right up you, right up your fucking cunt, you dirty bitch.'

As it hit me, and I felt the molten liquid rise up my penis, I thought I heard Lorna say she hated me but I didn't care. I'd got the pressure out of my balls. I collapsed down on top of her, panting hard with the exertion and laughing with relief. I was barely at the end of the final twitches before I was unceremoniously pushed off and up against the back of the sofa as Lorna tore from the room like a clap of thunder.

After the rush died down I reflected on what had happened. It was like I'd been taken over by some kind of demon. I couldn't believe I'd come that close to raping my wife. To my horror it had felt great, too. Lorna's reluctant capitulation was the only thing that had saved us from crossing a disastrous line in our relationship. Would I have really forced her, had she not resigned herself to giving in? Would I have committed a heinous criminal act in my own home? I suddenly feared I might be losing control such had become my need of intense experience. As soon as I was struck with the horror of what I'd done, I also registered my aching need to confess. I needed absolving, and only you could grant me release from the guilt.

The remainder of the evening was spent with Lorna practising her repertoire of withering looks every time I did something that annoyed her. And it didn't take much: the wrong serving spoon for the vegetables; the wrong bottle opener for the wine. I went out of my way to show impeccable manners at the dinner table, even though the conversation was perfunctory at best. I poured her wine and she didn't thank me. I told her the casserole was superb. Silence. I asked after her mother. I hung my head in shame and promised to make it up to her with a fantastic holiday and a new wardrobe, pleading a mystery surge of desire that was ironic in the face of being 53, but none of it softened her attitude one jot.

I changed tack, and made a serious attempt to talk about what I saw as the disintegration of a fundamental part of our marriage, but she wouldn't converse or engage with the subject at all. I felt some physical relief at finally managing to unburden my load, but my relaxed body language only served to annoy her even more. I apologised profusely, saying I didn't know what had come over me, but I was not going to shoulder all the blame for my actions. I laid out the bare facts: that a man cannot be denied a sexual life for months on end. I expressed concern that she seemed unable to let go sexually these days, telling her I couldn't remember the last time she'd had an orgasm. I got a sharp retort that it was none of my business and the atmosphere in the living room was so frosty that, after dinner, I retreated to my study for the remainder of the evening, listening to Dvořák and Schubert's sonatas to find a bit of calm.

When I retired to bed Lorna already had the lights turned off. I slid in beside her and immediately felt her flinch. She was trying hard to pretend she was asleep but I could tell she was fuming in the dark. I apologised for my behaviour once more, blaming the stress of the job, and I suggested investigating counselling but I was talking to the silence. She spoke only to tell me that we were having Sunday lunch at Sarah and Robert's, her voice projected at the wall. I could face this all with a lighter heart, however, because *you* had got in touch. I'd received a text while I was in my study: you had agreed to let me take you out on Monday. I had feared you might opt for a swish eaterie like Nobu but you said you'd prefer somewhere old school and discreet like Wishton's off Haymarket. I was relieved.

I must say, you are a constant surprise. Even the educated women in the House seem irresistibly drawn to celebrity tittle-tattle and status dining, but not you. You seem above it all, your concerns elsewhere. Oh, Miss Caine, next time we meet I'm going to have you.

Friday saw an early start. My voice coach had been round for a breakfast session at 8 a.m., working on exercises to improve communication, which seemed ironic, given that Lorna left the house mid-lesson without so much as a goodbye. The coach had me running around my garden to get my blood pumping and delivering lines over and over using different levels of 'presence'. Her techniques are unorthodox but I felt invigorated and almost happy after an hour of having her complete attention focused on me.

It was a bright day, and blustery, and I went for a walk on the Downs at lunchtime between my surgery sessions, pondering the state of things with Lorna and promising myself I wouldn't force myself on her again. She kept telling me it should be a woman's prerogative to say no, but for how long can a husband give good grace? Lorna has turned into such a nag and a grouch since I got my position, and I'm sure any man would be driven at least once in his marriage to demand some physical contact. If I was getting sexual satisfaction elsewhere then Lorna's frostiness wouldn't bother me so much, but I've been driven to distraction, what with your teasing, not letting me touch you, and then getting her cold shoulder on top. I've been desperate.

I set my sights on Monday for going after you. I had the idea that I would buy you something nice – something very feminine, so I texted you to ask what special lingerie you liked. I felt like a teenager as I got a text back from you that saying that oyster satin French knickers would be your favourite. Your favourite knickers – what a magnificent thought! To be able to present you with something as intimate filled me with elation. I reached into my pocket and my hand closed around something black and soft. Your gift from the other night. Oh joy! I strolled across the Downs, feeling myself stir once more as I held your panties to my face. The deeper I inhaled, the more elusive the scent, and I almost wept with the need of wanting to get close to you once more.

8 Supper with Madame

There's been a bit of an upset. I met with Ian in the Freemason's Arms on Friday and suggested we cool things for a while. It dawned on me why he'd come to my flat on Wednesday evening. It wasn't to hand-deliver some billet-doux of enduring affection but to catch a look at you. He'd expected that I would have taken you back there. It was an intrusion into my sanctuary, even though he hadn't got past Gordon. Thank goodness for him! I faced Ian with my deduction of his sneakiness and he didn't deny it, just deflected the issue in the usual fashion and tried to make a joke of it. He was already two pints into a session when I arrived and it irritated me that he had allowed himself to drink so early in the day, especially when he knew he would be meeting me, and knew how much I hated drunkenness. It also annoyed me that he had company when I arrived, so for the first five minutes I had to make small talk with some boring guy I was never likely to see again.

Things were pretty frosty in the early stages of our discussion. We went over old ground. He regards my friendships on the fetish scene as derisory and shallow but I think his opinion reflects his insecurity. The one time I took him to a party at Gareth's he was grumpy and nervous of the camp elements. Ian doesn't do camp, and I've even accused him of being homophobic, which of course he denies. He's the biggest pervert I know, yet he displays no deviant plumage. He should flaunt it, I tell him, but he shrugs and mumbles about his profession – his perpetual get-out clause.

I'm the only flesh and blood access to the extreme sexual games he enjoys. That we both enjoy. But it frustrates me that he won't look elsewhere. I told him he needs to find other lovers, to lighten the load from me. Of course this was a non-starter. He's never going to place a contact ad or chat up some yummy mummy in Waitrose. I do understand how much harder it is for men. There are such expectations. He kept asking why I so readily started playing these games with him again after such a long gap. Why, if I wasn't interested, did I 'go back' to him? This infuriated me. He should know, if anyone does – with his twenty years' experience of psychoanalytical practice – that it's all the reasons we do things we know are bad for us. It's laziness, convenience, ego stoking. And our unique mutual delight in being able to act a part and find liberation through experimentation.

I hadn't intended to start having sex with Ian again. When Dad died two years back it threw up some issues of abandonment for me. I needed to pour out to someone who already knew the whole story. I couldn't face telling my whole history again to a new therapist, so I went back to Baum. I didn't imagine for a second that we'd pick up where we had left off some twelve years previously but, by only the third session, we had reverted into the old roles that had served for us so well when we first met. He'd lost some hair and he was drinking more since his divorce but his intelligence was as sharp and enviable as ever, and that's what had turned me on. I'd been missing that irreverence. I found myself sitting on his sofa, aching and wet, desperate for him to make a move. I was weak. He was weak. But now it's making him unhappy and me irritated and it's time to call it a day.

We talked for three hours. By early evening he was pissed and I was fighting to stay sober, as I'd drunk three large glasses of red wine. I fed Ian the story I'd concocted, saying you'd called off the arrangement. That you'd refused to believe I wasn't some kind of exotic sex worker with a heavy pimp who was going to extort money from you. I couldn't believe how easy it was to effect the right intonation in my voice, to sound completely convincing. I felt bad about lying to Ian but it seemed essential to get myself some peace. I happily joined in his cursing of politicians, but it was a bit of a blow for him that there was no going back to his after one more drink.

We left the pub at that hour on a Friday night when optimism was in the air and London's working millions were making their way home or going out. The bar had started to fill up with groups of friends meeting for dinner and drinks, and the noise levels were increasing so that by six o' clock it was too much for Ian. I kept wishing I was with you instead – that you would buy me dinner and I could read from your diary. Then I would humiliate you into losing control and see you punished. You wouldn't dare get drunk in my company. You would be well behaved, certain to please me, eager to let me know that my touch was longed for but not expected as a right. Still, I knew I would not have long to wait. We had already made an arrangement to meet.

Ian asked me about ten times if I would go home with him. Being drunk, he couldn't understand my reasons for why I didn't want to, especially as you were out of the frame, but I remained strong, promising him it wasn't anything like a goodbye, just a little rest. After fifteen minutes of platitudes and gentle coaxing he took a taxi home. We parted on good terms although the situation is far from resolved. It's Monday now, and I've already had three emails, none of which I've replied to. There are more pressing demands – one badly behaved, filthy-minded public servant is about to find out what an affair with Miss Caine entails.

I'm walking along Jermyn Street, where the trappings of upper-class England are at their most pompous; where quality and standing are realised through a fine cologne from Trumper's and the cut of a pair of bespoke hunting trousers, in mustard corduroy, of course. And Jermyn Street in the autumn rain has a smell about it that is comforting and redolent of the dominion of men of the Old School: the damp Burberry mac over a pair of broad capable shoulders and the musky leather satchel that holds everything from a gentleman's brie and chutney sandwiches to his naughty copy of *Janus* magazine. Jermyn Street is, indeed, permeated with the scent of older men of stature and breeding.

It is no small irony that along this street devoted to all things masculine and respectable you walk next to me wearing the softest oyster-grey French silk knickers under your pinstriped suit. You texted me this afternoon to tell me you had bought my exquisite gift but, ever alert to keeping you on your toes, I insisted you warm them for me. I demanded evidence of this the moment we met in James's Park. You arrived dressed for the autumnal weather and I pushed you into some undergrowth to see if you had been wise enough to comply with my request. It's as much the thought of you changing into them in the Commons' men's room as the feel of them hugging your privates that delights me. Already you are pandering to my perverse whims. I could never do this with Ian Baum. It wouldn't be right. He's the lambswool jumper man; you're the pinstriped suit.

The rain is still spattering and we are under the protection of your large golfing umbrella. I feel the warmth of your body radiating from your suit as we walk closely beside each other. We are about to enter my favourtie place to dine in London when I'm in the mood for reliable service and an exemplary fish supper. The staff know me well; ever discreet, when I arrive with a new friend they always remember to remark how long it is since they've seen me. This evening they are marvellously attentive; my preferred seat has been reserved – one of the banquette booths at the back where we can speak freely without the sound of our conversation drifting to the next table. I wouldn't want to alarm anyone, as I may let slip out loud my opinion of your recent habits on my living-room floor or comment on your penchant for self-pleasure and the wearing on your head of the musky undergarments of fine ladies.

They take your raincoat and umbrella and we are shown to the booth. The tables are beautifully laid with the crispest whitest linen and the glasses are polished to a squeaky clarity. I ease myself onto the padded bench seat, feeling the glossy susurration of my stockings as I shift along. You smile awkwardly; no doubt the silky material of the underwear causing you a strange conundrum as it eases into the crevice of your buttocks. I suddenly realise that it might well be rendered somewhat tight on you, given the extra girth and weight of the masculine equipment. How silly of me not to take this into account when I ordered them to fit a little snug. Still, you're toughing it out, and I make a note that your comfort is being compromised for my pleasure.

It would be the most natural thing in the world to start behaving towards you in a familiar manner, making general conversation to break the ice and relating to you as a friend. But I feel we did too much of that at the Japanese restaurant. Friendly is how ordinary citizens converse, and we are not ordinary citizens. We are engaged in a power dynamic, and I am obliged to be the custodian of a strict rule book. In order to preserve the intensity of our arrangement, I make a huge effort to keep a professional distance. We are not equals and I must remind myself to treat you as a subordinate at all times.

You ache for my attentions but this evening may test the limits to which you are prepared to go. Yet I am not the only one playing a role. You are not all you seem, either. I have been conducting a little research. Your Gieves & Hawkes suit may be of a quality stitch and your nails clean and buffed but you are in fact a miner's son who did well at the local grammar school. Your origins are humble, and under the political correctness and southern lifestyle lurks a northern working-class heritage that must make what I'm doing to you all the more unnerving and exotic.

I scrutinise the wine list. We both know that I will be choosing. Your salary and appearance may allow you to move in elevated company now and then, but you are not a sophisticated man, and your knowledge of wine is more befitting one who operates a public omnibus. I was taught wine appreciation at my finishing school, and had plenty of opportunity to put this into practice mixing among the art set in Paris. You would make a buffoon of yourself and an embarrassment of me if you were to order, and that would never do. You wouldn't be as gauche as to request anything German, but I would genuinely raise an eyebrow if you opted for something other than a known Australian brand.

When the waitress arrives to take the drinks order I effect a supercilious smirk, revelling in the knowledge that without me you wouldn't have a hope of making a good choice. My exasperation of the dearth of your cultural knowledge is tempered slightly by a tweak of amusement for your haplessness when it comes to matters of taste. Too much time in your formative years spent in the company of bullish trades-union men – all Yorkshire bitter and Embassy Regals. Times have moved on, and even your lot has learned what to do with a vol-au-vent. I can see you are a little uncomfortable with sophistication, but you *are* trying, I'll give you credit for that. Your eyes dart to mine immediately after ordering, to check if your pronunciation was up to the mark. There was a little hesitation, but at least no stuttering or any disastrous recourse to pronounce the French in an overly English accent.

Things are easier with the menu. It's a foregone conclusion: the lady will have a dozen oysters. And you will be allowed one or two, at her discretion. It's a light supper, as it's best that we approach the evening without full stomachs. You'll thank me for it, when, in roughly an hour's time you are on your knees and under my heel. We are discussing my ten favourite films – another list I sent you in response of your request to know more about me – when the wine arrives. I sit up slightly in anticipation of how you will perform your first Task of Subservience. As the waitress pops the cork you raise your hand.

'Please, pour for the lady to taste. My divine companion is much more fluent with quality.'

There is the flicker of a knowing look across the waitress's face, but she does as requested and the pale liquid is poured into my glass. I sip and swirl as I notice that both pairs of eyes are downcast, no doubt waiting with tense anticipation as to the response from the 'divine companion'. I am pleased with this reverence and approve the wine with good grace.

'You remembered,' I say, referring to my list of tasks. 'So much the better for you.'

You shift in your seat and are obviously apprehensive as to how the evening will progress. My congenial manner lulls you into a false sense of security as I continue my discussion of one of the films on my list: Buñuel's *Phantom of Liberty*.

'I love it when the businessman who is getting thrashed in front of the other hotel guests calls out that the monks should stay and witness his punishment. This is the most perfect expression of inappropriate behaviour.'

'He was fond of that, Buñuel,' you answer, having at my insistence researched my favourite director. It's not enough that you can repeat parrot-fashion that he wanted to get up the noses of the Church. I want you to understand the full measure of how the inappropriate is grist to the sexual mill – the liberation of perversity made with good humour; outrage with the best intentions. Is it too much to expect you to embrace the artistic expression of transgression? I am patient, and I believe that one day it will all fall into place in your psyche. I'm enjoying raising the bar a little, provoking discussion of things you've never previously considered. You see, I think you can continue the progress of your liberty. And how much more combustible the chemistry for having been suppressed so long.

I order our oysters, taking care to mention that you will be allowed one or two, as if you were incapable of deciding for yourself. Such a satisfying reversal of protocol, don't you think? There is no doubt as to who is calling the shots here; yet equally predictable is that you will be picking up the tab. It's the least you can do. Your salary is coming out of the public purse. With all the fine conversation and company you are getting I would say our trysts are doing wonders for your cultural self-improvement. Now you can wow all your chums in the Houses of Parliament with your knowledge of the femme fatale as a motif of male sexual panic, and the use of metaphor in Bataille's novels. Well, maybe not, but it's got you thinking.

I'm keen to see that diary. There'll only be a few days' entries, but I want to see how many times you have masturbated, and where. I want to know everything, Charlesworth, and if I think you are withholding those details I will have to deny you what you crave so much and you will go home without having had your just desserts. So, much to your discomfort, I order you to hand the notebook over to me, while I savour the contents of your fevered mind and those of the large oval tray that is making its way towards our table.

I love the sight of a plate of oysters in front of me; they are a silent announcement of my status as a sensualist. I know what people are thinking: a couple, a plate of oysters, no surprises as to what they'll be getting up to later ... but they won't be even halfway near the mark. Of course, it is difficult to measure their effect on the libido when there are so many other factors to account for, such as knowing that the delicate satin of the finest underwear is folding ever more snug around your genitals, but the association with aphrodisiacs lingers in the national consciousness. I can tell by the fact that fellow diners always turn their eyes fleetingly to the person who has dared to order this most luscious of foods. Would they like to have sex with them? Is their order justified by the recipient's attractiveness? People are so predictable, yet each thinks himself so unique.

I relish the texture of the shell against my upper lip as I open my throat to receive the silky flesh. I love the briny scent – so unadulterated – and, most of all, I love to roll the meat around the back of my mouth for a few seconds, grazing the plump flesh with my teeth and allowing the flavour to erupt. I squeeze the lemon over them while you reach into your bag for the notebook that, if it found its way into the hands of your colleagues, would see you in the tabloids overnight. You have made a good start, and your handing over of this information speaks of trust, which doesn't go unnoticed.

You move closer to the table and I grant you the privilege of tasting your first oyster. You sprinkle a little Tabasco sauce on it and I watch as you enjoy the sensation of luxury slipping into your mouth. I do likewise, then wash it down with a few sips of wine and begin reading random entries.

9 September

I feel as if I have a sexual version of Tourette's or something. I want to say things most women are shocked by. Only KC knows how I feel. I've started to think about where this all began in my life. I remember tiptoeing along the landing in our old house when I was about nine or ten, spying on my auntie changing into her nightie. I stole evenings away from my studies to sneak into adult cinemas back in the early 70s. I loved the films with the words 'flesh' and 'devil' in them and I would masturbate in the back row, but it was never enough. It never has been enough. And now I'm 53 and my only true release has come under KC's ministrations, but tender they are not. I wasn't happy about the sodomy but I think I understand why she had to do it. And now things have moved on a little and I am being led down some very intriguing paths.

I can see right through you, Charlesworth. You are trying to flatter me. I know that your thoughts are baser, more puerile than this example. I read on.

Becoming consumed with the thought of making XXXX watch me wank off. Want to drag her into the gents' loos and have her see it up close as I beat myself off, make her touch my balls and show me her tits as I spurt onto the floor. I bet underneath that posh exterior the little bitch wants a right good porking. Instead I fight with these thoughts at an inner-city sports and recreation meeting. Can't concentrate. Right after the meeting I deal with the huge erection I've had on and off all day. Pull my trousers down as I sit on the toilet, stretch out my legs, and bring myself off violently, being careful not to get spunk on my shirt.

Well, well. That's certainly no language for a respectable MP, is it? Trying to smarm and charm and be the respectable politician on live TV when you've a head full of expletives that can't be deleted. No wonder you look so awkward, living with that need and having nowhere to express it. I flick through some of the other entries and, without exception, they express this burning need to be vile, yet with no thought to the consequences. I raise my voice just a little as I sound forth with a remonstration: 'You are a grubby little schoolboy,' I announce. 'You are obsessed with toilets and genitals and four-letter words. And I thought I was in something approaching refined company.'

You shift about in your seat again and tell me quietly, gaze cast downwards, that it was me who demanded honest details. I have already caught the eye of one of the other diners, whose ears are now cocked rigid towards our table.

'And I suppose the very act of writing this down precipitated a certain ... carnality?'

He nods. 'I just need to get it out of my system,' he says.

I know better. 'I'm afraid that is unlikely at your age. Once a dirty boy has a dirty mind it can never be got rid of, but there are some therapeutic ways you can exercise this revolting need and be absolved of the more distasteful effects.' I lower my voice to a whisper, as I have no wish to expose you. 'You are very, very lucky that you have found me. Carry on the way you have been and you would sooner or later run into trouble.'

My mind is whirring into action and, as I continue to prise the succulent oysters from their shells, I am planning something that will help to remedy your terrible conflict of register. You will have to learn some humility. I allow you two more oysters, but as you throw back your head to launch them into your mouth, I wheedle the toe of my shoe into your crotch. I sense your gristle is hardening, as it is so prone to doing, so I deftly remove my shoe and begin to feel around with my stockinged foot. Even the act of watching me read your diary has made you hard, you perverted dirty scoundrel. The feel of it on the sole of my 15-denier foot is achingly good as I absorb the energy of your arousal right up my leg and into my sex.

The shame burns through your eyes as you watch me finish the platter. Yes, I can do two things at once. It takes control, something you struggle with. I do not betray my desires with blatant language from the gutter; I have mastered a more refined approach. You go to stroke my foot but I snap at you sharply: 'Both hands on the table.'

I am dexterous with my foot, able to curl my toes to stroke the shaft of your penis underneath the tailored fabric. Your face is a picture. I take my phone from my Anna Sui handbag and text Miko, who is sitting in the car nearby awaiting instructions.

And after our little aperitif and taste of luxury, it is time for the second course. Not, you are disappointed to find out, to be ordered from the restaurant menu. I announce we are leaving and you have to leap into action with your credit card and bother with all the dull business of paying the bill. You complain that you are hungry but I pinch you hard on the thigh and you have to suppress a yell of pain.

'You can feast with both feet in the trough for all I care when you are on your own or with your dowdy wife,' I hiss into your ear. 'When you are with your Mistress, her needs are always top priority. Now cease your whining and prepare for an appointment with depravity.'

We exit the restaurant to find it has stopped raining, yet the pavements are damp and the lights of several gentlemen's outfitters are reflected on the street. There's that fresh smell of early evening in West London; an optimistic smell of money and excitement and it is a perfect moment when Miko strides across to greet us in one of her military uniforms. She is so charming and efficient, her petite frame shown off to dainty compactness. The fitted grey jacket and pencil skirt give her the appearance of a corporate miss, but the blue streaks in her long black hair and the industrial boots add a surprise element to the mix. A look of confusion crosses your face as you try to work out where she fits in the equation. I elucidate.

'This is Miko. She spent some time in the Japanese youth combat corps, special weapons division. Now happy to put errant clients into rope bondage that would vex the most gifted escapologist.'

I give a fruity chuckle as I watch the discomfort cross your face. It's a better yarn than saying she's a fashion student. Miko nods sweetly in greeting and you make some fumbled bow. We walk to my car that Miko has parked down a side street. As we get in the back she takes up position as chauffeuse, complete with leather gloves and requisite military cap. I am watching your face carefully to make sure your expression shows no inkling of disrespect to her. She is not your servant, she is your superior; she just happens to be driving this car because she enjoys driving.

Heady from the wine, I risk a little teasing.

'Mr Charlesworth is going to read us some beautiful prose later,' I start. 'All about how hard he gets when he thinks about trashy English sluts, and what he wants to do to them.'

Miko doesn't reply. To be honest, her command of vocabulary isn't fantastic, but she has perfected a lovely clipped accent.

I continue: 'You should hear what he says to his wife to get her in the mood for love,' I say, shoving my hand proprietorially between your thighs. As I thought, you are hard again. Your simultaneous embarrassment and arousal does things to me I would never admit to you, but I am perspiring with the need for absolute dominion over your body.

'Does he say sweet things?' asks Miko, turning into an underground car park where we have been promised an allocated space. 'I hear English gentlemen very romantic.'

'Such charming things,' I reply. 'You will not be disappointed.'

You lean over to me and whisper in my ear, sounding panicked. 'She's the waitress from the other night. What are you playing at? What's going on?'

I tell you everything is perfectly OK and to please learn to trust me. We enter the garage of an anonymous but expensive apartment block in Maida Vale that one of Gareth's generous wealthy clients owns. He lets Gareth have the keys while he's in New York and we often use it for scenes and photo shoots. The place is bristling with CCTV and you cover your face as we enter the serene modern foyer and take the lift to the top. What a threesome we make.

Inside, there is nothing heavy or fussy in a living room that is obsessively neat and beautifully styled – all the better for making an example of your indecorum. What you don't know is that cameras will be recording everything that happens here tonight. The footage will be grainy and our features barely distinguishable, but I like that effect. It's more real and more arousing than any slickly produced porn.

We walk into the spotless kitchen where Miko opens a bottle of white Burgundy on one of the polished marble surfaces and pours two generous glasses – one for each lady in the room. I nip to one of the bedrooms to change into a pair of boots that will have you drooling. Knee high with three-inch heels, their leather is buttery soft and just right for what you'll want to do to them when I've worked you over. I reach up to the hook on the back of the door for a collar and lead that I placed there earlier when Miko and I came to set up the scene. I re-enter the kitchen, walking up and down on the polished floor, clenching the leather and chain in my hands as you look shiftily about the room, and at my boots, moistening your lips. Your temperature has probably shot up a few degrees already. We know who's in command, don't we? I allow you to remove your overcoat and I take great pleasure watching you stand there flustered in your suit, unknowing of your immediate destiny. You thought you were getting close to me, but I have placed a new distance between us by introducing rogue elements into the mix: a beautiful Japanese sadist; an unfamiliar apartment; the promise of bondage. What's going to happen, dear minister?

I take my favourtie instrument of correction from a drawer and tuck it into my belt. Any nonsense from you and you will feel the kiss of Miss K's dragon quirt like a band of fire across whatever part of you I please to burn. It is also the signal for you to know the game is begun. I approach to stand within a metre of what you used to call your 'personal space'. Now your tormentor has encroached upon it, you can only feebly guess at what will be the next boundary she crosses. Maybe the oysters are living up to their reputation but I am aroused beyond the measure of any regular courtship. I conceal it behind small gestures: the flexing of the leather collar; the deep breaths I take. This time I pull you by your tie towards the centre of the living room and order you to stand there and behave. Miko follows, carrying the wine and the glasses. There is no glass for you; you surrendered all privileges as soon as you entered this building. But I want you to loosen up some, and more alcohol will help. I know how you lot can drink. I've heard such shocking stories from friends who work silver service at the Commons restaurants as to how MPs behave when they are off the leash. How very different things will be today when you are on it.

9 Kiss of the Dragon Quirt

Tonight you will learn how to behave from basics and to show some manners for Miss Caine and her accomplice. I open the door of a glass-fronted cabinet and retrieve a brown ceramic bowl. I place it on the coffee table next to our glasses so you can get the full measure of your status. 'Doggy' it says, and 'Doggy' you will be. I give Miko the signal, and she pours a generous measure into the vessel. You are craving for something more to drink and I can see the longing in your eyes. But you are not to have it yet. I flex my quirt and order you to take off your suit jacket, shoes, socks and trousers. You are complicit and you do look a lovely sight in my French knickers and shirt and tie. Unfortunately the tie has to go and your shirt is unbuttoned to reveal a man's singlet – the sort that my grandfather used to wear. It's hardly a fitting match for the La Perla knicks, but the contrast is almost touching in its guileless incongruity and I do my best to suppress a giggle.

'He's a lady boy!' jokes Miko, and you wince in your shame. I can see that feminisation is a very tricky area for you. Are there too many connotations of vulnerability? Does it alarm you that you can get aroused wearing women's panties? Is there a question mark over your sexuality? Or does it remind you that you are going to play the woman again?

The collar goes around your neck and your expression registers a flicker of alarm for a second or two, until you realise it isn't tight. The leash is clipped onto a D-ring and, although I can give you a sharp tug, I will not cause any marks. I am saving that little delight for other parts of your flesh. I bellow at you: 'Down!' and at once you drop to the floor on all fours, grateful to be assuming the position of the wretched supplicant. I nod to Miko and she places the bowl in front of you. You go to lick from it but I snap you back and demand an apology for your presumptuousness.

'Cease your vulgarian ways! You will wait for my command,' I hiss.

'Sorry, Madame K,' you utter, and a thrill runs through me as I hear you honour me with your now timid voice. Yet I worry that even in this ignoble position there is something of the swaggering alpha male about you. I don't like it all, and I know exactly the way to rid you of it. The pinny, I think. I hand over the leash to Miko, who immediately sets about prodding you with her boots, imprinting the soles onto your back. This must be unnerving, a sniff of the army cadet drill your dad wishes you'd had instead of all that Marxist drivel from the LSE.

Miko is so occupied with your panties that she doesn't see you lapping at the bowl and, as I emerge from the kitchen, I catch you face down sucking at the wine in a most undignified manner. You are such an opportunist, and you have no patience. I cannot let such flagrant insubordination go unpunished.

'Bring him to his feet!' I order, and Miko yanks the lead to have you at once standing with your chin moist from the wine and your hands crossed over your genitals as if you were about to guard yourself from a free kick. I cannot resist a little opportunism and lash at your buttocks with the quirt. You cry out. You have a long way to go; you should know how to silence the smarting pain with good grace and not make this terrible racket.

I do so love to dress a man in the garments of

subservience, and the kitchen apron is especially useful, particularly when it is as flowery as this one. I put it over your head and release the leash from underneath. And here's the bit I like. To pull the apron tags snug around your hips from behind, whispering into your ear what a beautiful docile housewife you make. I run my hands over the silky fabric that's gracing your buttocks and order you to your knees once more.

That's better. Now you look meek again. Who would have thought that such a fevered mind lurks beneath this spectacle of contrition? And here you are: a parliamentary package that is mine to chasten and exploit. I walk around you slowly, clockwise and anti-clockwise, making a close inspection of you from behind as Miko wraps the leash around her hands to hold you tight. You are staring at my boots, apprehensive yet in tremulous thrall to their potency. I lift the apron with the tip of the quirt to see the snug packet of your genitals pressed in their satin casing. I poke at them as if they were offensive litter, then harder at your buttocks. You are commanded to be poised there, looking at the floor as I squat down to speak into your ear, the gloss of my stockinged legs so tantalisingly close to your face.

'I think it's time for Doggy's diary,' I say. 'Miko wants to hear how romantic the English gentleman can be.' I reach into my bag and produce your notebook, flicking through it as I rest one high-heeled foot on your back. 'Here we are ... 10 September: "L doesn't know I have a secret porn stash and I spent a lovely hour looking at girls with hard nipples and big tits reaming themselves with huge dildos and making themselves come. I can tell they're really doing it because their skin has goose pimples. Other pictures show them getting facials and taking it in the arse. I especially like the picture that has the girl with the long socks up to her thighs spreading herself for a giant portion of cock."'

I affect a look of absolute disgust and, in a sorry voice, say to Miko: 'I'm afraid the gentleman's use of the English language is not what you'd hoped for.'

She shakes her head sadly. 'He's going to have to learn some nice manners.'

'You are absolutely right. We'll have no nasty little boys with their foul mouths here.' I turn to look you square in the eyes. 'This is a house for women of good breeding and taste, and the ladies who stop by here for tea and conversation do not want to hear a disgusting torrent of filth coming from the mouths of dirty boys. Do I make myself clear?'

You nod your head vigorously but I know you are going to act up.

'So, what have you got to say for yourself?' I tease you along further. 'What vile things did you do as you looked at the pornography?'

You lower your head. 'It made me hard. I had to masturbate all over the pictures.'

'Sit up!' I order. 'I can't hear you properly, mumbling like that.'

You sit back on your heels and the front of the pinny is protruding with what is straining inside your lovely French panties. I can barely stand to see this without casting aside my persona and demanding you fuck me on the floor, but I have to string it out, make it last.

'Go on, then. Show me what you do.'

We watch as you steal your right hand into the knickers and begin to rub yourself.

'Tell us exactly what you think about,' I demand. 'I want no detail spared.'

'I've been thinking about doing it in front of the younger women in my office,' you confess.

'Explain yourself ... doing what?'

'Making them watch, look at my erection, and telling them I'm going to do it all over their faces. I want to have one of them under me and spunk into her prissy, righteous, politically correct face.'

Miko and I look at each other as if we are assessing the behaviour of some reprobate from a problem estate.

'It really is shocking what some people vote in to their constituencies,' I remark. 'And what would these women do? Just take it as if they were brainless receptacles?'

'No, Madame, of course not. I would expect them to be shocked. I would want a bit of a fight, actually.'

'Did you hear that, Miko?' I ask. ' "A bit of a fight". I'm sure there would be a terrible to-do. Take off his leash. He's going to get what he wants for once.'

You are left kneeling up, touching yourself. I walk towards you and remove my skirt and top so my arms and legs can be unrestricted while I physically force you to submit. I am revealed to be wearing hold-up stockings, knee-high boots, snug underwear and a balconette bra. You are once again in thrall to my legs and you will do anything to get them wrapped around you. I walk towards you, remove your glasses then topple you backwards with one push of my boot. Sprawled on the floor you may not have the upper hand but your eyes are glittering with expectation. I pull you up by the neck of your vest and slap you hard across your face. You seize me behind the knees and pull me down to your level. Before you can make a grab for any intimate part of me, I have flipped you over and hooked one arm under your right thigh and locked it with the other arm that's under your left armpit, bracing my knee into your side. Unfortunately, your arms are free and you roll yourself sideways, releasing my hold and grabbing my wrists. I hop to a squatting position, where my suppleness has the advantage over what you try to put in motion – me flat on my back with you on top. Oh no, that will never do.

You have command for a couple of seconds before I get both feet tucked into your chest, heels down, and spring you away. You are sent sprawling across the floor with enough time for me to seize your arms and pin you to the ground as I straddle you. You are breathless with the effort and even laughing a little. With my crotch just inches from your face you are not complaining.

'Funny, is it, Cabinet Minister? Funny that you're rolling around a stranger's flat in a flowery apron, drinking from a doggy bowl? Funny that you're about to know pain of the likes that has not been administered since you were twelve years old, caned for cheating in school tests?'

'No, not that,' you cry. 'I'm not into whips and stuff.'

'Oh yes, that indeed. Miko and I are specialists in pain. And don't you think you deserve it, writing that filth and thinking such disgusting things about your colleagues? You, who are so high and mighty, Minister for Public Policy. Imagine your secret thoughts coming out during prime minister's question time!'

You make a lame attempt to struggle out from under me, but I know you are inhaling my scent and so, so grateful to have my sex near to you that you know, and I know, your efforts are all a sham. I love having my thighs clamped to your ears, and I decide to go one further. I lurch forwards so that I am completely covering your mouth and much of your nose. You are calling out your delight, although it is quickly muffled. You continue to touch yourself; I can feel the familiar rhythm of your hand pumping up and down behind me.

'You would be very, very foolish to think this is all going to go your way,' I warn, grinding myself onto your face. 'I am queening you not for your pleasure but so you can learn a little respect and humility. You are going to have to work very hard this evening. For a start, your schoolboy wanking can cease right now. Miko, the rope, please.'

I release the pressure for a couple of seconds, long enough to grab both your arms and bring them over your head by which time Miko is there with her favourite sash-window cord. She deftly and securely winds it around your wrists. She looks so beautiful in her sadistic concentration, her hair hanging down in that blue-black curtain.

'Nice and tight,' I say, sliding back onto your chest, and you groan at being denied your self-pleasure once more. 'We don't want any wriggling. You're going to stay exactly where you are while we play with you. If you move, you won't be sitting down for a week. Got that?'

You nod your head. 'I love having you on my face, Miss Caine. Can you do it again, please?'

'I'm not here to grant you your fantasies, Charlesworth,' I say. 'I'm here to teach you a lesson in respect.'

I get off you and stand by your side, then press a booted foot on your chest in a gesture of triumph. You are ordered to stay exactly where you are while Miko and I retreat to the kitchen for a quiet conference on your further humiliations. We have disgraced our MP by making him wear a collar and leash and a flowery apron, but it's all been quite gentle in comparison to what's about to occur – something that Miko loves and I love – but not before he's tasted the lash.

We stride back into the living room. I go to the table and continue drinking my wine. Miko still has on her military uniform. She stands astride you and looks down on you – this tiny fashion student in total command.

'I hear you like long hair,' she says. 'You like down there?'

'Oh yes, yes, please,' you say, and I notice how you

are being even more polite to Miko than to me. Could it be you are a little more scared of her than of me? Or that my familiarity is already breeding contempt? I'll have to change that.

She takes off her hat and lets the long sheen of hair fall down over her shoulders. Then she squats down and pulls aside the pinny, whisks off those darling oyster-grey satin panties, and flicks her crowning glory back and forth over your semi-tumescent genitals.

'Oh yes, yes!' you cry, throwing your head back in genuine rapture.

'You know agony and ecstasy today, Simon,' she says.

'I'm knowing only ecstasy at the moment,' you reply.

She grabs a fistful of shiny black hair and rubs it back and forth over your penis as you continue to lie with your arms bound above you.

'Not for long,' says Miko. 'You are here for punishment, not pleasure.'

She stands up to leave you erect and bereft and grabs hold of the leash, hauling you to a sitting position and finally to your knees. She drags you to the sofa and, with your wrists bound, you have to shuffle forwards with the pinny flapping in front of you. Once there you are bent forwards by Miko's firm hand on the back of your neck, your now bare arse revealed as a perfect target. Oh dear, for a minute back there you thought it was all going to go your way.

'What a very fine doggy you make, Charlesworth,' I say. 'Don't think that Miko here is the good cop to my bad just because she allowed you a little indulgence with her beautiful hair. Do remember the reason you are here.'

'What reason?' you demand, sounding all important and hard done by. 'I don't know where I am, who she is, or what. What do you want from me? Why are you doing this?'

'Such whining for a little doggy. Not used to not getting our own way, are we? Used to nice wifey doing everything for you? Having lackeys around you that will help you clear up your naughty business? Well, you can't spin and lie to us. We know your game and your filthy dark secrets and today you're going to get your nose rubbed in it. Time for the full force of the dragon quirt!'

I quickly pull my favourite implement of correction from my belt while Miko keeps you held in place. Your tethered arms are bracing you over the seat of the sofa. You are really not that uncomfortable and you have the temerity to complain. I know better-behaved gentlemen who would pay huge sums of money to be nearly naked in a luxury apartment with two such fine ladies. I think of all the conning and duplicity you are responsible for. Of the appalling betrayals of trust, the two-faced dodgy dealings with big business and for the big fuck-you to the people who voted for you, and I build up a loathing that will have your arse in tatters if I don't exercise my own restraint.

'Hold him still, Miko,' I say, and take a run from the door frame to rush at you, landing a stripe on the underside of your buttocks that makes you shriek in shock and agony. I repeat the exact movement, again and again, lashing into you with full ferocity. I am a safe, expert striper. I know to aim for the fleshiest area. It's your pride as much as your posterior that is being tarnished here.

You cry out your pleas for mercy but there's no stopping me. I am losing myself in the rapture of the moment, bestowing this wonderful punishment on you. Don't you want to be the centre of my attention? You should be grateful! In a moment you will come to know its benefits, as the endorphins spread their magic. Miko reaches down under the apron and finds your genitals, then digs her nails into your balls as you wince and tremble.

'He's still hard,' she says.

'Can't be that bad, eh?' I tease. 'I'll teach you to turn up your nose at my apartment, to think yourself superior, to suggest that I am a common prostitute. I want a full apology.'

'Sorry, sorry,' you bleat, gasping.

'Address me properly!'

I stand behind you now and begin to use a small riding crop to rain down strokes in rapid succession. They are short sharp attacks, done at close range, and not as searing in their intensity as the run-up beatings with the quirt but I am counting up to almost fifty now and your bottom is glowing nicely. Not only are you suffering unimagined agonies, you are also undergoing this cruel battery in the presence of a third person. Miko pinches and twists your genitals as she smiles at you and demands to see your wincing face. I wonder what is going through your mind, if you had envisaged the evening turning into such riotous assembly.

'Sorry, Miss Caine,' you plead. 'Please, stop.'

I stop for a few moments to come around to the sofa and squeeze myself next to Miko so I can see your pathetic face. You're panting, crying and beside yourself with the strange intensity of it all.

'Remember how good Doggy was at his place, worshipping Mistress's feet and taking the dildo?'

You hang your head on the sofa cushion.

'Head up!' barks Miko, yanking the leash.

'Yes,' you croak, looking at me, your hair dishevelled again. I do love it when you are undone like this. I bet you weren't expecting this when you daydreamed of our evening together.

'Mistress is going to let you worship her tonight if you are very good and learn to take your punishment stoically and gratefully.'

I can see that you want to swear at me and stop the play but you know that would be the end. If you called 'Tony' then the promise of getting up close to me would be obliterated in an instant. My scent is your addiction now. Ah, the power of the cunt! Ian was so right.

'Miko, it's time.'

Miko pulls your chain and you are hauled up from the sofa. 'Stand up. Time for walkies,' she says.

You are a sorry sight, naked but for your apron and vest, your backside on fire. And your thrashing has produced a most efficacious result – namely your penis is hard of its own volition, standing proud under the apron.

'You can take some succour, Charlesworth, from the fact that your fortitude has earned you a special treat,' I say, intoning my voice with enthusiasm. 'It seems your *invigoration*, let's call it, has proven you to be such a stoic and virile Cabinet minister! Not at all the lame sop we expected.'

That arse is as red as a London bus and will need some unguent applied to it. But not before you've undergone further depredations. Miko leads you to the bathroom. It is time for your ultimate test.

The room is large, with a black-and-white tiled floor, double sinks and a huge shower area that runs from one side of the room to the other. The shower stall is more than big enough for you to lie down in, which is exactly what is about to happen. You complain that your arse hurts, but we are deaf to your whingeing. Off comes the apron and vest, your hands are untied, and Miko pushes the plastic curtain aside to back you into the shower. You think you have come in here for a wash, but your imagination is sadly lacking. So now you are naked but for your collar.

'What do you want me to do now?' you ask.

'He's learning better manners, Miss Caine,' says Miko, 'but just you remember to say thank you. In Japan, manners are very important.'

She unclips the pair of handcuffs from her belt and swiftly turns you around, fastening your hands behind your back.

'You get down now,' she orders.

'I don't know if I can sit down. It hurts so much,' you complain.

'Get down!' I order. 'Right down on the floor.'

Once down on the granite base Miko clips your lead to an attachment in the wall. The flat's owner, being into heavy gay SM, has cleats and fastenings all over the flat and the bathrooms are no exception.

You look panicked. You are not going anywhere. 'No. No, don't leave me here, please.'

'Shut up or we gag you,' barks Miko.

The leash is long enough for you to sit or lie down, but for the time being you squat. I can sense your vulnerability – the best condition under which to perform a rare and unusual display of dominance. It's time for a little exhibitionism. I whip the shower curtain shut so you cannot see what's happening. Miko is stripping out of her uniform. Naked she is fantastic, like a little terror from a Manga comic. Her small dark nipples sit high on her pert breasts; her tiny pubescent-sized body is wiry and agile and, of course, that long black blue-streaked hair falls down her back. Without her clothes she could look vulnerable, so she keeps on her industrial boots. We giggle with each other. This is a rush for both of us and I am aroused beyond rational thought.

In case the discomfort of the situation and the pain

of your whipped buttocks making contact with the granite puts you in a woebegone mood, what happens next will rekindle the fires of your lust. I pull back the curtain to reveal us both in an embrace, kissing and touching each other. You squirm and ask for your glasses and I grant you this one small request. Miko fetches them while I poke at you with the crop, running its touch down your thighs. When she returns we resume our lesbian display.

We come down to your level, kneeling over each other and sucking nipples, caressing arses and rubbing pubises together. I position Miko so she is completely displayed to you, her black hair falling down her back. Your penis is hard again, but there is nothing you can do to relieve it. I prop myself against the doors under the sink unit and Miko lies back against me, her slender frame light like a boy's. I toy with her nipples, pinching them into dark points as she slides her tiny hand between her thighs. She is almost denuded of hair and takes great joy in showing herself to you. You are motionless, as if the smallest movement on your part would dissolve the spectacle. She is performing for you, being the cruel little exhibitionist she is, by revealing her moist pink sex to your gaze. Her diminutive stature is misleading. Men are too gentle with her, she complains. So she likes to show them what she can do to herself. She brought a dildo into the bathroom when she fetched your glasses, and now she is going to use it. She rubs it along her slit and teases herself. I move with her, caressing her body and playing with her hair.

Then she becomes more intense in her ministrations, at one point lying on the floor and ramming the object into herself with a violent passion. While the ten-inch length does its work, she takes to fingering her clit at the same time, her expression frantic and desperate. This slip of a girl, so needy and brutal, so aroused by seeing your beating – you have never known nor imagined anything like it. Your dick is purple and you are fit to burst, yet you are cuffed and unable to do a thing about it. I too am fascinated by her display of violent masturbation, although I've seen it several times. Enough to know carnality is mercenary and ungendered. Would you like to be the one to call her unfeminine?

One hand thrusts the dildo in and out, fucking her tiny sex; the fingers of her other hand are a blur as they rub and probe, bringing her closer. Her eyes are closed and she is lost in delirium. Yet suddenly she stops for a few seconds and propels herself closer to you, in your shallow granite prison. She braces herself against the edge of the shower stall so your face is only about two feet from the centre of the action. She lies back on the floor and prepares herself. For the first time she makes a noise – a series of gasps and purrs. I can't see her face but you can. You can see everything. There seems no end to your torture.

So here we are, two voyeurs and one exhibitionist: I watch you as you watch Miko as she plays out being watched in her head. Which of us is the most perverse? She writhes and abruptly stills – the delicious implosion is happening. Her head falls back, her hair thick and lustrous fanning over the floor, and her body arches perfectly as she thrusts her hips gently up and down in the throes. I have never seen such close attention paid to any one living thing as your focusing on Miko. After about twenty seconds she brings herself back to alertness and I crawl over to hold her naked body in my arms. We kiss deeply and I stroke her hair. I bide my time before embarking on the next depravity.

'Beautiful, isn't she?' I say to you. 'And so young looking she could pass for a teenager, don't you think? But you would be mistaken if you thought she was sweet. She can also be very cruel.'

'You know, Miss Caine,' she says 'after drinking that wine, I want to go to the toilet.'

'Me too,' I answer, 'but there isn't one in here, is there?'

In fact there is a toilet right in front of us but we are pretending not to see it.

'I really can't be bothered to leave the room. What about the shower, Miss Caine? We could use that.'

'A fantastic idea. But, oh, shame, there is someone already in there.'

'We don't worry about him. He make perfect toilet!'

I can see the expression on your face is one of total incredulity. That a sweet girl could be even thinking of such a perverse, bizarre thing to do, and that she is prepared to actually do it, is beyond your comprehension. But this china-doll beauty has a collision of impurities for a mind. Unbothered by Judaeo-Christian concepts of guilt and sin, she is an eager practitioner of amorality.

'Show him, Miko,' I say. 'Use him for the toilet he is.'

She stands up and gets into the shower stall with you. You cower at her feet and that's just the way it should be. You are confused by an avalanche of emotions: from arousal to revulsion in one fell swoop. You issue one tiny word – 'no' – but the magnetic pull of her dark folds means you cannot help but stare up at her. It is only a matter of seconds that you are held in dread-filled suspense before the merciless outrage comes gushing. You try to avoid getting it on your face, but she kicks you down with her big boots, raises her leg and releases it all over you. You make an inhuman noise, neither words nor expressions of disgust but something like the sound of bestial pain. Get used to it, Charlesworth, because I'm coming in for some too.

Miko, serene as a samurai having dispatched some usurper, washes herself at the sink, then gathers her clothes and retreats to the living room. Now we're alone and it's time for my indulgence. I am so inflamed by the sight of your drenching that I fear I won't be able to pee as I am too swollen. I too am wearing nothing except my stockings, bra and pants and boots. Always the boots, the shoes ... the weapons of your mass destruction, Charlesworth. I look at you in your pathetic state, your arms braced behind you, your legs kicking out under you, your chest, neck and face glistening with Japanese girl's urine.

'You as well?' you say, somewhat non-reverential considering the circumstances. Yes, me as well, because you need to become familiar with your mistress's intimate moments.

'Like that, did you, our little display?'

You nod your head. 'I'm so hard. Please do something. Please.'

'Oh. I'll do something all right. I remember the other night at your flat you were trying to look right up my skirt, were you not?'

'Any man would. You can't punish me for that. I've taken enough punishment. This is outrageous. It's gone too far.'

'Shh,' I warn, one finger on my lips before a stern rebuke. 'Someone like you can never say they've taken enough punishment. Every time we meet you must learn to stretch your boundaries. You must learn more humility, more natural truths, Mr Charlesworth, Secretary of State. You have a problem with the truth, don't you? Always being grilled by that nice Mr Paxman. Never answering his questions properly. Always squirming out of reach.'

You don't reply.

'Well, here's something that's real. Undeniable.'

I squat over you, within touching distance, if only your hands weren't cuffed behind you.

'See it? Take a good look at it. This is what you want so much, isn't it?'

'Oh God. Yes, please. Look at me. I'm so hard. Please, it aches. You know what you are doing to me, yet you don't offer me gratification.'

'I ache too, Charlesworth,' I say, plunging two fingers into myself. 'And gratification comes in many forms.'

I am wet and ready for sex, yet it must be denied me again. I take the juice and spread it under your nose. You inhale deeply, almost in tears with your need.

'You know what I'm going to do?' I ask.

You nod your head. 'I deserve it. I'm just a servant for you. A toilet.'

I'm so glad you have found the right words, playing properly, justifying my experiment to push your boundaries. I move myself into the corner of the shower and raise myself on two metal bars fixed into the wall. By this, I am able to take the weight on my arms, lift myself up, widen my legs and give you the total glory: an unrestricted view of the holiest of holies. You are whispering, 'Yes, yes', and wriggling. You want it, yet you don't want it, because it's strange and disgusting. I decide for you.

Out comes a hot pale stream, splashing over your face, your glasses, your neck, and then I move myself back and let it cascade in a steaming torrent over your groin. This atrocity, far from repulsing you, only serves to make your penis respond, flexing in a desperate plea for my total attention. I throw back my head and laugh like de Sade in Charenton as a full bladder-load is released. I feel triumphant in my transgression but understand there will have to be sexual release for both of us. We've earned it.

As the stream slows to a trickle, I flick myself of the last beads and stand back to regard you in your abjection – a picture I'll never forget. I tell you to be silent. I don't want to hear any moaning now. I want to be generous. I pull you up – you *are* in a shabby state for one usually so fastidious – and I reach to the sink unit for the key to the handcuffs. I release your hands, unclip the leash from the wall and tell you to shower, but I insist the collar stays on so you are reminded of your lowly status. It's moments like this when I am careful to display tenderness. It makes all the difference between out and out viciousness and caring control. By being a little generous, you are able to see that I am a good mistress, and will grant special favours where they are due. The least I can do is let you wash yourself.

When I think you've cleaned up enough I reach in and turn off the shower, handing you a towel. You are surprised but unprotesting when you realise what's going to happen. I pull a chair over to the edge of the shower and use it to prop myself onto. On your knees again, you are at the perfect height to give me oral pleasure. I spread my legs wide, my heels pressed down on the shiny tiles, and I pull your head between your legs. You grab around the chair to aid your access and suddenly we are into new territory.

'Do you understand how lucky you are?' I ask you. 'What a treat this is?'

'Yes, Miss K. May I touch your boots, please?'

'You can touch my boots with your hands and you can lick me with your doggy tongue. This is your special treat. You have ten minutes to make me come, and if you succeed in that time I will allow you your own orgasm. Don't make me regret allowing you this generosity.'

'May I touch myself while I am licking you, Miss K?'

'If you use your time wisely,' I grant. 'You have ten minutes to give your mistress her moment of ultimate ecstasy. If you spend it all grubbing about with your nasty doggy dick for your own pleasure then she will use the dragon quirt on you once more, is that clear?'

'Yes, Miss Caine. I don't want that.'

And so you set to work, and I'm surprised by how gentle you are for one who has been frustrated to such a point. But tenderness won't get us anywhere, so I pull your head more firmly into my sex, telling you I need it harder. That gets you aroused again, and you have to make a fist for yourself, if only for a few seconds. You don't know what you prefer most: the familiar but essential sensation of your penis finding the tried and trusted home of your hand, or the reward of your hands sliding around the leather-encased legs of the woman you are learning to worship as a goddess. You seem to be opting for the latter as I continue verbally abusing you.

I grind myself against your face. Your hesitance to get right in there tells me you either haven't done this for a long time or close proximity at last with the object of feminine power is too unnerving. I sense you are nervous of not doing it right. Well, it's time for some practice. I spur you on with reminders of your deadline. You come up for air but one thing I won't allow is for you to look me in the eye. The exchange would be too intimate, too much like lovers. This is work for you, you hound!

I berate you. I pull on your hair. I wrap my legs up and over your back, crossing the ankles so your face is totally smothered. It's a good angle, and I am able to get better friction, using you as little more than a human vibrator, albeit a very low-powered one. I know you will be encouraged by some cheap nasty talk, if your diary entries are anything to go by.

'That's it, go at me with your tongue, that lying little tongue. I'm going to cream in your face like a whore and you're going to lick it up. You're going to make me come, you dirty dog. You're just a servant, a slave, a toilet. I'm using you how you are meant to be used. Got your dick hard, has it? Make you want to spurt it out all over the floor?'

I love abusing men and, when treated to contact as intimate as this, they love being abused. You are no exception. Despite what I'm calling you, you are iron hard. You lean back for a second to play with yourself while the clock is ticking. Two minutes left. I know I am going to make it but what am I going to do about you when I'm done? Ian's words ring in my mind. You'll only be pliable while I am denying you power over my sex. He's right. I must not give in to nature. I cry out for more, telling you I'm nearly there. You dive back in and go to it, sneaking a hand in there when you fear the time is getting close. I should punish you for it, but right now I want it and allow it. Someone should have done this to you decades ago, taught you from an early age what it is to worship and respect the female sex. Too bad the women in your circles were all too terrified of their own sexuality. Too bad they lacked the imagination to step outside of tedious debates about sexism to take control and teach men like you a lesson. They thought prohibition would be enough because their menfolk were middle class. Did they really think they could keep the beast at bay? The wiser woman will allow her man his grubby indulgences – but carefully and compassionately rationed, and accompanied by confessions and punishments. But their loss is my gain, as there are so many like you, begging for permission to explore the viscera and the vice. I shall not disappoint. I take hold of your head and rub myself frantically up and down over your face, flexing my leg muscles to enjoy a firmer contact.

'Try sounding smug now, Cabinet Minister,' I tease.

'I'm going to come on your face. Don't you think the PM would like to see that?'

You make some a muffled sound of acknowledgment.

'Do you know how lucky you are, that you are making me do this?'

It builds so slowly, so teasingly, when it's not under one's own control. No man is ever firm enough in his touch, but I do understand; the female genitals are such a labyrinthine puzzle. One always gets the flicky little tongue when one wants the industrial machine. But I'm there, I'm there and, when the moment hits, I pull you in by the collar and make sure your face gets a grinding. I fall back gasping, enjoying the sensation of my back stretching over the seat as you are left with the soft fluttering of my sex against your face – the explosions exquisitely shattering inside me yet their physical manifestations so subtle; the perpetual mystery of woman.

You are left with your pressing need. You haven't asked for permission, but you have fallen onto the floor and are caressing my boots, fiercely pumping yourself. I recover enough to see the game through to its end with my majesty intact. I tread my feet all over your chest and arms, grazing you as you try to hold my legs still. When I have my feet on the floor again you rub your penis against them.

'What do you think you're doing?' I ask. 'Did I give you permission for that, you wretch?'

'Please, Mistress, I have given you an orgasm. Please let me have this one treat, please.'

'And do you not understand how generous a gift that was? You should be falling to the floor in thanks for being allowed such close proximity to my ultimate moment. You have just known contact with divinity yet the first thing you can do is think of your own disgusting needs.'

'I'm sorry, I didn't think … It was wonderful, of

course. Thank you, thank you for allowing me to do that.'

'Do you not still have my scent under your nose?'

'Yes, Miss K, and it's wonderful. Please, while it's still there, I too want to know my ultimate moment.'

Your genuine desperation is touching.

'Are you saying you would like freedom to be able to express yourself?'

'What?'

'Freedom, Charlesworth. It comes from trust. In order for you to have the freedom to climax I have to trust you. I need to grant you that liberty. You can't just take it.'

'I shouldn't have to beg for this. Can't you just allow me this one thing, please?'

'You'll learn to beg for everything soon enough!' I spit. 'I'm sick of hearing your sense of entitlement. Who do you think you are?'

'I'm a man with needs.'

'A man who cannot control himself more like.'

'Just this once. I beg you, Miss Caine.'

'Don't want to be cuffed again, do you? Don't want to find yourself in a position where you have no choice?'

'No. No, Mistress.'

I sit back on the stool, prolonging the anticipation. You are holding my leg, your head resting on my shin. You are stroking the leather as if it were the most priceless material. Good. Soak up the phenomenon of this experience for it is unique and overwhelming. You cannot find this level of attention with anyone else and you and I both know it. I am allowing access to incomparable sensations, getting under your skin and into your unconscious.

'You need to remember that an orgasm in my presence is a privilege, not a right, do you understand me?'

'Yes Miss K. Sorry, I forgot.'

'God, you need training! Very well then, show me what you can do with that frightful appendage.'

I actually love the sight of you rubbing your impressive unsheathed size over the leather of my foot, to know I can so easily make you perform this act of debasement. I insinuate the toe of my right foot under your balls and press the heel of the left foot hard into your thigh. You cry out then twist yourself onto your side so you are sliding lengthways against the full impact of the leather, where the ankle meets the calf. You don't care about your ungainly posture. You just need to know your own crisis.

I'm being too generous but I feel I have done well not to throw you back on the floor and fuck you. You are so needy, so well endowed, and so strangely attractive despite your age and lack of sexual intelligence that I have to fight down my own desires. I am undergoing the torments of Tantalus. The arrogance of the politician seems to have disappeared at this moment. It's times like this, when you reach an altered state of consciousness, that I will allow you to know bliss without condemnation. I ask you just one thing: to offer up your orgasm as a dedication to me. And as it comes jetting out of you, firing in an arc over my boots, you croak, 'I dedicate this to you, Mistress.'

It's your first communion.

I take your clothes to the bathroom. Before I leave you to clean up and dress, you beg to be allowed to embrace me and I cannot refuse. I allow you to press your body against mine even though it's not ideal to let you get too close. After a few moments of caresses I gently push you away. Your eyes are filled with tears. And then it all comes out. You break down, splashing tears of relief onto my boots, your shoulders heaving.

'This happens sometimes, don't be embarrassed,' I say.

'I don't know why it's happening,' you answer, choking through the sobs. 'I'm really grateful. That was amazing. I ... don't know what to say.'

'Makes a change from those TV broadcasts then. I thought you always had plenty to say.' It's an off-the-cuff quip but it seems to throw you into a crisis.

'What am I doing?' you wail. 'All the shit I have to deal with. For what? What's the point?'

'Your choice,' I say. 'No one forced you into it.'

'I know, I know, but it all seems so meaningless; Christ, it's only Monday evening. If you knew what I had to face tomorrow ...'

You trail off, quietly crying and feeling for me again to put my arms around you like a parent.

'Kirsten, this is the most real thing that's ever happened to me,' you blub. 'I don't know ... when I'm with you, about to ... you know, come, and you're so powerful and everything, I feel like I ... love you. I want to worship you.'

'That's exactly how you should feel,' I say, pulling back some hierarchy. 'You are beginning to properly recognise me as your mistress. Not in the sense of a "having an affair" type mistress but as your sexually superior mistress. You are finally realising how sex can be cathartic. It's not just boobs and dicks and porno – that's fine if you are going to operate on the most basic level, but there are other levels too. Levels that can take you out of your body. How do you feel psychically?' I ask. 'I mean, you've been pissed on and beaten tonight. And this is more real to you than romantic love?'

'That's what I don't understand,' you say. 'How can *that* make me feel good? I feel amazing, even though my backside is on fire. And you must know how good it makes me feel otherwise you wouldn't have done it.'

I laugh. 'You'll be proud of those stripes tomorrow,' I say, pulling you over to the mirror and showing you the red welts. You gasp and smile. Not the reaction I would have expected but this is important – it's your first glimmer of pride over your battle wounds. I've marked you.

I reach for an expensive balm from one of the cupboards.

'What I'm doing with you will change you forever,' I say quietly. 'And when you're sufficiently trained I'll release you to the wild.'

You stare at me, wondering what the hell I'm talking about, but too in awe to counter me with logic or questions.

I turn you round and apply the scented fluid to the welts already rising on your buttocks. It is my first touch of tenderness on your intimate person.

We drive you back to your Bayswater apartment. Miko tunes the radio to a soporific music station and we glide through the London night in a post-orgasmic drift as you sit passively holding my hand like a child whose heart is full of wonder, having seen some magical dream-inspiring movie for the first time. I have got you to agree to the next step of the process – a day out at a country house with some special friends of mine. Surely even you cannot now imagine it will be in any way orthodox. You get out of the car, and we agree to pick you up from Pimlico station on Saturday. It seems you're not spending much time at home these days.

10 **A Day at Madame Edwarda's**

As we approach Pimlico station from the Lupus Street end, I spot you waiting beside the Paolozzi sculpture. I tell Miko to pull up the car for a few moments so I can observe you from a distance. A middle-aged man in a grey suit on a Saturday morning standing outside a London tube station. What could be more uneventful? Perhaps you're going to a meeting of football executives; you might be attending a business self-improvement course, learning the '23 secrets of highly effective managers' or some such waste of mental exertion. And you've probably attended such courses, haven't you, where everyone pretends they don't have genitals or night terrors, while underneath they're twisted into a misery of conformity and denial? Anything to avoid the blood and guts challenge of a raging, authentic life.

'Look at how perfect he is for us,' I say to Miko through the open glass partition that separates the front and back seats of the car. We sit watching you with the engine purring. 'I can almost smell his apprehension. He's even looking at his watch. He's so trained to be precise and businesslike, poor thing, but timetables and routines are no substitute for ecstasy and paradise. We're so glad to follow a left-hand path, aren't we?'

'Traffic warden of Westminster borough,' says Miko, ever practical, glancing in the rear-view mirror.

'Bastards,' I spit, loathing the slothful gait of this particular breed of petty officialdom. Mostly obese, sweating into their unattractive uniforms, they're the scourge of every decent person who just nipped out to pick up a newspaper. 'Probably never read a book in his life. Look at him ambling about, sucking his teeth and making his quotas.'

'In Japan, at least they look good,' says Miko, as she puts the car into gear and we glide past the station, honking the horn before pulling up round the corner. You break into a trot – the first of many today – as if you think we're going to drive off without you. Just take it easy, Charlesworth, there's plenty of time.

Miko gets out and takes your bag, to place it in the boot. She is keeping an eye out for anything untoward, but the coast seems clear. You open the door and get into the back with me, bringing a draught of fresh air with you. You can barely look me in the eye, so consumed are you with embarrassment of what happened earlier this week, and concerned as to what awaits you today.

'There is no need for shyness,' I announce, holding out a gloved hand for you to kiss. You rub your thumb over the soft kid leather. No doubt you are imagining what it would feel like curled around your penis. Like all men, you are ever the dirty dog opportunist. You, Ian Baum, you're all the same.

'You are very lucky that the house we're visiting today is a rare playground of deviant delights,' I begin. 'You will be at home there, with others undergoing initiation for the first time.'

You look alarmed. 'Don't you think I've undergone enough initiation?' you whisper harshly. 'And why does she have to be everywhere with us?'

'"She" allows me to concentrate all my attention on you,' I declare. 'Imagine if we had to bother with taking trains and mixing with the general public. It would be ghastly. Miko is my chauffeuse extraordinaire, and just you be sure to stay on her good side. As my chauffeuse she can focus on the driving while I focus on your filthy mind. And that's what you really want, isn't it?'

You resign yourself to a grudging acknowledgment.

'Well, I do hope you are going to cheer up a bit. No one wants a long face at the party.'

'It's a party?'

'Not exactly, and please stop being so literal. It's a country house. Our hosts are fabulous ladies. There will be refreshments. That equates a party in my book. Madame Edwarda and her partner have devoted all their creative energies to the running of their unique establishment. There are only a couple of places like it in the country, as far as I'm aware. England is trailing behind when it comes to institutes of correction.' I add extra pronunciation to the last three words.

'Surely people will recognise me,' you fret, all panicky.

'Stop worrying, for God's sake,' I say, rolling my eyes and pulling the gloves tight over my hands. 'Cameras are strictly verboten and no one uses real names. You have an exaggerated idea of your own importance, Charlesworth. You're not prime minister yet, you know. No one will know or care who you are. They will all be far too self-obsessed and consumed by their own performance.'

'I'm not sure I'm ready for this,' you whinge. 'I don't know what I'm getting into here.'

'Then for once just go with the flow and learn to enjoy yourself. Surrender your responsibility to me. All you have to do is obey orders. I'd have thought you would be used to that.'

Miko heads for the South Circular and you settle back into the seat. I love looking at you as you sink into your discomfort. I know what's occupying your mind: you should never have come today; someone will expose you; you are crazy for going along with the game to this extent. Yet if you had not showed up, you would have risked this being the end of these delights which you have come to crave and need. You are bedazzled and prepared to suffer. The pull is strong and it does not rest. The forbidden grail that has eluded you is within sight. Your contradictions are tormenting you, but not half as much as I will.

We pick up speed as we head south, past Croydon and its grey sprawl. Sibelius is on the CD player and you are attempting polite conversation around subjects in the general news. Even you realise the futility of that, as our relationship is predicated on far less mundane activities than making small talk and, after a few minutes, you give up and begin looking at me with lascivious intent. You gaze at my legs, neatly crossed in fully fashioned stockings – a nude colour but with a black seam – ending in a pair of black high-heeled Charles Jourdan shoes that button at the sides. How much you want to run your hand over my foot, my ankle, and work up, up . . .

But you know that's not allowed. You are swallowing often, with nervousness, and moistening your lips. You glance fleetingly at my face for some sign of how to progress, but all I give you is a Gioconda smile. Inscrutable, displaying curiosity but not what would be termed 'affection'. I want to see you in a state of such humility as to be begging for that. I know only too well that if I gave in to my desires now – and indulged yours – we could not drag out the delicious longing. It's something we share. I've learned that much about this thing we have started: neither of us wants it to be over too quickly. Are you even aware of how much self-control I am exercising here? Maybe not. You are such a novice around people of my disposition. Still, that won't last for long, as we have our fun day out at Madame Edwarda's Academy for Adult Miscreants.

We pull up at a major junction and some God-awful creature tries to squirt water onto our windscreen. He is snarling at Miko, brandishing a squeegee. Miko immediately starts up the wipers, firing our screen wash three feet in the air, and making it impossible for this wretched individual to gain purchase. With her imperial gaze behind those mirrored aviator shades, she is not to be trifled with. I've seen her get out of the car on more than one occasion and once, to my delight, slap some rodent-faced beggar around the face. She is such a little treasure! My uncompromising vitriol has you wincing, but you know in your fake, bleeding liberal heart that I'm right.

Sexually I am in as much of a state of anticipation as you. I can barely wait to have you ready; to take to your arse again with the dragon quirt or with any one of Edwarda's fantastic implements. I make myself breathless just thinking about it, and between my legs I am swollen and slick. I need to start up a little playful exchange with you and I make a sudden movement to clamp my gloved hand over your mouth, and whisper in your ear: 'I know what you want, and what you're thinking. You want dirty boys' pleasures, don't you?'

You nod your head.

'But you'll not have your disgusting desires matched that easily, my Right Honourable friend. I will have your bollocks bursting with the strain of containing yourself before you will be allowed even a caress from me, do you understand?'

You make some suffocating sound behind my hand and I draw it away sharply, not wanting to get your spittle on the kid leather.

'I want you now,' you say pathetically, but make no

movement to approach me. I sit back against the seat and trail one finger from your shoulder to your knee, pressing harder as soon as I touch your leg. I need to see you trussed and desperate, your penis bulging and ready to blow. I am suffering too, and if you knew the lengths to which I'm going in order to prolong your pleasure you wouldn't display your weakness so readily. Our journey lasts just under two hours. I am in such painful rapture imagining what it will be like to finally take you inside me that I spend long periods in silence, gazing out of the car window with one hand on your groin, every now and then twisting you into remembering who's in charge.

En route I have you on the floor of the car, watching pitifully as I pleasure myself. I am wearing the most exquisite coffee-coloured French knickers with a pistachio-green trim, yet such feminine fripperies belie brutal and cruel intentions. My gloved fingers dive deep into my sex. I make you suck the juices off, your glasses steaming up and your penis hard as a ramrod in your trousers. I read more of your diary extracts, aloud, to shame you into red-faced embarrassment. I quiz you about your filthy thoughts and make you repeat humiliating lines for my amusement. And then, when neither of us can stand it any longer, I allow some mutual touching. I indulge myself by laying my gloved hand on your straining erection. Then, your greatest treat yet – I lie back along the length of the seat and guide your trembling hand to between my legs. I whisper instructions and you insert two fingers past that fabulous lace and inside me. We look deep into each other's eyes at that moment. I have never witnessed such rapture, nor felt such total control over a man's pleasure. It is an awesome moment for you, finally feeling the smouldering slick vice of my interior. It's all the mystery and the magic you crave and need in one instant.

'I want to fuck you,' you croak, unable to speak with anything like the voice you use for TV broadcasts. I love it that the feel of my sex holds such power it can dissolve the command of your vocal chords.

'I know,' I say. 'But the circumstances need to be exactly right. Don't think for a second that I'll allow such an astonishing liberty to be taken on the back seat of my car.'

'You know something, I thought you might say that,' you answer, and it looks as if you are learning to play the game, and wait, wait for your heavenly reward.

'But you may pleasure me. Prove to me what you can do!'

You begin working diligently, cautiously, circling your fingers over me as I tense my leg muscles and raise my pelvis up to meet your touch, which is unbearably soft. For all your gutter talk and porno peeping you are timid and almost too reverential. I have to whisper to you to make it harder, and apply pressure to your hand. Your head rests on my shoulder, like a real lover's, and I know I have to ignore this discomforting closeness if I want to reach orgasm. And I do. I hold on to the hand loops stitched in the car's roof and hiss instructions at you.

'Just keep making those circles; make me come, you fucking servant. Worship me and know that your pleasure belongs to me. You have no rights of your own.'

I make you tell me a confession as you touch me, of how you are forced to play with yourself as your wife denies you sex. How you've sat in your car masturbating in the dark; how you want to drive to a place where couples show off; how one night a couple might allow you to join them and fuck the woman while the man watches. I need to have the details of the feeling of your own crisis. I need to hear it: about the spunk shooting up the shaft, about your balls tight and ready to blow, about your cock so hard you could rape the nearest woman for her cunt.

You look mortified. That last phrase is something you are very uncomfortable with but it doesn't stop you grinding yourself at me in desperate need. You should know I'm punishing you with such extremes because of your inability to come up with effective dialogue of your own. Your own attempts are too feeble and middle class.

'Say it!' I hiss, and hold you tight around your neck. The combination is too much. I feel the fires gathering and ready to ignite the pyre of this indecent desire. Oh, mighty conflagration. I am there, panting and swearing at you to look at me, as I plunge daggers of pure lust and loathing into your putrid soul. This is the Dark Age of love, my little Westminster love rat, and don't you forget it.

We journey on towards the countryside. The streets are emptier, the driveways longer and the affluence more evident. Edwarda's place is naturally well concealed behind tall trees. There are high walls and security gates and state-of-the-art surveillance equipment. She has a couple of security guards monitoring the property from a control room. They are beefcake from the SM nightclub scene, and they know better than to spill the beans on the likes of us. They know we would exact revenge upon squealers that would involve torture on a scale enough to make Pinochet weep.

You have been hard four times by the time we arrive, and still you haven't been allowed release. The cruelty. The longing. You are almost raging with your need and I cannot conceive of withholding the ultimate reward for much longer. A security camera swivels on us as we approach the gates. Miko lowers the driver's window and presses a code into the metal panel on the wall. The gates open to let us cruise up the long driveway and towards the grand house. The scene is one of tranquility and order. A gardener is raking some leaves. The only sign this may be a somewhat irregular establishment is that he is wearing leather chaps with no underwear. On seeing the car he drops to his knees in supplication until we have passed and pulled up beside a number of impressive vehicles belonging to the other dominants. There's a distinctive Lotus and Frau Gruber's Kübelwagen, which has had a respray in matte black, setting off the flags of the Reich handsomely. You blurt out something about swastikas being illegal but I sharply reprimand you not to be a party pooper before stepping from the car as Miko holds the door open.

You go to climb out too, but you are in for a shock.

'You stay there until told,' she orders you, pushing you back, and us two fine ladies walk to the main entrance, leaving you behind like a forlorn pet watching through the window. We don't have to ring the bell. The door is opened immediately by one of Lady E's sissy maids clad in an old-fashioned black dress with a white half-apron and lace cap.

The entrance hall is airy and light, furnished in classical style, with beautiful flagstones covering the floor and white-painted wrought-iron tables at either side, on which balance marble figurines of Eros and Aphrodite. Eddie is very fond of Victoriana, and the gardens have been landscaped to the style of that period, boasting statues of Pan and other pagan deities, a grotto and a beautiful gazebo by the pond.

There is the sound of chatter coming from the main drawing room and then Lady Edwarda's magnificence fills my vision. Statuesque and marvellous as ever, she is dressed today in a ladies' riding outfit, with jodhpurs, a black brocade jacket that flares over her hips, a high-necked white blouse and her hair is in a chignon. There is something of Catherine Deneuve about her, and her grand personality could lend sophistication to the blandest of events. Equally, if she is in one of her frosty moods, you would want to clone her and put her in charge of the nation's hospitals and prisons. That would see things run shipshape for a change.

'Madame K and Miko,' she welcomes us. 'How wonderful you could attend today.' She kisses me on each cheek and shakes Miko's hand. 'It's so windy out there. Where's your doggy?'

'He's waiting in the car. Boy, has he got a shock coming to him,' I say.

'It's always something of a sharp surprise for them,' she says, as if a headmistress receiving a child on their first day at infant school, 'especially the rescue hounds, or the ones who are used to being given a long leash. I will particularly enjoy the initiations today. Frau Gruber has brought a pet female barrister who will spend most of the afternoon in big blue gym knickers and not much else, although she doesn't know that yet.' She gives a chuckle and leans into me. 'Probably thinks it's some kind of spa or something.'

She emits a hearty tinkling laugh as she tightly twists her hand in the hair of her maid, eliciting a small whimper. 'We have our own kind of spa here, don't we, Hyacinth? No Jacuzzis or any of that nonsense. We prefer a more natural approach, using the resources Mother Nature has provided us with, such as the birch and the icy lake! But you must come through to the drawing room. There's champagne, and so much to do!'

She commands Hyacinth to fetch champagne for her new guests and we are announced in the drawing room. The room is a splendid size, understated in tones of mustard and cream, with a large fireplace and four pale settees. There is also alcoved window seating that affords a view of the lawn, where, in inclement weather, mistresses can watch their charges being put through their paces while they partake of an aperitif in the warmth and trade discipline tips with other dominants.

There's quite a gathering of masters and mistresses as it's a 'mixed initiation' day. Eddie caters for both male and female doms and subs, although the gay men have their own establishments run to a more purist military theme. No matter how spartan some of the scenes get, a frisson of frivolity is never too far away when Lady E and her ladies get together. I've been to banquets here, recreated to emulate those in Huysman's *Against Nature*, although, of course, Eddie is very much *for* it. She believes in nature's invigorating and humbling qualities, and delights in putting men through their paces using natural resources. I saw her reduce a high court judge to tears one night in the gardens. Left by the fountain, trussed in the full moonlight with only a garland of thorns about his distended midriff, he too came around to reciting Eddie's chorus to the Celestial Mistress. He wasn't allowed release until he had dedicated his emission to Selene, the moon goddess. What a wonderful night that was! Her pagan sensibilities and love of stark punishments do not, however, preclude a penchant for hedonism. A lover of fine food and wine, Eddie is never happier than when in her cups, surrounded by friends, about to partake of some leisurely feast.

There are some seven or eight doms here today, not including Miko, myself or Lady E, so that means there will be enough 'serviles' – as the inductees are called – for some particularly humiliating sports later on. It's always such fun to see the sissy maids' three-legged race or the 'no-panty leapfrog'. I recognise about half the people in the room. Everyone is friendly and done up to the nines. There are three butch doms in sharp suits, two masters in black who look as if they cross over with the occult circuit, and a brace of dominatrices, both a little haggard looking but tall, and bristling with paraphernalia. I can tell from the glassy look in their eyes and their over made-up faces, designer handbags, Swarovski-studded mobiles and lighters, that these women are in it for the cash. Their fantasies dwell in Sloane Street couture and airport-lounge posturing. One of them is wearing leather trousers and a fur gilet, for God's sake. Miko adds a wild, culty edge to the proceedings in her pink military suit and lace-up boots. Together we turn heads as we walk over to the butches to break the ice. One of them steps forwards immediately.

'Dagmar,' she says, shaking our hands firmly. 'This is Frankie and Lon. We're all down from Manchester.'

'Took the first-class carriage on the train, didn't we,' the one called Lon piped up. 'Right fucking laugh. Us three dressed like this and the tarts in their little skirts. Should've seen the ticket inspector's face.'

'Actually, it were quite funny,' said Dagmar. 'I could tell exactly what he were thinking: which one belongs to ... which one? You could see the confusion.'

Out the corner of my eye I am watching the black-clad warlocks speaking quietly to each other, pulling on their satanic little goatees. From their body language one would imagine a conspiracy of hermetic secrets is being shared. More likely they are discussing the latest computer software. The maid brings two chilled bottles of Moët on a silver tray and everyone partakes. I wonder where the charges are, and I'm just about to ask when Madame E breaks off from speaking to Frau Gruber, who is dressed fantastically, in what looks like SS uniform, and claps her hands to attract everyone's attention. I think of you, sitting forlornly in the car, and cannot help a winsome smile crossing my face. Then I reason there's a very good chance you will be playing with yourself in

there. If I find you've made your horrible mess in my car I will be livid. I should have warned you against it.

Eddie tells us what's on the agenda. In a moment the serviles are to be lined up outside and given a dressing down before being taken to the showers, undressed, hosed down, and made into abject apologies of their former selves. They will wear costumes: humiliating French maid, schoolgirl outfits or baby-doll skimpies for the girls (depending on their master's or mistress's preference) and a type of old-fashioned prison uniform for the men. There are also harnesses and collars and cock rings and all manner of leads and chains and blindfolds to play with. Doms have already filled in a questionnaire as to their preferences, whether or not their charges can be marked, and what level of punishment they can take. Eddie thinks of everything.

A buffet lunch will be served after sport, and there will be lessons and games to round up the day until seven o'clock when people will depart. It's a day you will never forget and one I will relish. I'm not sure where the other charges are being kept but Eddie's 'nurse' Bronwen is already leading a couple of shivering young things onto the lawn. I laugh out loud as I see you being dragged by the ear across the path by a sissy maid in a starched pinny. A marvellous sight, as you come face to face with the others of your sexual rank. What on earth are you feeling? I wonder. No doubt your ego is still vainly trying to best your psyche. You are one of only three males today, and there are lots of girls – lucky you, you think, but I don't want you getting ideas above your station. There will be no fraternising on a sexual level with the other serviles. The last type of man they will be interested in is a submissive wretch like you. Even if you pick a heterosexual one she'll want the firm hand of her dark master, not the damp sobs of a grey civil servant. By the time you've been put through your paces, you'll be begging for me to kiss it all better. You are broke and I *will* fix it.

One by one the other serviles are led to stand in a row on the lawn. The wind is blowing the long hair of one or two of the girls, and the swirling leaves and fast-scudding clouds add a dramatic detail to the proceedings as the bizarre sentry forms its order. We all troop out, champagne glasses in hand, to listen to Nurse Bronwen announce a chilling 'welcome'. She recites the ten main rules of the house, and they are beautifully annunciated in Eddie's old-fashioned style. It is a moment of foreboding – and it harbours echoes of the last rites read at the scaffold: the unfurled document; the impending doom; the unamplified voice carried on the chill wind and into the trees . . .

1. Serviles are not allowed to address any master or mistress by their first name. They will have their method of respectful address already decided, but Edwarda and Bronwen will be known as Lady or Madame or Mistress Edwarda and Nurse Bronwen.
2. Serviles are to eat and drink only when allowed by their master or mistress.
3. Serviles are to thank anyone of higher rank who sees fit to bestow the privilege of divine punishment upon them. In light-hearted moments, when not occupied by drudgery, maids may also make sport with the serviles, being one rank above them.
4. Serviles shall not make unseemly gestures or noises. Decorum should be maintained at all times. It is a rare thing to be granted this opportunity of bettering oneself and tasks should be undertaken with good grace and pain borne with stoicism.
5. If a servile needs to visit the lavatory, he or she

shall raise a hand until a superior sees fit to attend to them. Do not assume your relief will be a private affair. The grounds are spacious and urination can easily be absorbed by the borders and the grass. If your needs are more substantial, a maid will escort you to a bathroom.

6. Serviles' opinions count for nought. By coming here today you have placed yourself in exalted company. You should have nothing to say other than grateful thanks to your master or mistress.

7. Serviles will refuse orders at their peril. Know that we take a very dim view of insubordination. Not only do we have a collection of the finest instruments of correction at our disposal, we also keep a fully equipped dungeon and are not shy of using it to its full potential.

8. If a servile is unable to control his or herself and is found masturbating or having had an orgasm without permission, he or she will receive fifty strokes. On the bare.

9. Serviles are not to go wandering off around the grounds as if they were at some holiday camp. The grounds are for the aesthetic contemplation of Mother Nature and you may visit only accompanied by your master or mistress, who can be sure you show the correct respect and decorum at all times.

10. Whining is not to be tolerated. Know that today is for your own good. Without your master or mistress to keep an eye on you, you would probably be spending today in idle putrefaction. Here you will get fresh air, exercise and quality time with your superiors. Enjoy yourself!

While reading the rules, Nurse Bronwen takes a good look at her charges, sizing up who can take what. The women are on average about fifteen years younger than the men. I doubt there is a girl here over 30, apart from Frau Gruber's barrister, who is about 35. Each one of them is an egocentric, needy, vain creature – the warlocks' playthings, especially, and I smile as I notice Bronwen registering the same conclusion as me. Young women generally bore me, with their disingenuous body paranoia and self-obsession, playing at being edgy. Give 'em ten years and they'll be living in Clapham with husbands and babies and goodness knows what other bourgeois inconveniences. That's one thing I do admire in you ... your deep-seated loathing of small children. Until they make babies with pointed snouts and thick fur, I'll stay light years away from all of it.

Nurse picks out her charges at random and grills them on the fine detail of each rule. Looking more closely, as is our prerogative, one or two of the girls are very decorative in a Gothic way – little Marilyn Manson Red Riding Hoods with raven hair and heavy silver jewellery answering very politely that 'Yes, thank you, they deserve divine punishment.' But I am suspicious they are in it for little more than the pose. They are certainly not here to purge a lifetime of lies and smarminess like a certain person I know. They want a baroque operetta, whereas you need to writhe in purgatory. This said, I doubt Frau Gruber's little Fräulein will get off lightly. With her blonde hair in pigtails and bare arms and legs, she's already looking in desperate need of a fleece and a mug of hot soup. The baby dykes are toughing it out with a countenance of nonchalance and Dagmar's girl gets a sharp tap on the buttocks from Lady E's crop for sounding half-hearted about correct address of rank. Frankie's girl, with her 50s blonde-bombshell look, is stacked against the breeze and upholstered well enough to cushion the blows and she will make a fetching dishevelled femme.

Almost invisible against the pretty faces are the three men. Two belong to the professional dominatrices. One is soft-faced and nondescript, although I suspect deep intelligence. The other is an older balding fellow about your age, and then there is you – the most uncomfortable of the whole sorry platoon, standing there in your dark raincoat over your shirt and chino-style trousers. You look as if you've come about the insurance.

You are looking doubtfully at the bristling birch rod Nurse Bronwen is holding. And with good reason. Each of the serviles knows the merest infraction of the rules will have it lashing down on them, and Nursey doesn't look as if she goes gently on anyone's arse. They will soon all be out of civvies and finery and butt naked in the showers. And then the fun will start – when we get to see what each wretch is made of. You'd better not show me up. I know you are worried about being recognised, but none of these apolitical dandy girls know who you are. And as for the others, well, there are no snitches here. There is honour among scene players. But that's not something you know much about. Here you will be truly denuded of your protective layers but no one is a sneak.

Bronwen points at the three males and marches them back to the house. They are to be put through their drill first. Lady Edwarda motions the rest of us to follow. We're a good crowd – twenty at least, not including the maids. We troop downstairs to the changing rooms in the basement. I am ahead with Miko and Frau Gruber, and the dominatrices, warlocks, dykes and their girls bring up the rear. The room is basic, with cold lino and the communal showers of 1960s school changing rooms. We are seated on three low wooden school benches. The faint disinfectant scent is redolent of institutions and all around are accoutrements devoid of luxury: mops and metal buckets; scrubbing brushes; floral aprons hung on rusty pegs. A maid skitters in to charge our glasses with more fizz – an incongruous treat in these spartan environs. Nurse Bronwen barks at the three men to strip. Clothes are folded, and shoes neatly placed in lockers; there is no room for slovenliness anywhere. Once naked, the serviles' buttocks bounce meatily as they are led into the showers, of which we have an open view. Each of the men is handed a bar of Wright's coal tar soap and discovers the showers don't warm up much beyond the tepid. Bronwen looks every inch the school matron as she parades up and down the edge of the porcelain shower stall. She barks at the serviles to wash their backside holes vigorously and to ensure that the entire private area is cleansed and rinsed at least three times. Armpits, feet and all the other problem male areas are scrubbed and fastidiously attended to. There is to be an inspection of grooming later, and woe betide the wretch who is exuding a musty scent from any part of his private person.

After the ablutions, each man is thrown a rough towel – no soft, fluffy numbers here. Anyway, since when did men become such girls? They get one minute for a quick rub down before being led to the communal changing area on the other side of our seats, for being fitted into the Drill Chain. The Drill Chain has been fashioned exclusively for Madame Edwarda. It is a long length of metal to which easy-release leather collars can be attached by the links wheresoever a mistress pleases. In this way, serviles can be made to stand very close together – always amusing to see if erections result from the close contact to their fellow submissives. In this case, the serviles are allowed to have about two feet between them. The collars, of course, are omni-functional. The metal connectors act like karabiners and enable mistresses to tether their charges to other pieces of chain that exist around the house and the grounds.

With hands cuffed, it is possible to leave a miscreant outdoors in the rain, naked, or prostrate on the floor if he has been particularly disobedient.

Ah, the warm flood of pride that shoots through me as I see you fitted into the Drill Chain for the first time. The other serviles are equally alarmed, it too being their first time, and the exchange of emotions that occurs between the ladies and their pets is not dissimilar to that experienced by mothers watching their little darlings perform in their first school play. Not one servile is looking at anyone other than his own mistress; yet his mistress is watching all three serviles, each wanting her own little wretch to be the best behaved. The pro-doms are engaging poker-faced with this theatre. Contrary to Eddie and Bronwen's spartan aesthetic, these women are impressed by luxury, avaricious with their need for the business-class lifestyle. I can see it all: Austria for Christmas and Verbier for the ski season. Portly rich gentleman clients showing them off at the opera, a Louis Vuitton man-bag on one arm, a lady in her late forties dripping jewels on the other. They're walking like spectres through a fading fantasy of old Europe. Cakes and coffee and tiny exquisite trinkets. Lapdogs and broadsheet newspapers in the lobbies of grand hotels. The swish-swish of the Mercedes that takes them to Kärntnerstrasse for a little heavy shopping. Brandy warmed and platinum coated, they feel impervious, but the clock is ticking, *mein liebchen*. Indulge yourselves before it's too late. Before the expanding European Union welcomes Yemen as a new member state and brings the foot soldiers of the caliphate to your doorstep to behead you, infidels.

I'm happy to be more closely aligned to Eddie and her Victorian English bent. Her preference echoes the Swinburne school of discipline, of young men and women taught in the old-fashioned way: Latin recitals and strict elocution; starched grey tunics and trousers and no nonsense in the classroom.

And here you all are, in your spartan display. There is something both horrifying and fascinating about full-frontal male nudity in its flaccid state. The male is so much more exposed than the sleek, seemingly 'castrated' female. With his equipment waggling at the world there can be no pretence at grace or modesty. All smooth lines stop there; the Grecian ideal of muscular form is undone with that bulbous tangle. As a young girl in the convent library I would stare at the plates of classical statuary and ponder the site of the controversy. Where was the thrust and excitement I'd heard so much about? Male genitals in represented form always seemed so confusing: the testicles not like balls at all; the penis a shrivelled rubbery tube. And the alarming sight of my first circumcised cock was a revelation, but I got more used to it over the years I've been allowing Ian Baum to do what he does. The vulnerable, almost spherical appearance of the unsheltered glans still strikes me as peculiarly disturbing. Masturbation is never as gratifyingly lewd as with a traditional Anglo-Saxon model.

Of the three serviles, it is only you who are not cut. And out of the three of you, you are easily the most appealing figure; at least your genitals look normal and penis-shaped, loaded with promise. Your head of wiry grey hair and trim body show the world that at least you take care of yourself. Your arrogance lends you good posture; the other two are slouchy and cowed and there is nothing about them that intrigues or excites me. But the two doms are professionals and I sense that money will be changing hands at some point today, so they don't need to look attractive. Theirs is a business deal. I'm so glad I can do this for love.

Now tethered, you are all made to kneel on the cold floor. A couple of the girls are giggling, but surely they must realise they'll be undergoing their own form of drill very soon. They are as bad as the sissy maids – so ready to laugh at the humiliation of others, yet apt to yowl and protest when their own time comes for moments of desolation and despair. Bronwen comes into her own during this session, making the serviles prove their loyalty and admit to their wretchedness. She has strapped some kind of miner's lamp to her forehead. The sight of seeing you naked and humbled for this audience of perverts is most satisfying, especially when Bronwen makes a thorough inspection of you, spreading your cheeks and illuminating your intimate crevice to check for any traces of unsatisfactory showering. It occurs to me that this is some world away from how you might otherwise be spending your Saturday.

Eddie comes to make her inspection, walking up and down the line of kneeling men and prodding at them. This is her domain, and she can call the shots. She has each of them bend forwards and kiss her shoes. I watch with rapt attention seeing you brought so close to your favourite fetish and you look over to me as you plant a kiss on the leather. We know very well, don't we, what you like and what you want? And I want it too. Before this weekend is out I will be taking things even higher. I just need to make sure everything is perfect.

She asks Bronwen if they have cleaned themselves to a high standard, and Bronwen invites Eddie to look for herself. She has the men stay bending over, foreheads on the ground as she takes a look. Without warning, she lashes her crop onto the arses of the three men, who all squeal in shock. Shame. You've not quite healed since Monday's larruping. Still, your buttocks will be toughening up nicely.

'Clean within a reasonable degree, but too hairy to be sure,' she declares. 'We'll be removing that without delay. Hyacinth!'

The maid responds to her name and immediately wheels in a trolley on top of which is a vessel heating hair-removing wax – the kind beauty salons use.

'I cannot believe your mistresses have tolerated this outrage for so long,' she starts. 'They are obviously far too lenient. Well, today you are going to learn what it's like to serve a sterner mistress. You will be denuded not only of your arrogant ways, but also of backside and testicle hair. I will not have men running around in my grounds hairy-arsed! It's an insult. Now keep your heads down and proffer yourselves well.'

The shackled men remain bent forwards and the audience goes on to enjoy a right to-do of protestation and complaint as Nurse Bronwen and Hyacinth take spatula after spatula of golden hot wax to each of the men's bottom creases. They lay the strips of linen in place and pull vigorously. There are howls of pain, feeble stuttered excuses as to why this shouldn't be happening and faces reddened in indignation and discomfort, yet all three undergo their enforced depilation to the end.

Once it is done Hyacinth takes a good fingerful of soothing cream and massages it liberally into the crevice of each now smooth-skinned victim, sliding a finger here and there wherever she wants to go. She cheekily winks to the audience and mimics buggery out of the range of the men's vision, making sport of their indecorum. Even the warlocks raise a laugh.

'Right, that's better,' says Eddie. 'Time to be fitted with your uniforms, and now it's the girls' turn.'

There's a lot of squealing from the other benches as the men are released from the Drill Chain, retaining their collars, and ordered to put on their prisonlike uniforms. Being an establishment catering primarily to female doms, all the men are fair game; and anyone may have access to their indignity. The female subs' humiliation – stripping for the showers and the like – is not for the view of the male subs, however, so the three female doms are asked to leave the area with their charges. We have about 45 minutes of leisure time, which we can spend wandering the grounds or retreating to private quarters. All participants are expected to stay in character, though, and I hope you won't let me down with dismal chat about work or your wife. Miko opts to stay and watch the girls being put through their paces, so I clip your leash on and take you for a stroll around the estate. I have a bag of tricks with me, containing a blindfold, a ball gag, some penis rings, a paddle and, my old favourite, the dragon quirt.

I lead you upstairs and out to ground level again for a mooch around the perimeter of the house. My shoes crunch satisfyingly on the gravel as you hop like an invalid in your bare feet, trailing behind me to the fullest extension of your leash.

'This is ridiculous. Kirsten, why can't we just spend some proper time together?'

'Will you stop whining!' I yell, in full bitch-mistress mode. 'You are lucky I'm not making you *crawl* around the house. In fact, that's a very good idea. Take a closer look at your mistress's shoes, my finest Charles Jourdans. Now drop to all fours. Do it!'

You look confused, exasperated, injured and intrigued all at once. This *is* cathartic for you. Can you remember the last time you felt such a riot of lively emotions?

'Why here? Why can't we go inside? It's warmer there.'

I size up the pros and cons. There is a conservatory that looks inviting at the back of the building.

'Very well,' I say. 'But you are crawling there, Charlesworth.'

11 An Incident in the Conservatory

To my delight and amusement you drop down and crawl on your hands and knees to the conservatory. I turn the handle and enter, making sure you follow me in doggy mode. The still atmosphere recalls the Victorian hothouse at Kew – one of my favourite environments – only in miniature. It is beautifully decorated with wide cane chairs, plenty of foliage and statuary of satyrs planted on the marble floor. It's aesthetically perfect. In a large cage over by some palms sits a grey parrot. His beady eyes alight on us the moment we enter and I don't doubt he thinks of us as intruders in his domain.

I feel instantly elated by this tranquil sanctuary.

'Now, if I take off your leash, you can show me what a well-behaved doggy you are. Will you do that for me?' I say playfully.

You nod your head, eyes downcast. You are better behaved than I had predicted.

'Good doggy.' I take a step towards you, to bend down and unclip your leash, but before I can continue our mannered sparring you have grabbed me and pulled me down onto the floor. My high shoes don't allow me to keep balance, and I fall on top of you. I'm incandescent with anger at this undoing. Before I can right myself you flip me over, holding both my wrists in your hand, your eyes full of venom.

'Why are you doing this to me, you bitch?' you hiss.

'Just be real for a minute, will you, and listen to me. I'm crazy about you. Not a night goes by without me waking up in a cold sweat wanting you. I've got the bloody party conference in a week's time but I can't concentrate on anything I'm supposed to because of you.'

I know I should struggle to regain dominance and continue the play, exacting harsh punishment for this impertinence, but I begin to enjoy your display of raw emotion more than the subjugation I was planning. It is evidence of your unravelling reserve. Not so supercilious now, are we? You go on.

'I can't take any more of this. Do you know what it's like, what you've turned me into, with your teasing and buggery and Christ knows what?'

'I've brought you closer to living an authentic life,' I say, managing to speak calmly considering I am in the ignominious position of being flat on my back. I will remain in control verbally, even though you temporarily have the upper hand physically. You continue your vitriol.

'You've turned me into a monster, planting all sorts of unthinkable thoughts in my head. Do you know what I did to my wife? I raped her. I raped her. No man can ever have been driven so hard, so far without . . .'

'Without what?' I ask. 'Being able to stick his obscenity where he likes?'

'If you want to put it like that, yes. It's not natural to withhold this. Don't you want it, Kirsten? Don't you want me? Feel me, feel what you're doing to me.'

You release my arms so I prop myself up on my elbows to see you pull your hard penis from the pyjama bottoms then slide back down on top of me so you remain in the superior position.

'Oh, let me, let me now. I can't stand this,' you plead. 'Not after everything in the car.'

From a practical perspective I am fully clothed, even

corseted, and a long way from being easily accessible, so you have no chance of getting your way. Emotionally I am serene. Everything will happen on my terms and not otherwise. You know you can't do what you want without a terrible fuss ensuing. Not only would you be roughed up by the security, you would be taken to the dungeons and be lucky to escape without a serious lashing or even a branding on your arse. How would that go down in the parliamentary showers? Eddie and Bronwen play safe and for laughs on these weekends, but they are no strangers to the dark side of the scene, and are fully equipped to take it to any level they require.

But I am undergoing a crisis of my own. I am aching for you. Aching to be fucked but not daring to risk it. You would be intolerable, swaggering, arrogant. I cannot let you top me. I need to string out your longing even further, although I am swollen and ready for the most-needed fuck of my life. I want more than Gareth's little porn stars can give me. I want something other than the cloying familiarity of Ian Baum, playing the neurotic for him. I want something magnificent and new and complicated. Yes, I want you. But I will put you through hell before I let you know it. I summon all the strength within me and tumble you onto the floor in a flash. In the struggle your glasses come off and you are vulnerable enough for the time I need to get the cuffs out of my bag. There's no finesse now; no safe words apply. I am using the pure rage of frustration to teach you a lesson. My knee goes hard into your kidneys and your arms are pulled back and cuffed. A nice trick I learned from my SFPD friends.

'You bitch, you're sick. Let me go,' you protest.

'You're the sick one, Charlesworth,' I spit, 'for what you did to your wife. And you're very foolish to think you can undignify *me*. You failed. And you will end up worse for that. You're lucky I don't make you crawl on broken glass for penance.'

I now take delight from knowing how I will make you really suffer. I press down on your neck so you are curled into a ball. You try to stand from this position but your 53-year-old knees are too creaky to spring you to a standing position, so you crumple.

Just as I am reaching for the ball gag I see Miko walking towards the conservatory. She notices there is a struggle going on, breaks into a run, and is there in seconds. I want to howl with fury and really lash into you but I ease myself back into the play with extreme control.

'Miko, it's time for the amazing Japanese rope trick,' I say, a little breathless.

'Is he not behaving well?' she asks, her ever-regal face creasing into a sadistic smile.

'Not at all.'

Hilariously, the grey parrot has come to life, issuing a series of whistles, clicks and a perfectly enunciated 'naughty boy'.

Miko and I register the irony as you continue your serious intentions.

'Look, I didn't mean –'

Before you have time to utter your flimsy excuse Miko has cracked you around the face with a stinging slap that surprises even me.

You shout obscenities of genuine rage at this. We agree you'll have to be gagged. I hold your hair back tight and your mouth falls open a little at the shock of what's happening. Miko grasps your nose and forces you to open your mouth wider to breathe. It's then that I stuff the rubber ball in and clench the fastening around the back of your head. Your protestations are now rendered unintelligible, your desires thwarted once more.

'I get rope from the car. You hold him,' Miko orders. Her enthusiasm for bondage is completely genuine.

'With pleasure,' I say, running my hands over you in a proprietorial manner.

The others begin emerging from the basement and trooping onto the lawn. The girls are now done up in their costumes and very pretty they look, too, in their French maid and schoolgirl outfits. I can see Eddie looking at her watch while a couple of the sissy maids refresh everyone's glasses.

'You've brought this on yourself,' I say with venom, speaking closely into your ear as my heart beats rapidly in my breast. I press myself into your back. The thin material of your pyjama uniform allows intimate contact and I sense you arching back to increase the pressure. I want to visit such infamy upon you that I feel almost supernatural in my power. I quickly steal a hand into my knickers and gather the essence of my juices.

'Look, the others are having drinks now. What a shame you can't have any. If you'd learned to behave and kept your mouth only for pleasing me and being courteous, then you could have had a reward, but instead you are going to be trussed like a chicken and not given a thing expect the touch of the lash. And this.'

I rub my fingers across your face and you inhale deeply to breathe of the scent. Within a few seconds you begin swelling in your pyjama bottoms. You try to make yourself understood but it's no use as the noise just comes out as a frantic hum through the ball gag. Even though I am incensed with your behaviour, you are completely beholden to me. Kneeling behind you with my arms and legs unhindered I am able to touch any part of your body. An autumn wasp bounces against the glass panes of the conservatory, and my head reels with the idea of capturing it in a jar and introducing it to your privates. I could bugger you here, under a statue of Pan. I could stand up, remove my knickers and piss on you. I could savage your backside with a strop or deliver you to Eddie to be taken to the dungeon. Instead, what arouses the greatest voluptuousness in me is simply to toy with you as my prisoner.

I do not approach the handling of your genitals with anything like a sense of wanting to please you, though. I am sure to let you know that you are now being violated. My hands go where I please. These are not favours. This is impropriety, outrage, defilement. Oh, you wretched creature, you are as immoral as I am! You are tethered and in no little discomfort but you are hard and your balls are full. I can feel them. How does it feel, as I manipulate you? Is it a relief to have a hand on you at last? But I shall not catch your tribute in my mouth or allow you your favourite treat – my feet. I am going to make you into a sight of ridicule.

I know how to handle a man like you, by alternating between fondling your testicles and applying firm strokes to that ample rod. You are still uttering futile whimpers through your gag. The muscles of your flanks are constricting. What a fine little sex machine you are. There is no going back. I am taking you headlong into such an atrocious debauchery yet you are complicit in the outrage. The urge is so strong that you are temporarily suspending all concern for the consequences. Now this is no state for a Cabinet minister to find himself in, is it – so easily persuaded to corruption? You begin to issue sharp snorting breaths through your nose as the flexing of your buttock muscles increases. I rub my hands under your sac once more. It's tightening. Your penis is rolled back and engorged to its maximum condition. Up and down goes my hand, gripping firmly all the way, my other hand intermittently wiping my scent under your nose. Still I continue to whisper obscenities in your ear. What a thing to undergo in such delightful surroundings!

Your straining muffled cries have got louder and increasingly more desperate. Isn't human communication a wonderful thing? You cannot issue a word yet still I can tell your crisis is urgent. I bet you wish you'd exercised more self-control because it is upon you now. As I feel the eruption bursting up the shaft I watch in rapt horror and elation as you release yourself into your trousers. Miko re-enters the conservatory holding a coiled length of rope, making a curious juxtaposition with the tranquil environment.

'Naughty boy!' she exclaims, sounding just like the parrot. 'I tell Madame what happened and you already in trouble. But look at you now!'

'He's a complete disgrace,' I say with resigned calm. 'A total mess. How am I going to hold up my head out there today with such an impossible slave?'

'You come now anyway,' says Miko. 'Out on the lawn.'

You shake your head violently but it's no good – there is no hiding place from exposure. The ramifications of your shame are about to happen, dear little minister. And in front of all those nice young girls, too. You should have thought about that before you let yourself go.

You are shockingly embarrassed, even though you cannot speak. I can see your skin has coloured and there's a pitiful look in your eye. You are no doubt fearing what's about to happen. And with good reason. I stand up and pull you up with me. You are a little unsteady on those legs. If you think you've already undergone a bit of a trial, it's nothing compared to the punishments that await you. I reach over and pick up my bag of tricks as Miko takes over your lead and walks you, gagged, cuffed and disgraced, out of the conservatory into the assembled colourful throng of deviants.

'I'm afraid we've had a little tantrum,' I declare, getting back into role as everyone turns to stare and point. 'And then a little accident. It seems the sight of his mistress was just too much for him. This naughty boy just cannot learn to control himself.'

The doms all break into laughter.

'He needs a taste of the whip!' says Frankie, raising her glass.

'To the whip,' shouts Lon, and everyone joins in, clinking glasses.

'What a disgusting display,' shouts Bronwen. He needs his arse tanning! Let's see it then.'

'Too right,' pipes up Miko, learning some English vernacular. 'He is absolutely vile, spraying all that nasty stuff into his outfit.'

'Get those trousers off him,' Bronwen orders. 'We'll have him naked.'

You are rolled over and debagged of the scandalous evidence, your depilated arse on display for all.

'On all fours,' I order, 'like the beast you are.'

With the others around I can release you from the cuffs, knowing you dare not try anything mutinous. I then pull you down on the grass and have you walking around on all fours, following me to heel like a show dog. There are guffaws all round and, worst for you, the other male subs laugh loudest.

'I think it's time for the paddle,' I say. 'Just for the crack of it.'

I pull a bifurcated leather strop from my bag and rub it sensuously, almost tenderly, against your backside before building up a head of loathing for your inability to play by my rules and then I lash down on you with full force.

'What's he made of?' shouts one of the warlocks. 'Fifty on the bare!'

So there you are: secretary of state for public policy, ball-gagged, stripped and upended on an English lawn in front of a motley collection of perverts, getting the right royal larruping you deserve. You are silent and terrified, but you haven't yet cried 'Tony', so we won't be going home just yet. Everyone is cheering but I am almost in tears of sexual frustration. You still haven't learned to be contrite or respectful of my role in this arrangement. You still think you can get your way; that somehow I am going to turn into this vanilla lover who will embark on a romantic affair with you. Keep dreaming, Charlesworth.

After I've tanned your backside to a glowing ball, it's Bronwen's turn. The sight of this matronly lady striding towards you with her arm raised is an image I will savour in future times when you are getting a little high and mighty. Next to having my hands on you, watching a woman of formidable build and countenance such as Bronwen let loose to exact some discipline makes a rewarding spectacle. After it is over, your head is bowed and you are finally subdued, shivering half-naked on the lawn. I have a few private moments with you, asking you questions to which you reply with nods and shakes of the head and promises to be better behaved. I finally release you from the gag. How mournful you look. You don't want to be put in that again in a hurry.

You are given a fresh pair of trousers and the entertainment continues. No sooner are you getting used to freedom of movement once more than Miko makes good with a display of *kinbaku* on you. She explains its history and place in the samurai tradition, where this elaborate bondage was used to bring captured rogues before justice. Her skills earn a round of applause from everyone, and I see Eddie and Bronwen put their heads together in conversation. They are sure to employ her for one of their more elaborate dinner parties. A couple of the girls are doing cartwheels, cheekily flashing their knickers, and there is movement afoot for the afternoon sports.

Trussed into Miko's military bondage you are fair game for the maids to poke fun at. I am laughing, engrossed in watching them have their fun and relieved of the desperation I felt earlier. Suddenly I feel a hand on my arm. It's Eddie. She wants a quiet word.

'Kirsten, that is Simon Charlesworth, the MP, isn't it?' she asks rhetorically, knowing full well she's guessed correctly.

'Yes. I've bagged myself one of Her Majesty's public servants,' I say with a laugh. 'You don't think anyone else –'

'No, of course not. They are not political creatures. At least, no one has mentioned it to me, except Bronnie. The thing is, you see, he's local. That's how we recognise him. His constituency isn't far from here. And he's been in the news recently, the bastard.'

'He's on TV a bit these days,' I say. 'They always wheel him on to talk about new transport schemes and private finance, and all that boring nonsense. But why "bastard"?'

'He's the arsehole who's okayed the plans to tear down Broxbourne Wood.'

'Really? I've not heard about that.'

'No, well you wouldn't have. It's hardly national news. This is the sort of thing that's going on all over – the tearing down of ancient woodland for fucking supermarkets. There's a conspiracy not to report it like they used to. Gets too much support. Now they put a media gag on it.'

Eddie has raised her voice and is bristling with

passion. I've heard her talk about Broxbourne before. I'd forgotten your own constituency is round here and you have matters to attend to there as well as in the Cabinet job.

'Where is Broxbourne Wood?' I ask.

'About twenty miles from here. It's survived Norman invasion and two world wars. It's a Saxon wood. A sacred place.'

'And he wants to build a supermarket there?' I ask.

'Supermarket, housing estate and what he terms "modern amenities". We know what that means, don't we? Plastic multiplex cinemas, retail parks and fast-food monstrosities. The scourge of the modern British land-scape. On a Saxon wood! It's one of our special places, isn't it, Bronnie?'

Bronnie nods her head and chips in. 'I played there as a child and it's a truly special place. A magical woodland.'

'So, what should we do?' I ask, knowing already that they will suggest I have his ear.

'Use your formidable powers of persuasion any way you can,' says Eddie. 'And if they don't work then use force! But don't worry – we shan't let on we've deduced who he is. I'd like to take him downstairs and flay him alive, personally, but we can't show we've sussed him out. We have to be professional.'

The others are starting to get a bit raucous. Frau Gruber is swigging wine straight from the bottle and the dykes are snogging each other.

'I'd better get back to the sports,' says Eddie. 'But let me know how you get on. Think about what that two-faced shit is doing. Broxbourne is important to us. We do rituals there. It's a place of power.'

My mind whirrs into action. I'm so disappointed in you that I feel nauseous and I'm tingling with rage. You wouldn't have thought for a moment that I could have found out about this. You think I'm some privileged bitch with a head full of designer clothes and city living. You wouldn't know that I spent a good part of my twenties fighting to save ancient woodland under threat from developers and their oleaginous political allies. You wouldn't guess in a million years that I've firebombed the headquarters of construction companies, set light to advertising billboards and protested against multinationals. It really doesn't go with my new image. I may have polished my appearance since the firebrand days; I even own a car now, so I am something of a contradiction, but the destruction of England's natural landscape is something I'll still stand in front of the bulldozers to prevent. It goes against my principles to use blackmail, but if I have to in this case, to save that wood, then so be it. I regard you now with a new loathing. You are not just a grey-hearted bureaucrat, you are a two-faced, money-grubbing liar. Yes, I still want to fuck you, but I'm going to hold that privilege as collateral.

Miko has released you and I see that everyone is moving round to the back of the house. Eddie and Bronwen have arranged a start and finish line on the big lawn. Eddie shouts the orders: 'Get your charges down here ready. Hurry.'

Bronwen announces the obvious: the serviles are to line up and get ready for their sporting trials. The winners get a prize each – a bottle of champagne and their master's or mistress's choice of the latest new sex toy to use on them. Second and third place get minor treats, with the rest suffering varying humiliations on a sliding scale of where he or she comes in the race. My job is to keep record of the performances. Bronwen hands me a pad and pen. Apart from the Fräulein barrister and buxom Katie, the girls are shivering or complaining. Frau Gruber is still drinking from her wine bottle, her face getting redder, and there's more booze lined up inside for us to share at the end.

'Right. First race is the clothed free form. One end to the other. This is the easiest of the three races.'

I see the girls look at each other in disbelief. They never imagined they would be running about in the cold in their skimpy baby-doll outfits. The men look less perturbed, but they don't know what Eddie has in store for them yet.

'On your marks, then, you bunch of weak-willed infants,' yells Eddie. 'I want to see those legs moving. Remember there will be appalling punishment for the wretch who comes last and glory only to the winner.'

'This is like fascism,' you complain. 'It's like the Nazi Olympics.'

'Oh, shut up,' I spit, an image of you shaking hands with some supermarket CEO inflaming me to a fury. 'I bet the Nazi Olympics were a damn sight better organised than what awaits us in 2012. Think you can get the transport sorted out by then?'

I couldn't resist such a jibe, and I crack you one on the arse with the quirt to let you know who's boss. You jump in the air with the sudden pain, then take your place in the line with the others. I notice you are slyly ogling the barrister in pigtails and old-fashioned schoolgirl tunic.

'Remember,' Eddie shouts, 'you are doing this not only for your own sense of self-worth but also for your masters and mistresses. It is up to you whether or not you put in a good performance but I wouldn't like to be in the shoes of the servile who comes last.'

One of the smart-arse baby dykes whispers to Katie, 'None of us are wearing shoes.' Bronwen hears this and immediately has her out of line and dropping to do ten press-ups. The girl protests but is used as a warning to the others not to cheek those in charge. Frankie apologises to Eddie and Bronwen for the insolence of her girl, and announces they can use her later for dildo practice. The shocked girl is red in the face – from exertion and embarrassment.

'Are we back in line now?' shouts Eddie. 'Good. Nurse Bronwen will count down, and then you'll be off.'

I can see you looking pretty confident about your chances, even though a few moments ago you were decrying the whole thing as fascism. Bronwen counts down and the first race is under way. The doms cheer on their charges, only the stone-faced warlocks remaining silent. These overly serious scene players dare not show themselves to be team-spirited; it would undermine their aloof style. But they are outnumbered in their reserve by the hearty back-slapping butches and the fiercely competitive pro-doms. Bronwen is pretending to be serious about the whole thing, but I can see her smiling. Eddie is at the halfway point, shouting encouragement. The baby dykes are all slender, so get a good sprint up. The men too get off to a good start but I'm pleased to see you are ahead out of the three. Gruber's girl is in the lead, with Katie second, but the girly Goths are a dead loss, mincing along pathetically, arms all over the place, tripping over their feet.

It's hilarious watching all the participants wearing such serious expressions in their fancy dress as they come back towards us doms, who are sharing a drink and a joke at the finishing line. The bald man is slowing to a jog, and is even caught up by the Goths. Katie and you are fighting it out for second place but Paula is the first one back, beaming with schoolgirl pride to throw her arms around Frau Gruber. Eddie is cantering alongside the winners, and I am delighted to see you running in your little prison pyjamas, bringing in second place. You seem to have cheered up a bit, and the intensity of the conservatory seems to have been dispersed by the fresh air and exercise.

'I thought I would make it then, to first,' you say, panting and gasping for air. 'I'm sorry. I wanted to win for you.'

'Plenty of chance to make up for it,' I say. 'Unencumbered by clothes next time.'

'What?' you say, panicked. 'You mean . . .'

'Well done, well done to the first three. Damien and Gisli, you should be ashamed of those girls,' Eddie says to the warlocks. 'They're a disgrace. They need some proper training. Look at them.'

I can't believe the girls are actually walking back. They don't know what's in store for them later. And neither do you. For now, it's the done thing to join in with the fun.

'Get ready, back to your positions,' shouts Eddie. 'Time for the men's Spartan race. You know what this means . . . butt naked!'

To my surprise you strip down without any further complaint. That beating seems to have bucked your ideas up a bit and I'm feeling quietly confident you can win this one. Off strides Eddie, back to the halfway line and Bronwen calls for the off. Those bare backsides are jouncing again as the three men head towards the 200-metre mark. You are neck and neck with the studious-looking guy but something seems to have changed in you. You suddenly get a competitive spurt on, your breath steaming in the chill air. This is as much a health-giving exercise as anything. You turn around and make it back in first place, your strong legs powering you to the finish line.

In a moment of magnanimity I stretch out my arms and allow you to run your cold body into the warm protection of my coat. Again I feel the sensation of improper access. It is unusual that a fully clothed woman dressed for a bracing outdoor pursuit would know the sensation of embracing a naked man, but there it is. Eddie's weekends are full of such moments – when things that feel so wrong also feel so right.

'So you won! That's brilliant,' I say, being sure to show no indication of what I've learned about you. You'd take off at the slightest hint of suspicion.

'Shades of cross-country at school,' you reply, then bend over to rest your hands on your knees and take a few deep breaths.

'Well, it seems to be doing you good,' I note. 'And good to have a target, too. Imagine how awful it would have been for both of us if you had come last.'

I point over at the pro-doms who are stern-faced, laying into their serviles with their crops.

'I can't take any more today,' you say. 'I'm fifty-three.'

'That's no get-out clause, Charlesworth. I thought you were the thrusting man of party politics, you can't use your age as an excuse. Which reminds me ... your party conference is in Brighton, isn't it? Not too far from here, in fact.'

'Yes, it's next week.'

'I've got a lot of friends in Brighton,' I say. 'I'm due a visit. Maybe we could hook up.'

'Well, I've got to be discreet. Lorna will be there as a party member.'

'Discreet is my speciality. It'll make it all the more exciting being furtive. Look, I've been thinking ... you've been such a good sport today. Taken such a beating! I want us to get a hotel room. I can't stand the waiting any longer either. You can sneak out and visit me. I love Brighton for so many reasons. The weird thing is, I always feel really horny when I'm there.'

'Really?'

I can see you're already hooked. This is my first confession of arousal, given so casually, and you are putty in my hands. Hands that I run over you.

'I have to give a speech this time,' you say proudly. 'I'm taking the platform the same day as the PM.'

'That's *very* exciting,' I say.

There's no time for any more conversation, as it's time for the blindfold race. Frankie and Lon are fitting black velvet masks onto their baby dykes and the war-locks are doing likewise with their Goth princesses. Things aren't quite as pretty for the male subs as each gets a burlap sack over his head. There's a good deal of squealing and confusion as all the serviles are pushed to the start line and read the rules by Eddie, still mag-nificent in her riding gear. Everyone cries it's not fair, it's demeaning and other feeble protestations, but Bron-wen counts down and they're all off, the men still naked among the fancy-dressed girls.

This time all the doms run alongside the wider flank of the course to shout encouragement and get the best view of the fun. The studious guy and one of the Goths have already hit the deck and the bald man and the other Goth girl are treading so gingerly they'll get to the finish by next week at this rate. Eddie has zeroed in on you, as you have gone wide of the course. She runs up alongside you and lets fly with her crop, striping you on the back. You cry out and run faster, but are going in the wrong direction, heading for the shrubbery to the left of the halfway line. Either Paula or one of the dykes looks set to win this competition, as they are the only contestants on course.

If I don't stop you, you are going to land somewhere uncomfortable so I head towards you. Face on you make a terrifying sight – a naked middle-aged man running with his head a crumpled mass of burlap – but I call your name and you slow down. I grab you and turn you round, shouting instructions.

'Caine, you're cheating!' shouts Eddie. 'We'll deduct points for that.'

I run back to the finish line but it's already over by the time I get there. Lon's girl wins. It's time for tea. The exertions of the day have worked up a good appetite. The serviles are allowed back to the showers to wash and freshen up, but must put their outfits back on to assist with the serving of drinks and food from the buffet that has been laid out in the drawing room. Masters and mistresses are given their food first, of course. The French maids come into their own and the Goth schoolgirls look very decorative in the servant role before they are permitted to sit at their masters' feet and pick at the occasional vegetarian snack. Gruber handfeeds Paula, who kneels fetchingly like a little lapdog while the baby dykes are permitted to sit on low stools. The male subs get the worst deal, eating from doggy bowls under the tables.

As you did well in one of the races you are allowed a stool, but I decide to nominate you in charge of refreshments. You barely get a chance to swallow a couple of sandwich quarters before you are dispatched to the kitchen with the sissy maids to brew an urn-full of tea and coffee. Naturally the maids take the opportunity to order you around and a lot of protest and yelping issues from the kitchen to accompany our feast.

By the time you re-enter the drawing room you have been put into a maid's outfit and everyone cheers when they see you have been enforcibly feminised. It's your worst nightmare. You want to be the man of the world, but you've been reduced to the maid of the high tea. That Hyacinth does have such a wicked streak! Once again you are wearing a pinny, and this time it's to serve a selection of refreshments in bone china cups and saucers. Your trolley is laden with 1930s crockery and the spread is decidedly retro: there are fondant fancies, doilies, silver forks and spoons, sugar bowls and jugs of milk and cream. Each dominant must be served with impeccable manners and you know better than to make a single error. Thing is, you are not used to wearing women's shoes, and your teetering and swaying as you wheel the trolley around the room is simply hilarious. You've taken a lot of punishment over the past week, and I'd have doubted whether you could take any more without a rebellion but you know better than to protest in the present circumstances. There are people here who would make mincemeat of you. It's a wonderful touch from Hyacinth, who is allowed to berate you with a crop as a special treat for being so inventive. The sight of you in a dress and blonde wig with a starched white cap and apron is the cherry on the cake of humiliation after such a day of weird and wonderful adult fun.

The remainder of the day is taken up with a demonstration of equipment in the dungeon. The pro-doms are impressive, and one even uses a bullwhip on her client. The balding man is wired up to some electrical stimulation toys and we all gasp to see the use of pegs on his nipples. The dykes aren't so enamoured by the Gothic trappings of the dungeon but the warlocks and their girls love it. Frankie, Lon and Dagmar prefer the sportier end of things, and love using the paddles and strap-ons. Each in his or her own way has a wonderful time. I demand you put on a display of foot worship for the others, which causes you immense embarrassment, dressed as you are.

When all the punishments, fun and games are over, there is tenderness, laughter and conversation as the couples pack up to leave. The serviles get dressed again in their day clothes and there's time to explore the grounds, which look stunning in the autumn evening light, especially as the leaves of the sumachs and rowan trees are turning to flame red and burnished copper. I manage to have a quiet word with Eddie, and find out precise directions to Broxbourne Wood.

'That sacred grove must be saved,' she says, taking hold of my hands like a favourtie auntie. 'We're on the protest committee but they're too much of a gentle shower of liberal humanists to get anything done. Saving Albion from the ravages of the corporate monolith requires shock troops, not bearded Christian geography teachers. Still, this is a gift from the goddess. We couldn't have dreamed that one of our friends might be in a position to help stop it.'

'I promise I'll do what I can, Eddie,' I say. 'By the way, do you still have those animal masks we used that time we did a pagan scene in the grounds?'

12 **Into the Woods**

Twenty-five years I've been coming to these bloody things and finally, this time round, I'm taking the stand with confidence. Last year was the dry run; this year I'm going to be the toast of the hall. There's no going back. I can rightly say I'm primed for success. I'm the man who has put private finance initiatives back on the political agenda for the party. In this age, no one can afford to ignore business in public policy. The speech is written and I've had extra voice-coaching lessons to get it pitch perfect. Jason has put together a fantastic PowerPoint projection to display while I'm on the podium and it's going to knock the conference on its arse. I know I'm looking good. Maybe those stupid races at that bloody country house for perverts have contributed to me feeling so fit. I might even take up running again. All I have to do is get through one more day of it and I'm there.

I've had to endure four days of rank and file hectoring from what's left of the old guard. They're all so quick to judge and sling names, but I couldn't care less. They're on the way out. If we'd left it to their lot we'd never have got back in power at all. Our PR team has been a shining star on every campaign since we modernised. No more wilderness years. Christ, when I think back to my first conferences, forming a bloody line with Kinnock and singing 'The Internationale', I could cringe with embarrassment. It's like another life. And that's exactly what I've been given – a new life; a new opportunity. All the hard work of the past ten years has paid off. Of course, the anti-war lot are still making a noise but who cares when the economy's this strong. They're duped if they still think they can build some kind of utopia. We're long past that. We were right to go to war. Sometimes you have to do the strong thing, even if it goes against your previous ideals. What's done is done. It's the future I need to think about. And my present needs.

The speech is set for eleven o'clock tomorrow morning. The chancellor is up at noon and then the PM takes the stand at three o'clock. And I'll be sitting on the podium the whole day. No more grubbing around with the flotsam and jetsam in the audience any more. It'll be me, Simon Charlesworth, up in his rightful place with the big league.

And not only am I confident about party matters. I'm seeing you tonight and we're on course, finally, for the real thing. I've never been through anything like that bloody day at that place with those freaks. Is this the price I'm paying to be assured of the kind of sex I've only dreamed about? You're right, though, to tell me to be wary of those polished women who are obsessed with status and who will betray me the moment they get a sniff of money from the tabloids. You're a strange woman but it's not like you've tried to tap me up for expensive gifts and you've never shown any interest in shopping, which is a relief. I've proven to you that I can play your games, make a fool of myself, worship you, take punishment and be your dog, as you call me. I don't care, because it's an escape from the pressure of everything else. For all the bizarre antics I've found myself in with you and your little Japanese sidekick I always get a strange sense of calm afterwards. I feel fitter than I have done in years. I've lost weight and I'm being careful about what I eat. And, although it's weird to admit it, I'm proud of the marks you've left on me.

Lorna hasn't seen them, of course. There's been barely

any contact between us since I forced her to have sex with me, although she hasn't mentioned it again. She's just given me enough dirty looks to know that the personal side of our marriage is a dead loss for the foreseeable future. She even booked a hotel room with twin beds this time. I don't know what future we have together. I don't want to think about the inconvenience of divorce. I know she'd plead the injured party and take me for everything I've got and it's my wages that's paid for that house. Maybe we'll settle into a comfortable arrangement. I'll lead my life and she can lead hers. If she won't even discuss sex then I can't see how things can be made better. I'll just keep my head down. Worry about it if and when the time comes.

I know that once you've let me make love to you it'll be the end of the stupid role playing between us. Then we can embark on a proper affair. I still think of how wonderful you would look on my arm walking down a Parisian boulevard. I'm quite taken with the idea of you letting me worship your boots in some luxury hotel suite. It'll all be on expenses, of course. Still, if we can't have Paris for just now, there's always Hove, where I'm to meet you in your hotel. Lorna's going out with her female friends from the old days, and there'll be no questions asked as to where I'm going. She's given up bothering about my life. If the worst comes to the worst Jason will cover for me. I've told him I'm meeting a diplomat – all hush-hush – and he gets the drift. If anything crops up in an emergency he can reach me on the BlackBerry.

The rest of the day drones on with speeches from the health and pensions ministers and finally I am free to prepare myself. I've spruced up in a Hugo Boss suit and tailor-made shirt, silk tie and handmade shoes. No more maids' outfits! Whatever ridiculous circus I found myself playing with you last weekend, tonight it's my time to call the shots. I look good. I feel great. And I'm going to set the style. This evening will be sophistication and old-fashioned seduction. I dab on some cologne and brush myself down, then swirl around a mouthwash and I'm downstairs in the lobby in a flash as soon as reception buzzes me and lets me know my cab is here. My heart is racing. Finally it's going to happen.

As we travelled back to London last Saturday you were so proud of me. You let me lie with my head in your lap as you stroked my hair. I do like it when you do that. You brought me off with your hand in the back of the car once more and it was wonderful to know for once the tenderness of your touch, rather than your cruel whip hand. You whispered to me of your desires. How you'd been apprehensive of letting me go all the way. How other powerful men had hurt you. How you'd forgotten what it was like to be able to trust someone. All these things have proven to me that you are not looking to sell your story; you're looking for love, just like the rest of us. And because I'd been such a good sport you're going to grant me the ultimate privilege, you said. No caning or beating or humiliation – just worship and long leisurely lovemaking in a hotel room. What I wanted from the beginning.

You embraced me after you dropped me off at Sloane Square. I invited you to have dinner with me but you wanted to wait until we were less tired, when dinner could be the prelude to a wonderful evening. Oh, your perfume as you pulled yourself close to me! I wanted to drown in it, buy you a lifetime's supply of it. And you told me then such naughty things: how you want me inside of you; want to feel me spunk into you; watch me come and know that moment as we look into each other's eyes. How powerful that will be! And that moment is about to happen.

I sit in the back of the car feeling ready for anything the world can throw at me. The lights are out along the promenade and it feels like they're out just for me, in glorious preparation of tomorrow, when I show the country I've got what it takes to be a dynamic minister. Who knows, after this one, the senior members may even be looking to me as a party-leader-in-waiting. And what a leader-in-waiting deserves is a bloody good fuck!

Here it is ... your hotel. It's small and trendy. The lobby is about the size of my study and I sense immediately that the ownership is gay as I make my way up the stairs to find your room – number eight. I knock on the door and my heart is going like the clappers. It's so exciting to be doing this just down the road from Lorna and her boring friends. You open it and there stands a vision of the like I have never seen. Your hair is down, long and lustrous against a cheongsam of midnight-blue satin. You have on the tallest shoes I have ever seen – they must have cost a small fortune – and the room is permeated by that perfume I have come to adore. You are bringing a much-needed feminine touch to this house of gay men and their guests.

'Oh, Kirsten, look at you!' I say.

'I've been doing just that for the past half an hour, Simon. What do you think, then? Is that something you'd like to get on top of?'

Oh, joy, you are still in the mood for me. That's an invite if ever I heard one.

'Is that a daft question or what?' I say, entering the room and closing the door behind me.

'You look pretty sharp,' you say. 'Scrubbed up well for the conference, huh?'

'I feel like we're Humphrey Bogart and Lauren Bacall, trying to outsmart each other with wisecracking lines. I've scrubbed up well for you, baby,' I say. 'Here ... I got you something.'

I extract a small box from my pocket. I remembered you like to be surprised with gifts. You're not insisting on the usual terms of address. I seem to be getting away with calling you by your real name, by terms of affection.

You tear into it with nails that are polished an even darker shade of blue than your dress, almost black with an iridescent sheen the colour of bluebottles. You open the box and extract a necklace.

'I bought it for you in the Lanes today. It's antique.'

'It's beautiful, Simon. Put it on for me,' you say. 'I want to wear it immediately.'

You hand it to me and turn around. I clip the necklace in place and then I can't wait. I have my arms around you, over you, running up and down the sides of your satin-covered body, feeling the curve of your waist.

'I'm crazy about you, Kirsten,' I whisper in your ear.

You fall back into me, undulating your hips slightly. It's heavenly torture as you rub yourself against my crotch. I'm getting hard already but I know I have to prove to you how restrained I can be. I daren't put you off with a gauche display of adolescent groping. After all I've been through, after all you've made me do, I deserve this reward. And, oh, baby, you seem to be giving me what I want. But I can't rush it. Mustn't go for speed over quality. Have to take it easy. Still, I can't help moving things on just a little.

'Look at the nice big bed you have. Shouldn't we lie down?' I suggest.

'Sure. But let's have some champagne first. Sit down, of course.'

It's then that I notice there's a magnum of champagne on ice in a bucket by the window.

'Absolutely. This is a special occasion, right? One I thought might not happen.'

You smile that imperial smile I've seen so many

times. 'Take off your jacket. There's a hanger in the wardrobe,' you say. 'Don't want to the get that lovely suit all crumpled.'

As I hang it up I hear you pop the cork. It's funny, but after the whole range of outrageous things you have done to me, I feel more apprehensive of tonight than any other. It's like a first date. I excuse myself into the en-suite bathroom for a few minutes. When I come out you are handing me a champagne flute full of fizzing liquid.

We drink a toast.

'To your beauty, Kirsten,' I say.

'To your conference speech,' you say, having read my emails about how important it is for me, how you must tune in to it tomorrow when it's broadcast live. 'May both these things go down in history.'

And we quickly get through two glasses each as I speak to you of how crazy the past few weeks have been.

'I know I've said it before, but I've never met anyone like you. Not even in the wild nineteen-seventies. I can't imagine where you got your views on the world. You don't seem to be concerned by the things that bother other people. I really can't work you out.'

'You'll die trying,' you say, which unnerves me slightly until you smile and lay your hand on my leg. I guess you're just what the Americans call a kooky kind of girl.

'You are here alone, aren't you?' I check. 'I keep thinking Miko is going to jump out of the bathroom or something.'

You laugh and assure me we're going to be completely undisturbed, although it means I won't get a lesbian display tonight. You stand next to the bed, between my legs as I sit on the edge and run my hands over you.

'May I touch your breasts?' I ask. I sense that we are

not in role tonight, but it's best to check anyway. I've been trained so well!

'I'd love you to touch my breasts,' you say. 'They ache for you to touch them.'

My hands feel like magnets drawn to them, they are so perfect. But your beautiful dress is tantalising me. I can't get at you properly, skin on skin. I want to bury my face in them, suck on them, come all over them.

'Then take your dress off. Please.'

'You do it. Unzip me from the back.'

I stand up and do as you bid me. To unwrap you from your silky sheath is a delight. There you are, in exquisite lingerie and stockings, waiting for the best I can give you. You won't be disappointed.

'Oh, Kirsten, if you knew how long I've fantasised about this,' I tell you. 'You've had a spell over me. I don't know what planet you come from, but if their women are all like you, then book me on the next spaceship.'

I put my glass down and fall back on the bed. The lights are dimmed and I think I'm about to enter a heavenly place. Now you're crawling over me and this is truly paradise. You're all legs and breasts and I cannot believe my luck. Here I am in a gay hotel room in Brighton, dressed to the nines with the most drop-dead gorgeous woman on top of me and I think after this I can die happy. If only Lorna could see this, she'd realise what she's missing. Still, it's not Lorna I want. It's you. And so very, very badly.

You plant kisses on me and undo my shirt. Your hands run through the hair on my chest and you scratch me lightly. Your hair falls around you. Fantastically, it cascades over your breasts and I reach up and play with it, then pull you down so those baps are in my face. I'm so hard I could burst the zip of my fly.

I chuckle out loud. How d'you like this, Robert? Stuff this for your family values!

'Hey, Kirsten, it's your turn to unzip me, baby,' I say and, to my total delight, you sit back and do it, millimetre by agonising millimetre. Then, praise be, that mouth is on me. It's over me, working me up and down and I call my delight out loud in the room. Finally, after all the waiting, after all the stupid games and crazy shenanigans I'm finally going to get to do what I've wanted to do since I first laid eyes on you in that bar. Good things come to those who wait, it's true.

I start flexing my buttock muscles, pushing into your beautiful mouth for all I'm worth. But I've got an embarrassment of riches here. I don't want you to stop, but I want to show you what I can do. I want to lick you and feel you and lose myself in you. God, I feel amazing. It's like I've been supercharged with some incredible aphrodisiac. I can feel a rush of something travelling up my spine. I am breathing deeply and with each in-breath I feel more animalistic, more brazen. I feel like I want to run naked through the streets, showing my erection to the world.

I pull you off my penis by your hair and up towards my face. Now I'm kissing you deeply, tasting my own flesh as I run my hand over your fancy knickers. I spin you over and the sudden movement makes me a little dizzy. That champagne has gone to my head on my empty stomach. I feel like I'm going to faint but I've got to deliver the goods here. My hand is on your breasts and then between your legs. Oh Christ, it's extraordinary. After all the weeks of torture you've put me through, I'm finally getting what I want. I ease my fingers under the leg of your knickers. It's humid down there. You're slick and ready for me, you beautiful bitch.

My suit trousers are working their way down my thighs. I must remember to put them into the trouser press tonight. I kick them off and giggle at their reluctance to leave my legs. Now I'm ready.

'Socks, Simon.'

'Huh?'

'For Christ's sake! Your socks. Take them off!'

'Oh yeah, sorry.' I giggle. To think that such a small thing would cause such a stern reprimand. Still, women are funny about that sort of thing, so off they come. Wow. I sit up and the room seems to tilt a little.

'That champagne has gone right to my head,' I say. 'I must be so excited that all the blood has rushed downwards.'

You lie serene and exotic on top of the duvet. Hopefully there won't be any more demands. I can just find my way inside you. It's happening in about one minute, baby. I crawl back on top of you, taking your wrists in my hands and pinning your arms above your head as you've done to me several times. The joy of feeling your female form beneath me is incomparable. This is what I wanted so badly in that conservatory. Finally, it's real. Those magnificent orbs of flesh are pressed underneath me, and your hot moist cunt is under my hand. It's all too much.

'Can I?' I ask. 'Is this the moment?'

You nod your head, surprisingly subdued considering your usual demonstrative persona with the crop and the rope. I'm not sure which I prefer. This new you is very mild in comparison, and I've kind of got used to being given orders, but, oh my God, I'm not complaining. I stroke your hair and bury my face in it. As I close my eyes I can see a firework display of starburst colours behind my eyes. You really have put a spell on me. But I'm not wasting any more time. I ease your slithery, silky knickers down your legs and brace myself fully up against you and prepare to plunder the uncharted territory.

'Oh, yes,' I cry, feeling your liquid velvet close around my cock. 'Oh, Kirsten, I'm fucking you, I'm really doing it.'

I brace myself on my arms as you curl your legs around my back with your shoes still on – a nice touch. I begin to pump inside you, fearful I'll come too soon and be a disappointment. It suddenly strikes me that I haven't pleasured you and I worry about your orgasm. I'm sure you would rather come first. Ladies first, that's what they always say, isn't it, whoever 'they' are. Who are they? Who is anyone?

I suddenly realise I've stopped. I'm not fucking you as much as writhing around like some kind of snake-hipped dancer.

'Everything OK?' you ask.

'Er, I'm not sure. What about your orgasm?'

'What indeed, Simon Charlesworth,' you say, and the mention of my name makes me feel strange. The sea-front lights are shining a dazzle of colours into the room and everything looks very pretty. It's crazy, but I feel like I want to be outside; to go for a run along the promenade. I shake the thought from my head and turn back to you.

'Take your time, Cabinet Minister,' you say, but I don't want to be reminded of my job right now. I feel there's something more important going on.

'Tell me what you want, Kirsten,' I say. 'Be like you've been with me up until now. You know, stern. Make me beg for you.'

'Oh, we can do that again, soon enough,' you say.

I look into your face. It's extraordinary. You've taken on the appearance of something otherwordly. I can't believe I'm fucking this otherworldly creature. And doing it in such a conventional way. You've got such lovely, silky legs. Maybe you are an alien. I have my hands under your buttocks and over your thighs. You're gorgeous. I've waited so long and now I'm finally here. Silky, silky ... just like your hair. That's it, let me play with it ... so soft. That perfume. OK, I'll put your knickers on again. You are funny. Room service ... more champagne. I'm giggling. Spinning. Those lights ... they're dancing. Getting brighter. Now they're in the room. Whoosh! I'm just going to lie down for a minute. For a min ...

Good idea ... some air. Such a lovely evening. The lights. Sea. Must just lie down again. Everything's OK. Always OK with Kirsten. Ms Caine. Mistress. Lovely to lie back, see lights speed by. Rippling. So funny. Warm, moving along. Don't want to move. Everything else move ... music and lights. Going up ... into the dark. Lights gone but still warm ... still Kirsten. Oops! What's that? Can't. Not upright. Too difficult. Just, let me ... lie down, please. Ow! Let me ... that's right. You carry me. I'll be all right if you hold me. Soft. Dark. Going to bed now. Corridor is soft like carpet. But it's dark. No doors. Funny noise. Snap! Where's the bed. It's dirty. Say something. Can't think what you saying ... so tired ... must lie down ...

Well, the evening has taken a rather strange turn, hasn't it, my darling? Looks like I've lapsed back into my old ways. I tried, I really tried to be a sophisticated well-groomed lady but I guess there's only so much playing the game I can take. I entered your world and now it's time for you to know something of mine. Marvellous here, isn't it, when the moon is fat and the nocturnal creatures are rustling in their hidey-holes? Can't you feel the whole of nature strong in love and death all around you? Don't you feel the galvanising force of the moonlight streaming over you? Doesn't it give you power? It does me, as I crawl over your partially clothed body, doing what I want with it.

It's gone midnight now. I built a small fire to occupy myself while I waited for you to come back to consciousness and it's glowing all warm beside us. Your rag-doll head righted itself about ten minutes ago and you wondered where you were and got scared, especially as you couldn't move your arms and the first thing that greeted your blurry vision was a boar's head, tusks and all, staring down at you. I think you tried to scream, but it came out as a croaking bellow of fear in the dark. Poor thing, it must have been a bit of a start. You were very woozy at that point, and I don't think you knew it was me in a mask. I'm so glad to be able to let you know a little primordial fear. It'll do you the world of good in the long run. If I was really cruel I could have abandoned you at that point and left you alone to the mercy of the forest and your fevered visions but I need to talk to you, to tell you why the evening's romantic tête-à-tête has taken such a curious diversion.

I made a flask of coffee in the hotel room for our journey, and I added a little drop of whisky to aid your recovery. I helped you drink it like an invalid. I've even placed a blanket on the ground beneath you so you aren't in too much discomfort. I can wrap it around you so you don't freeze, but what I prefer is to cover you with my body, straddling you the way you straddled me in Eddie's conservatory. I'm wasn't sure if you'd be able to perform in your condition so I crushed a whole bunch of Viagra pills into the coffee which will have you ready for me in about half an hour.

I'm so glad I could bring you to Broxbourne Wood. I'd have hated for you to have missed out. Such a shame your suit got all messy. At least one of us had the foresight to be prepared for the environment. I'm wearing a tight-fitting long-sleeved catsuit that's perfect for all the stretchy movements I needed to make to bind your hands to the branches, and I've got on my big black army boots that enable me to clamber over logs without twisting my ankles. You were passed out on the bed when I changed my clothes. I don't think you remember Gareth coming in and taking those lewd pictures of you, either. You did pose so provocatively as well, wearing my stockings and panties and smiling for the camera as I tickled you. That was so much fun for the boys. They came in and had such a laugh at your expense. It was handy they were there to help me get you downstairs and into the car. Of course, the proprietors are Gareth's friends and they turn a blind eye to the many bizarre antics they witness, running a hotel in Brighton. It's not unusual for someone to arrive or depart their premises in a variety of inebriated states.

I'm so glad I did a practice run to these woods the other day, according to Eddie's instructions for finding the sacred grove. I sat here in the autumn afternoon, as the low sunlight illuminated the moss to a glowing emerald green and the golden leaves trembled and shimmered in the breeze. I was moved to tears soaking up the power of this special and ancient place, and I resolved then to do everything it would take to protect it. I sat and thought about how different we are, and how our world-views have come to collide.

I've travelled the world to connect with nature. I've seen illuminated octopuses on night dives in the coral seas of the Caribbean, neon tetras darting through cerise tendrils of elegant anemones, and giant turtles in the Indian Ocean tuned to the magnetic fields. I have stood under the Northern Lights in Hammerfest and curled up in the cloud forest with anteaters licking my toes. I've felt the passion of the tigress calling for her lost mate in the jungle and the booming solitude of the blue whale adrift in the ocean, with a heart as big as a car.

And you have dedicated your life to party politics.

I can't change your history. But I can influence your decision about the fate of this wood. And now, in the depths of night, this place is electric and alive. The chittering yowl of the foxes makes even me jump, so goodness knows how you must be feeling. It's as if all the trees of this magic wood are on my side, wishing me to succeed. I don't think you'll be building any supermarket here, Charlesworth. Not when you know the ammunition I have. I knew there would be the inevitable questions, and I have to suffer a barrage of protest, whining and disbelief after you woke up. But still I sit on top of you, licking your nipples, planting soft kisses up and down your chest and stomach – an inappropriate response to your vitriol. You try speaking in that reassuring tone of voice you've heard in movies, where the cop tries to talk down the psychopath into dropping the gun, but it isn't going to work with me. I'm too smart for that, but I let you go on. I'll let you exhaust yourself with the nicey-nicey 'please let me go' pleas. I sit close to you, occasionally mesmerised by the flickering flames of our little campfire.

One little word keeps issuing from your greedy lying lips: 'Why?'

Finally, I answer: 'Because you need to be returned to the wild.'

'What are you talking about?'

'You needed taking back to a primordial state. You've known it, in some of the games we've played. You've known ecstasy in oblivion.'

'This is going too far, though, Kirsten. What you're doing is illegal. This is kidnapping. You drugged me once before and I let it go. But not a second time. And why are we here, in this forest? Why do we have to be here?'

'Do you remember a few weeks back, when I said the challenge of the subversive was to reintroduce the over-civilised human to a more primitive reality?'

'No, I don't remember. A lot of what you say goes

over my head, to be honest. Can't we go back to the hotel? This is horrid. It's cold. We could be in luxury.'

I seize a burning piece of firewood to light up your face.

'You're too used to luxury,' I hiss. 'You're overcivilised, like so many of your ilk. You're divorced from your natural self and, as the wise know, that does a human no good at all. Leaves him unprepared to cope in the wilderness.'

'We don't need to be in the wilderness,' you wail in desperation. 'We *are* civilised.'

'That, I think, is a point of contention,' I answer, stroking your hair the way you like it before working my way down your body, giving attention to your penis, tonguing your balls and sucking on you. As earlier in the hotel room, I'm giving you the thing you crave – the closeness of contact and the feminine touch. I'm being soft and sensual.

'I want to do it in the outdoors, Simon. Do it with you in the dirt. Does it excite you to know you can finally fuck me?'

'Of course, of course, but this is too much for me. Too strange.'

'Strange for you, maybe at the moment, but you'll get used to it. This catsuit may cover my body but I can release my breasts,' I say, 'like this.' I pull at a Velcro strip and out they fall, those beauties, rubbing softly against your chest. 'And I have the same thing here, between my legs. Oh God, Simon, you know, having you as my prisoner makes me so horny. I want to fuck you now, so badly, here in the woods. I like to play games of prisoner and kidnapper.'

I can finally feel something stirring between your legs. It's too good to resist. I slide down and take you into my mouth. Slowly you unfurl and harden. The combination of drugs is putting you in a perfect state for sex – that of aroused languidness, as if you were some laudanum-saturated young gentleman of the fin de siècle decadence. I roll my tongue around your meaty length and rub it between my lips and over my face. You forget the confines of your circumstances to groan your appreciation into a night air that's musky with the fungal scent of autumn. It'll soon be time to ingest of the sacred mushroom. Now that's something I'd love to see – you crawling around in a state of psychedelic wonder. Maybe that time will come. For now, I need to finally take this wonderful thing inside me.

Your penis has overridden your rational mind and, like a horse, you have come to full erection in the face of a threat – with a little help that you don't know about, of course. You probably think you're some kind of a stud to be able to get hard even in circumstances of such adversity. I won't dispel the illusion. I rip the Velcro pad from between my legs and reveal myself, wet and ready for you. I turn about face on all fours and show you the pink, plunging my fingers into the moisture and giving you the old favourite – my scent under your nose. You are blotting out the reality of your situation to give yourself over to desire. You beg me to untie you but I don't think that's necessary. There's still work to be done here.

I turn around and face you, the firelight flickering. You are bucking your hips towards me and you're needy of my touch. With one knee on the ground and the other leg bent with my foot on the floor I am able to rise and fall down on you at will, my wet sex the only part of me touching you. I ease myself down on to your thick shaft. It's so good. At this moment we hate each other, but we're making a good go of it all the same. You thrust up to meet my plunging descents – each envelopment to the hilt bringing an expression of delirium to your face. I slide myself up and down, occasionally stopping, which has you in groaning need and panic.

'Take me all the way, please,' you beg. 'Let me come in you.'

It's been a long time, my little parliamentarian. I want you to know why you crave this oblivion so desperately. To look at you in your moment of raw need is to know you are nothing more than any beast propelled by its instinct. But you are one of the species that ravages the world of resources and contributes little but an increased burden of toxicity. Six and a half billion human fuckers, most of them consuming, shitting, fighting and exploiting without a sense of humility. For as long as I participate in this life I shall do it with awareness of the debt incurred and alert wretches like you to the abominations you commit in the name of progress.

'Admit your insignificance,' I say. 'Admit you are nothing in this universe.'

'I'm nothing.'

'Admit you're just an animal – a filthy lying dog. Say it!'

'I'm a filthy lying dog.'

'You want to fuck your mistress?'

'I want to fuck my mistress.'

'You want to come, to spurt your load in my beautiful cunt?'

'Let me come. Let me spurt my load in your beautiful cunt. Oh, yes, oh, yes.'

You are working you way to orgasm. And it's going to be so excruciating this time as I tease you to the very edge then stop.

'No!' you wail. 'Please finish me off.'

'If you make me a promise.'

'Depends.' I grind down on you and you gasp and pant. 'Oh, oh, please.'

'Promise?'

'Anything. Just please let me, oh, my God, please, I'm going to –'

'You sure? I'll not release you if you don't.'

'I'm sure. Yes, oh God, please. I'm coming now, oh, yes.'

I squeeze my muscles around your cock. Ian Baum told me I constrict a man's penis tighter than anyone he's known. I like to use this talent to its full advantage. You are pumping at me for the final strokes but still I raise myself up to the tip. I'd love to see your cock spurt its milky tribute but instead I keep my side of the bargain and ease down on you one more time.

'Oh, fucking yes. Yes, I'm coming in your cunt. I'm coming inside you.'

I throw back my head and enjoy the sensation of full mastery over you. Finally, we've both known the moment.

Afterwards I help you to drink from my water bottle, and I wrap the blanket around you then go to sit by the fire.

'So ... can you release me now, please?' you say quietly.

I don't answer your question.

'Do you know where you are?' I ask, poking at the fire.

'No, I bloody don't. Are you going to tell me?'

'We're near Brighton, Simon. We're in Broxbourne Wood. Does that mean anything to you?'

'Well, er ... yes. I mean, it's part of the redevelopment scheme locally. Why are we here? What the hell has it got to do with you?'

'Can you not imagine?'

'You're not one of those ... tree huggers are you? One of those environmental terrorists? Nature First, or something?'

I stay silent for a few moments, then give you a little philosophy.

'There you go again, using pejorative terms. You see, my dull little member of parliament, the universe offers us the opportunity to realise ourselves as part of nature and the cosmos, but most of us don't bother. It's too vast for our puny imaginations. We prefer to live in a small narrow world where we can strut around being important, making money and destroying things. You want to turn our ancient sacred island into a bland-scape of monotony. Car showrooms, business parks, burger bars, casinos – all the soulless clones that stand in monolithic arrogant opposition to anything colour-ful, vibrant or enhancing. Our most profound emotion is not that of achieving power or riches, Simon Charles-worth. It is the sensation of the mystical. And Brox-bourne Wood is a place where mystical things have happened for a number of people. They say it's haunted, you know. Some people swear they've seen the headless ghosts of Saxon warriors slaughtered by the Normans. They use to hunt wild boar here too, and there are reports of spirit hunts here on full moon nights. But it's also a very beautiful place. A powerful place. I know that very unpleasant things will happen to anyone who organises its destruction, but of course, that's not going to happen, is it?'

'You're out of your depth. You're talking rubbish. I can't spend time thinking about nonsense philosophy and ... nature worship, I'm dealing with progress. Let me go. Christ, I mean, you're very sexy and everything, but I could get you arrested for what you've done to me tonight. I'm done in. Kirsten, please.'

'Nonsense is it? I wouldn't be so disrespectful if I were you. You are at something of a disadvantage at the moment. I would actually like to see you try and get me arrested. I'd make my one phone call that would have

JPEGs and MPEGs of you sent to the tabloids faster than you could say "Tony".'

'What JPEGs and MPEGs?'

'Footage from the flat in Maida Vale, for a start. My friends there use cameras for their sex games. They're a bit kinky like that. It's a bit grainy, but there's a lovely sequence of you getting the dragon quirt, wearing my knickers. One can tell it's you, all right. But my favourites have to be those of you wearing my underwear and stockings earlier tonight, in the hotel room. Oh, poor thing, you probably don't remember.'

'What! This is illegal. How dare you!'

'You came there of your own free will, Charlesworth. It would be your word against mine.'

'You bitch. You wouldn't tell the tabloids. It would go against all your principles. Or are they just lies? I knew it would come down to money. You're all the same — women — just after one thing.'

'You see, your devious little brain can't imagine that someone would be passionate about anything other than money. This is not about money, not for me, anyway. Reverse the decision to build here, or I'll have those pictures in the tabloids by Sunday.'

You're defeated and exhausted. You're trying to weigh up what would be the greatest loss. Your Cabinet post. Your cosy domesticity. Your backhander from the developers . . .

The fire crackles and I kick at the branches with my boots. 'You know, Simon, I feel confident you're going to make the right choice. You did promise.'

'You fucking bitch. You're mad. You should be locked up.'

I almost say, 'I was, once' but instead I remind you of your promise. 'No song and dance . . . no police . . . no sneaky phone calls. Think about it. You try to get me arrested and it would be your word against mine. I can prove all the things we've done together. It wouldn't be that strange for us to sneak out to the woods for a little fun. I would tell them it was your thing; that you'd heard couples come here for dogging. Picture the court scene ... I could wear my Chanel suit, my Charles Jourdan shoes. There's my address in South Kensington. Do you think they'd believe you, that I was a tree-hugging freak who'd drugged and raped you? Bit of a long shot, I'd say. They could call your wife as a character witness, like that other fragrant lady. D'you think she'd stand by you, after what you've done to her? How's it looking, Simon? Not brilliant, is it?'

You concede. You know you are defeated. I've played a huge bluff. Of course, you could run me in and they'd find out immediately that I have a criminal history, but it's not going to happen. I whisk my Swiss Army knife from my bag and slice through the ropes. You're free. I throw your clothes back at you and you make the best of tidying yourself. Our games are over. You want nothing more to do with me but still I say I'll drive you back to Brighton. Drop you in the town centre. You grunt a grudging acknowledgment, then, without asking, snatch the flask of coffee and gulp down the lot. There's enough Viagra in it to keep you up for a week. I wouldn't want to be in your trousers for the next 24 hours.

13 **Undoing and Redemption**

I tuned in to the live conference the next day, after a long soak and a leisurely brunch with some of my 'pervert' friends. I thought you might be a little lacklustre but what transpired was nothing short of a scandal. You were stuttering, inept, ashen-faced and barely able to read your speech, although, because it was prepared days earlier, you were able to recite it parrot-fashion from the page, enough to just about get away with it. You dragged out the speech, and cutaways to the audience showed people bored, asleep and exasperated. But from the looks on the faces of your Right Honourable colleagues, something was definitely wrong with the secretary of state for public policy. The lectern hid your embarrassment to most of the audience while you were speaking, but it was plain that everyone on the podium was staring at you and whispering. A number of photographers and reporters had gathered near the edge of the stage and were taking shots of you, then they walked away at a brisk pace, laughing. You were obviously reluctant to leave the podium, but when you were finally ushered off by the chancellor you looked nervous, holding your papers in front of your groin.

The next day the papers were full of it. Ribald jokes covered the tabloids, with the offending protuberance in your trousers circled, with arrows pointing at it in the way that gossip magazines highlight fat, spots and cellulite. It was a first. An erect penis – albeit covered – gracing the front page of the papers. No one could take you seriously any more. Whenever you were wheeled out for soundbites after that it was plain to see the interviewers trying not to smile. Satirical programmes and publications made a meal of it, and speculated what you would do during the next general erection.

News of your divorce came just after Christmas, accompanied by Lorna Charlesworth's famous interview to a daily paper in a 'new year, new woman' feature about living with her parliamentary porn-addicted husband who forced her into degrading acts. The priapism had been the final straw, she'd said, especially as she'd campaigned against pornography in the 80s. That, and your returning home the night before the conference dishevelled, drunk and reeking of sex. She seemed like a misery and I hated her for betraying you in that way with nothing to gain but money for the feature. I could have made a packet with the pictures I still have of you, but you see I'm a woman of my word.

As soon as we heard Broxbourne Wood had been reprieved I sent you a text of thanks and commiseration on your circumstances as I had heard you'd stepped down from the Cabinet. I've not heard back from you ... not yet. I continue to work on freelance design projects, still walking between several worlds. I've seen Ian a couple of times since September and we're on good terms but I haven't gone back to playing sex games with him. He's asked me several times whether Simon Charlesworth was my MP and my reluctance to show emphatic denial keeps him guessing. I might tell him one day.

We celebrated the saving of Broxbourne Wood at Eddie's, with one of her legendary banquets held in her drawing room to celebrate the spring equinox. The daffodils were blooming around the fountain, rabbits were running across the lawn and all felt good with the world. We gathered in the conservatory to drink a toast to Pan and the spirits of the woodland to keep us always gleeful, spiritual and unusual, before tucking into a feast of organic lamb and roast vegetables. She mentioned you still hold your seat in your local constituency, but there's been something of an about-turn in your principles. In fact, it seems you've embraced green issues.

She handed me a press cutting from that week's local paper showing you standing in the high street shaking hands with the representative for 'celebrate small businesses' week and you've recently instigated a newer, more efficient recycling campaign. You look relaxed in the picture, happier than you used to under the media glare of questions about transport and public policy. Despite your public shaming, it looks as if you're better off. There were rumours locally that you'd had a breakdown but you fought back against the accusations by saying it was all due to the stress you'd been suffering. I'd read somewhere that you were planning to write a piece for a left-leaning magazine on the impossible demands of public life and the importance of 'finding one's true desires'.

The article mentions you've moved to a smaller property nearer to Broxbourne Wood and you cycle to your office most days. In fact, you're getting a reputation as something of an eccentric. Eddie has heard that at weekends, apparently, you're often seen walking across the Downs in something of a trance, holding a scrap of black satin to your face.

Visit the Black Lace website at
www.blacklace-books.co.uk

LOOK OUT FOR THE ALL-NEW BLACK LACE BOOKS – AVAILABLE NOW!

All books priced £7.99 in the UK. Please note publication dates apply to the UK only. For other territories, please contact your retailer.

THE MASTER OF SHILDEN
Lucinda Carrington
ISBN 0 352 33140 2

When successful interior designer Elise St John is offered a commission at a remote castle, she jumps at the chance to distance herself from a web of sexual and emotional entanglements. Yet, as she sets to work creating rooms in which guests will be able to realise their most erotic fantasies, she finds herself indulging in fantasies of her own, about two very different men.

Blair Devlin – overtly sexy and self-confident – is a local riding instructor. Max Lannsen – the Master of Shilden – is darkly attractive but more remote. All they seem to have in common is their hatred for one another. Then, when Elise's sensual daydreams become reality, she discovers that each man's future depends on a decision she will soon be forced to make. To which of them does she really owe her loyalty?

Coming in October

EQUAL OPPORTUNITIES
Mathilde Madden
ISBN O 352 34070 3

David thinks his love-life is over when he is left unable to walk after a car accident. But then he meets kinky Mary, who finds the idea of a boy in a wheelchair too sexy for words. But is their affair just based on satisfying Mary's kinks, or something deeper? As David's scars begin to heal, soon both of them are having to face questions about what their attraction to one another really means.

DARKER THAN LOVE
Kristina Lloyd
ISBN O 352 33279 4

It's 1875, and the morals of Queen Victoria mean nothing to London's wayward and debauched elite. Young but naïve Clarissa Longleigh is visiting London for the first time. She is eager to meet Lord Marldon – the man to whom she's been promised – knowing only that he's handsome, dark and sophisticated. In fact he is depraved, louche, and has a taste for sexual excess.

Clarissa has also struck up a friendship with a young Italian artist, Gabriel. When Marldon hears of this he is incensed, and imprisons Clarissa in his opulent London mansion. When Gabriel tries to free her, he too is captured, and the young lovers find themselves at the mercy of the debauched lord.

Coming in November

DARK DESIGNS
Madelynne Ellis
ISBN 0 352 34075 4

Remy Davies is under pressure as the designer for an opulent gothic wedding. There's the over-stressed bride, a trinity of vampire-obsessed bridesmaids, a wayward groom, and then there's the best man . . . Silk looks like he's been drawn by a *manga* artist; beautiful, exotic, and with a predatory sexuality. Remy has to have him, in her bed and between the pages of her new catalogue. Remy is about to launch herself into the alternative fashion world, and Silk is going to sell it for her whether he knows it or not. But Silk is nobody's toy, and for all his androgyny, he's determinedly heterosexual. Pity, since Remy's biggest fantasy is to see him making out with her Japanese biker, sometime boyfriend, Takeshi.

ASKING FOR TROUBLE
Kristina Lloyd
ISBN 0 352 33362 6

When Beth Bradshaw – the manager of a fashionable bar in the seaside town of Brighton – starts flirting with the handsome Ilya, she becomes a player in a game based purely on sexual brinkmanship. The boundaries between fantasy and reality start to blur as their relationship takes on an increasingly reckless element.

When Ilya's murky past catches up with him, he's determined to involve Beth. Unwilling to extricate herself from their addictive games, she finds herself being drawn deeper into the seedy underbelly of Brighton where things, including Ilya, are far more dangerous than she bargained for.

Black Lace Booklist

Information is correct at time of printing. To avoid disappointment, check availability before ordering. Go to www.blacklace-books.co.uk. All books are priced £6.99 unless another price is given.

BLACK LACE BOOKS WITH A CONTEMPORARY SETTING

☐ ON THE EDGE Laura Hamilton	ISBN 0 352 33534 3	£5.99
☐ THE TRANSFORMATION Natasha Rostova	ISBN 0 352 33311 1	
☐ SIN.NET Helena Ravenscroft	ISBN 0 352 33598 X	
☐ TWO WEEKS IN TANGIER Annabel Lee	ISBN 0 352 33599 8	
☐ SYMPHONY X Jasmine Stone	ISBN 0 352 33629 3	
☐ A SECRET PLACE Ella Broussard	ISBN 0 352 33307 3	
☐ GOING TOO FAR Laura Hamilton	ISBN 0 352 33657 9	
☐ RELEASE ME Suki Cunningham	ISBN 0 352 33671 4	
☐ SLAVE TO SUCCESS Kimberley Raines	ISBN 0 352 33687 0	
☐ SHADOWPLAY Portia Da Costa	ISBN 0 352 33313 8	
☐ ARIA APPASSIONATA Julie Hastings	ISBN 0 352 33056 2	
☐ A MULTITUDE OF SINS Kit Mason	ISBN 0 352 33737 0	
☐ COMING ROUND THE MOUNTAIN Tabitha Flyte	ISBN 0 352 33873 3	
☐ FEMININE WILES Karina Moore	ISBN 0 352 33235 2	
☐ MIXED SIGNALS Anna Clare	ISBN 0 352 33889 X	
☐ BLACK LIPSTICK KISSES Monica Belle	ISBN 0 352 33885 7	
☐ GOING DEEP Kimberly Dean	ISBN 0 352 33876 8	
☐ PACKING HEAT Karina Moore	ISBN 0 352 33356 1	
☐ MIXED DOUBLES Zoe le Verdier	ISBN 0 352 33312 X	
☐ UP TO NO GOOD Karen S. Smith	ISBN 0 352 33589 0	
☐ CLUB CRÈME Primula Bond	ISBN 0 352 33907 1	
☐ BONDED Fleur Reynolds	ISBN 0 352 33192 5	
☐ SWITCHING HANDS Alaine Hood	ISBN 0 352 33896 2	
☐ EDEN'S FLESH Robyn Russell	ISBN 0 352 33923 0	
☐ PEEP SHOW Mathilde Madden	ISBN 0 352 33924 1	£7.99
☐ RISKY BUSINESS Lisette Allen	ISBN 0 352 33280 8	£7.99
☐ CAMPAIGN HEAT Gabrielle Marcola	ISBN 0 352 33941 1	£7.99
☐ MS BEHAVIOUR Mini Lee	ISBN 0 352 33962 4	£7.99

BLACK LACE BOOKS WITH AN HISTORICAL SETTING

To find out the latest information about Black Lace titles, check out the website: www.blacklace-books.co.uk or send for a booklist with complete synopses by writing to:

Black Lace Booklist, Virgin Books Ltd
Thames Wharf Studios
Rainville Road
London W6 9HA

Please include an SAE of decent size. Please note only British stamps are valid.

Our privacy policy
We will not disclose information you supply us to any other parties. We will not disclose any information which identifies you personally to any person without your express consent.

From time to time we may send out information about Black Lace books and special offers. Please tick here if you do <u>not</u> wish to receive Black Lace information. ❏